IRREVERSIBLE
DAMAGE

THE KATIE SUAREZ SOCIAL JUSTICE SERIES

A NOVEL BY JL RUIZ

WPR BOOKS: LATINO INSIGHTS

CARLSBAD, CA

DEDICATION

This book is dedicated to the "Dreamers" and their families, as well as the many immigrants who have started families, made a productive and honest life in this country, are in immigration limbo, and whose families will continue to be in despair, deprived of the American dream. Something must be done.

THE BOOK CREATION TEAM

Cover Illustration:	Ignacio Gomez
Editing Assistance:	Sue Ann Painter, Kathleen Kaiser, and Flo Selfman
Marketing:	Kathleen Kaiser
ePub Creation:	Ana Patiño
Publisher:	Kirk Whisler

Learn more about JL Ruiz at www.JLRuizBooks.com

Copyright © 2019 by JL Ruiz
Printed and bound in the United States of America. All Rights Reserved.
ISBN 978-1-889379-91-3 (Hardcover)   **ISBN 978-1-889379-94-4** (ePub)
ISBN 978-1-889379-93-7 (Paperback)   **ISBN 978-1-889379-95-1** (Kindle)

Library of Congress Control Number: 2019905120

For more about books presented by WPR Publishing, please go to www.WPRbooks.com.

WPR BOOKS: Latino Insights
3445 Catalina Dr., Carlsbad, CA 92010-2856
www.WPRbooks.com   760-434-1223   kirk@whisler.com

TABLE OF CONTENTS

INTRODUCTION

I have been wanting to write this novel for the past thirty years. With that in mind, I have been saving experiences and carefully observing and researching the unexplainable condition of the Mexican-American community in the US. The recent wave of attacks against the Mexican-American community reignited my desire to write. But it wasn't until one of my coworkers told me about the terrible suicidal depression her niece was experiencing as a consequence of her uncertain future as a "Dreamer," that I realized how our inaction is allowing irreversible damage to be inflicted on these young people, and I felt obliged to tell their story.

When I arrived at this wonderful land of opportunity as a naïve, fresh-faced Mexican immigrant with a big American dream, I encountered an unexpected, pessimistic attitude toward achieving success by my new Mexican-America acquaintances, which I had not seen in Mexico City. Small episodes started to tell me a story I did not comprehend. For example, time after time, I saw people become awkward when asking me what my background was. "Are you Mexi…um…Hispanic?" with an obvious fear of offending me by calling me Mexican. Or the times when I spoke in Spanish to a person who I knew was of Mexican background, and they, feeling offended, barked at me, "I don't speak Spanish!" I was always curious as to why Mexican-Americans are so often hiding their identity, using every sort of alternative name.

I realized that while most Americans appreciate everything Mexican—food, architecture, art, music, parts of the culture–they don't feel the same way about the people. For example, I would hear nice people say during casual conversations, "I'm going to pick up some Mexicans to clean my front lawn." Or when my half-Mexican cousin welcomed me upon my arrival from Mexico saying, "Why do you want to move here? To be one more dirty gardener?" Or my other half-Mexican cousin telling the most offensive jokes about Mexicans, and then, straight-faced, arguing that he was white and his Mexican side was really not important. And the time when I applied for a faculty position at a local university and the head of admission told me, "Sorry, we don't hire faculty who are not US-trained," to later find out that the school had many faculty trained in Europe and Asia, just not in Mexico or Latin America. It took me a relentless two-year fight, to ultimately be allowed in.

The use of scapegoat tactics for political or financial gain is as old as time, and has been previously used by Nazis against Jews, Turks against Armenians, and many others throughout history. This is not the first time Mexican-Americans have been used as scapegoats for the financial and political benefit of unscrupulous people. This novel tells in human terms the harmful effects of these practices, and how they ultimately harm the entire community.

This is not just a Mexican-American story, it's an American story that acknowledges how, in this nation of immigrants, there is good and bad amongst all people. Without coming to terms with the past, there is no understanding of how it affects the present, and without action, will continue to repeat in the future. The multicultural cast of characters reminds us that a lack of respect leads to abuse and isolation, while respect and acknowledgment of our cultural contributions allow for a unity between cultures.

Sincerely,

CHAPTER ONE

SUPERPOWERS

Frowning and clearly overwhelmed, Katie Suarez struggled with all of the papers escaping from her backpack, trying to find her group history project. The sheets scattered in the relentless desert wind that sweeps across her high school quad.

"Here you go," said Blaire Carter, handing Katie a stack of paper. "Why my best friend is so old-fashioned, I'll never understand. Do you really need to print all of this junk?"

"How else to share with everyone?" replied Katie.

"On a computer," Blaire said, pulling her new rose gold MacBook from her Michael Kors tote. "Google Sheets, ever heard of it?"

"That's for homework. Most of the team never worked on the project, and I want to be sure they read what is being submitted with their names on it."

"Why? Are you the protector of the overprivileged Washington High students? Why do you always have to try so hard?" said Mallory Ochoa, one of Katie's close friends, approaching with more loose papers.

"For extra credits," Katie responded, as if it was natural for everyone to try hard. Mallory and Blaire looked at each other and rolled their eyes.

"Chill, Katie, school is almost over. We must enjoy it before it ends. You're such a nerd, I bet you don't even have a date for the dance."

"Come on, Mallory, give her a break. You know Katie. She's an overachiever, and thanks to her pushing us this year, I will have the best point average in my school history. Thanks, Katie, but Mallory's right. You need to chill, girl." As usual, Blaire felt the need to defend her friend.

"Miss Future Harvard Law is a nerd, but a brilliant nerd!" Mallory laughed as the class bell rang.

Katie fumed. "You don't get it. I have my best shot at getting an A+ in history, and that will help me keep my 4.0 average. Chemistry is killing me, and I may only get a B+."

Blaire and Mallory stopped and stared hard at Katie.

"Only a B+? My mother would give me an unlimited credit card if I got a B+ in Chemistry," said Blaire.

"Mine too—well, if she had the money," said Mallory, linking arms with Katie. "By the way, do you know who your brother is taking to the dance?"

"I don't keep track of Mark's conquests. It's hard enough competing with him—star athlete, Mr. Popular—not to mention, Mom's favorite."

Mallory started to say something, but Blaire touched her arm and exchanged a quick "no" shake of her head. Katie rarely spoke about her brother, and since both Mallory and Blaire had had crushes on him since elementary school, silence seemed the right response.

"At least Mark isn't a shining academic star," said Katie. "I want to show my mom I also deserve her attention."

"You are definitely better at schoolwork, and a nerd too," replied Mallory, laughing again.

"You bitches are just wasting time," said Blaire, trying to change the conversation, knowing her friend didn't like to be called nerd. "There are so many hot boys out there, and we need to socialize if we want to get invited to a few of the senior parties, which are all happening soon."

"Blaire, I hate when you call us bitches," Katie said. "Honestly, I am so stressed right now, I have zero desire to go to any party and waste precious study time."

Once in the classroom, her study group was settled into the back corner, heads buried in their phones. "Come on, guys, pay attention. Mrs. Smith said that if we turn in this project by Friday, she will give us five extra points toward the final," said Katie.

Whenever Katie got this intense about a school project, Blaire just smiled and went along. She couldn't understand what drove Katie, even though they had been best friends since childhood and lived on the same block of Paradise Valley. Blaire's dad was a partner at Phoenix's largest real estate agency, and her mom had been a Miss Arizona runner-up. Neither one of them was big on education, but were big on success.

Katie's parents were both lawyers; her mom worked for the district attorney. Since Katie was a child she dreamed of being a lawyer, and sometimes she dreamed she was a superhero. In her dreams, Katie had superpowers and with them, she would always save the lives of the people she loved. Katie was very kind to others, liked to tell jokes, and loved to make people laugh. She usually made an effort to make friends with the new students in class, because she knew they needed a friend.

Katie did not have an inflated ego; she just loved the idea of helping people. She thought that by becoming a lawyer, she would be able to help the weak and unfortunate. If she became a lawyer, she would be a third-generation lawyer. Katie had heard many stories of how her grandfather had helped and improved many people's lives as a judge, during and after the revolutionary war in Mexico.

Over the last few years, Blaire had watched Katie blossom. The shy, insecure but determined nerdy tomboy was becoming a beautiful girl, with thick, curly black hair, a perfectly shaped nose, and elegant eyebrows above her deep-set dark eyes. She was like a Mexican version of Scarlett Johansson. Blaire was confident of her own beauty, much like her mom, but she always felt a bit flat-chested around Katie. She truly loved her and often thought that if she had Katie's perfect tanned skin and sexy body, she would rule high school.

Most annoying was when boys asked Blaire to introduce them to Katie. She'd let the fools try, but their efforts were of no use. Katie's mind was all about school and she didn't care about any boys. At least none that Blaire knew about.

CHAPTER TWO

POPULAR

The small neighborhood of Paradise Valley, with its winding streets, multimillion-dollar homes and beautifully designed drought-resistant lawns, was the pride of Phoenix. The elite lived there. On any Sunday morning you could see its influential entrepreneurs, politicians, and celebrity residents drive through the well-manicured winding avenues in their Bentleys, Ferraris and S class Mercedes. The residents decided to incorporate and form their own local government in the sixties to keep separate from the neighboring cities, in order to maintain more exclusive standards. Paradise Valley was clean, safe, beautiful, and the population was 97% white. Residents of Paradise Valley liked to brag about this and say, "There is a reason why Paradise is in the name."

Phoenix in May could reach a temperature of 110 degrees, but regardless of the hellish heat outside, air conditioners provided the ideal temperature in the impeccably clean and bright halls of Washington High School. It was no ordinary high school: Students were polite, academic achievement was valued, and a good number of seniors were accepted to the top colleges and universities in Arizona and the country. After all, Washington High School was in Paradise Valley.

On that particularly hot and windy day two weeks before the end of school, the air was filled with the talk of prom, end-of-the-year parties, yearbooks, and plans for summer. Near the lockers on the east hall, Mark Suarez, Katie's older brother, and Zack Mackintosh, two of the most popular juniors at school, were having their usual friendly banter about football.

Zack, with a smile from ear to ear, sarcastically asked, "So how do you feel about your stinking Cowboys now? I just heard that John Patterson is in trouble with the law again, and may be suspended four more games. What the hell is wrong with your guys? They can't stay out of trouble. There goes your season."

Mark enjoyed the dig. "Dude, you're full of shit. With or without John, we are going to kick the Cardinals' ass badly this year. You can't even get a decent quarterback who will stay healthy," making reference to the previous season when the Cardinals had three quarterbacks play: Palmer, Lindley, and Stanton.

"Palmer is healthy, and we are going all the way, baby."

"Dream on, dude, your guys will choke, as usual."

Cole Jones, another varsity player who was eavesdropping close by, said, with sudden fury, "Mark, you are a fucking traitor. Why can't you root for our local teams? Romo is too old and beat-up to do anything anyway. Your useless Cowboys and their multimillion-dollar budget are going to embarrass themselves, again."

Mark, in the same fun, teasing tone he used with Zack, responded to Cole, "Screw you, Cole, what do you know about football anyway?"

But Cole did not take it as banter. He made it a personal insult and lunged for Mark's throat with his hands.

Zack saw the rage in Cole's eyes and put his massive arm around him, using the weight of his 6'3" frame to gently stop the much smaller Cole. "Dude, what's wrong with you? We're just bull-shitting here."

Cole, still under Zack's grip, responded, "I hate this mother-fucking traitor. He likes the Cowboys only because Romo is Mexican and his people always root for outside teams. What's next? Is he going to cheer for the Dodgers?"

"Hey, man, we are just talking about sports here. It is not life or death."

Mark was surprised to hear Zack, as he knew sports was his life.

"No man, this asshole has always been a traitor," shouted Cole.

Mark was shocked because he barely knew Cole. They had gone to the same junior high but had little interaction over the years, and he didn't know where his animosity was coming from.

Zack let go of Cole and said in a more serious tone, "Just shake it off,

Cole. You guys are both varsity team members. This shit can't happen between teammates."

Mark extended his hand out to Cole, but Cole gave him the finger, said "Fuck you," and walked away.

Zack looked at Mark and said, "What did you do to him?"

"Nothing. I barely know him."

Zack clicked his tongue and said, "He'll get over it, don't sweat it." Zack had no clue how wrong he was.

After Cole left, both friends were left with an uneasy feeling, the way people feel after they just saw a tragedy. They attempted to go back to their football banter, but they were both distracted.

Fortunately, the angel Savannah, her friend Paige, and two more girls from the cheerleading squad walked by, and as usual both boys' eyes were on them. Savannah was the girl every boy in the school dreamed about. She was tall, had perfect freckles, and walked with her head up like a model on a runway.

Turning to them, Savannah said, "Hi, Mark." Mark's and Savannah's eyes locked. He felt a jolt of electricity go through his body. He tried to respond, but the words did not come out, and all he could do was smile. And just like that, the beautiful girls walked away.

Zack's testosterone exploded the moment the girls passed.

"What the hell? She just said 'hi' to you! Am I freaking invisible?" The obvious jealousy dripped from his words.

"I think she has a crush on me," Mark said. Though he didn't believe it, he knew Zack liked her and knew the comment would piss him off.

"Screw you. You're dreaming." Zack shoved Mark and stormed off to his next class. Mark had always been a loyal friend to Zack, but he secretly envied Zack's coolness, good looks, and athletic abilities. He looked up to Zack, but like any seventeen-year-old boy full of bravado, he didn't want Zack to realize he looked up to him.

Zack was handsome, honest, and very likable. It didn't take long to know Zack was a one of the good guys. Zack's parents met at the University of Alabama, where Zack's dad, Tom Mackintosh, was the quarterback of the Crimson Tide, and Zack's mom, Anne, played volleyball on the school's varsity team. Zack's parents were not just great athletes, they were also good students; both got degrees in business administration from the University of Alabama. Anne was born in Phoenix and missed her family, so when they got married, they moved back to Arizona.

For Tom, moving to Phoenix was a big change because it was a modern city in the desert. He grew up in the small town of Abernant and had not experienced much diversity. Phoenix had a large population of Mexican and Mexican-American people, close to forty percent. And from what he could see, these immigrants from another country were capable laborers, gardeners, nannies, cooks, and friendly people. He ended up liking them, and always treated them kindly. Tom fell in love with the very popular Mexican food and adapted well to the hot weather. Once in Phoenix, and with a child on the way, Tom accepted a job as a lower-level business analyst at Geico, but using the leadership skills learned on the football field, he moved up. He was a force to be reckoned with and it didn't take long for him to become COO of the company.

Anne was equally successful as a top executive at Walmart. The Mackintosh family was devoutly Christian, went to church every Sunday, and raised their kids to have good values, to be respectful, and to help others. Zack's older sister, Jenny, was beautiful and wanted to help the entire world. As soon as she finished college, she enrolled in a church mission and moved to Zimbabwe to help as many children as possible get an education.

Zack and his sister grew up chasing and catching balls, so being an athlete was in Zack's blood. Since he was three, he was swinging a bat and Little League followed. Zack was excellent at every sport and he was usually much bigger than the other kids. When Zack was eight years old, he swung the bat and hit the ball so hard, it went straight into the young pitcher's face and the poor boy bled instantly. Instead of running to first base, Zack ran toward the crying pitcher and did everything he could do to help.

Later that night, Anne saw he couldn't sleep and said, "Honey, you have to go to sleep."

"Mom, I just feel so bad I hurt that boy," Zack said. Anne smiled and kissed him, and she knew Zack had a kind heart.

Zack's parents had their priorities straight. They organized their schedules to insure that one of them could take the kids to every Little League baseball, Pee Wee football, and AYSO soccer practice and game they could. When they couldn't, they had Socorro. Socorro was the Mackintosh kids' nanny during their entire childhood. As the youngest, Zack and Socorro shared a special love, and he called her Soco. She taught him Spanish and told him stories about her hometown, Tepatitlan, a very small pueblo in Jalisco.

Soco was light-skinned with very dark hair and green eyes. She told him that when she was a child, they didn't have electricity in her home in Tepatitlan, and some people still moved around on horses and mules. She told him stories about chasing rabbits, running in beautiful green fields, climbing to the top of the mountain, and looking at a beautiful valley with green rolling hills. Young Zack would listen and dream of this lovely place, and looked forward to hearing Soco's stories about Mexico. The Mackintoshes treated Socorro like part of their family. Socorro had two young girls of her own, and every once in a while she would bring them with her, and they would play with the Mackintosh kids. There was a lot of love in that home.

CHAPTER THREE

ELIZABETH

The Suarez family lived in a 4,000-square-foot, two-story Contemporary-Modern-style home in Paradise Valley. It was set in an artistically designed low-water-consumption front lawn. The interior decoration was simple, yet sophisticated. The entrance was wide and open; to the right, cantilevered stairs appeared to float in space. The walls were ivory and sculpted along clean lines. A small blue accent wall framed a bronze model of a rearing horse.

Elizabeth Suarez arrived home and looked happily at the shiny, light-colored granite floors, which reflected the light. She was a junior prosecutor at the Maricopa County District Attorney's office. It was apparent by her appearance that she had had a tough day.

As usual, as soon as she arrived, she heard the kids scream.

"Mooom, Mark has been bothering me all afternoon and not letting me study."

"Mark, stop making your sister upset. What is it with you?"

"She's so boring! Since she got home she's not stopped studying, and I've been trying to talk to her about this girl I'm in class with, and she's totally ignoring me."

Katie quickly replied, "Mark is in love with Savannah! But he's dreaming if he thinks he's got a shot at the most popular girl in school."

"I'm not in love, jerk," Mark said. "You only say that because she's too cool to talk to a book nerd like you."

"Maybe, but for your information, she told me that right now the only thing on her mind is getting good grades. She wants to go to the USC School of Cinematic Arts in Los Angeles, and only three percent of applicants get accepted, so she must get better than 4.0."

Elizabeth, exasperated with the bickering, said, "Okay, if you guys don't stop this childish behavior, I will…" she was interrupted by the short, high-pitched sound the front door alarm.

"Dad's home," yelled Katie, with a big smile.

Lorenzo Suarez walked in, wearing a well-fitted striped blue suit and solid honey-color tie. He was average height, very fit, and youthful for an attractive man in his late forties, with sharp features, dark skin, dark eyes, and a full head of hair. "I'm starving," he said, loosening his tie, and with an obviously tired look in his eyes.

He entered the kitchen, saw Elizabeth, and his eyes twinkled. She was a vision, still dressed in her navy-blue business suit skirt. Elizabeth was tall and with heels she was statuesque. Long, thick, wavy dark hair, light-brown almond eyes, and in her early forties, Elizabeth looked ten years younger. She was a stunning woman and Lorenzo felt very lucky. "Honey, you look amazing," he said.

Elizabeth looked at him and with a semi-tired tone said, "Thanks, Hon," and then with a commanding tone said, "Everyone! Let's go to the table and let's start eating, or this food will get cold."

Lorenzo, Mark, and Katie quickly prepared the table in the usual formal style, the way Lorenzo liked it. As usual, the food was delivered, from one of the local restaurants. Lorenzo had tried to retain the tradition of the fine Mexican families—to eat at a "properly set up" main dining table and have stimulating conversation. As the kids were growing up, this was becoming increasingly more difficult. Mark was especially resistant.

"Mark, how are you doing on your finals?" asked Lorenzo.

"Dad, can we just eat in silence for once?"

"I just want to know how you're doing. It's not about your grades." Lorenzo knew Mark was struggling with his grades. "Don't get so defensive, my son," said Lorenzo in a kind voice. "And you, Katie?"

"Dad, I had an awful day. Mallory was giving me such a hard time about the project I told you about. She just wants to chat about boys and wants me to do all the work, and on top of that she made fun of me and called me boring."

Lorenzo repeated one of his usual pep talk speeches. "I'm so proud of your drive to do well in school, my daughter. You know we Suarezes have been overachievers for generations. You cannot allow other people's laziness to affect your future. You come from a long line of hardworking, educated people in Mexico, who were dedicated to helping others. You have a responsibility to give back, as you have been given much."

"Daaad, now you're stressing me out even more," said Katie.

Visibly upset, Elizabeth said, "Lorenzo, quit putting so much pressure on your poor daughter, and don't start with your old Mexican ancestor stories."

Lorenzo loved Elizabeth dearly and wanted peace at home, so he happily obliged.

Elizabeth was of Mexican ancestry as well, but she was not attached to her Mexican roots. In fact, she never said she was Mexican to anyone. She was light-skinned and didn't look like the stereotypical Mexican; people assumed she could be any beautiful American mixture. When anyone asked, "What is your ancestry?" She would reply, "I'm several generations American, a mixture of Hispanic, and a little Spanish."

She felt saying "Mexican" would diminish her value. Her mom raised her to assimilate and to be an American. Her mother's parents and grandparents had been born in Arizona, and her dad was from a small town in Zacatecas.

Elizabeth's mom, Maria, was a third-generation Mexican and her family was not very cultured or educated. Maria grew up surrounded by stories of how Mexicans in Phoenix had never been allowed to have the good jobs, how it was virtually impossible for any Mexican to be accepted at a higher learning institution, and of the humiliation and abuse by older generations of Anglo-Americans.

Maria was very light-skinned and could have easily passed for white. She grew up in the Ponderosa neighborhood of Phoenix with a mostly Mexican population. Her parents and grandparents told Maria that Mexicans were not allowed to live anywhere else. The Phoenix city leaders did not want to spend any money improving the Mexican neighborhoods, so the streets were rundown, and crime was allowed to grow.

White neighborhoods had the idea that if they allowed Mexicans in, the community would lose value, and residents would never sell to a Mexican. Since the 1880s, when Phoenix was established, and for the next ninety years, Mexicans were segregated from whites and trained by the police and authorities to stay in their neighborhoods.

Just when the segregation was loosening for the Mexicans, Sheriff Joe Arpaio decided to boost his career by energizing people against Mexican immigrants. He used his police to do immigrant roundup by racially profiling Mexicans, mixing legal and illegal immigrants and even American-born Mexicans. Once more, Mexicans started to feel the need to segregate and stay in their neighborhoods, which was the safest place to be.

When Mexicans with money wanted to move to a better neighborhood, they had to hide their Mexican ancestry. As long as they said they were Spanish, Cuban, Chilean, or Turkish (anything but Mexican), no one seemed to have a problem. It is easy to understand why, during this time, Mexican-Americans were embarrassed and afraid to use "Mexican" as their ancestry, and started to come up with alternative names—Chicano, Latino, Hispanic, anything but Mexican.

Maria was surrounded by mostly Mexican people, some newcomer Mexican immigrants, and some Mexicans who traced their ancestry to when the land was still part of Mexico. Although Maria was born in the US, she spoke with a Ponderosa/Mexican barrio accent. Maria looked down on newly immigrated Mexicans and avoided speaking Spanish with them. In fact, if anyone talked to her in Spanish, she took it as an offense and would say, "I don't speak Spanish," even though she could speak a poor and uneducated version of Spanish.

Barely finishing high school, but because she was pretty and light- skinned, Maria was able to get a job on the white side of town, as a mail clerk at a large law firm. Making a couple of dollars above minimum wage made her feel proud. The first few years at the law firm were hard. She was regularly made fun of by her coworkers because she had a ghetto accent from La Ponderosa. They called her "Beaner," and spoke in distorted Spanish to bother her.

When she didn't hear something clearly, they would say, "No comprende?" (Don't you understand?) and when there was misunderstanding, they would say, "Tu no habla Ingles?" (Don't you speak English?). Finally, she cleaned up her accent and decided to never tell any new co-workers she was Mexican. She understood that the prejudice she suffered was not about the color of her skin, but about the fact that she was Mexican. Maria wished one day she could be seen as just an American. She felt the only way for a Mexican to have equality and value was to just be considered American.

At nineteen, she met Manuel, who was a tall, handsome Mexican newcomer immigrant—older than she was. Maria fell in love with him because he had better manners than the guys from the barrio, he was an honest man, and he had a stable job. They soon married, and Elizabeth was born.

Manuel had been a farmer in Zacatecas. When he arrived in the US, a cousin got him a job as a dishwasher at an Italian restaurant. With hard work, Manuel moved up and became a cook's helper. With time, hard work, and a natural talent for cooking, he moved up the ladder to become cook's help supervisor.

Unknown to him, his hard work and stability were instrumental to the success of the restaurant. Over the thirty years he worked there and ran the kitchen, the restaurant grew and grew. He was never the head chef, even though he was a better cook than any of the chefs hired over the years, whose names honored the menus. Manuel was always the Mexican cook hiding in the kitchen.

Manuel wanted to take Elizabeth to Mexico more often, but her mother, Maria, didn't really like Mexico. Elizabeth visited Mexico twice, once when she was five and again when she was thirteen. She fondly remembered her first visit when she met her sizeable Mexican family, who were so friendly. She loved the farm with beautiful horses, cows, chickens, and eating a lot of delicious food!

Unfortunately, her second visit did not leave good memories. She remembered the trip being long. She had to fly to Mexico City first, then take a different airplane to Zacatecas, the capital, and then get into Uncle Juan's van for the drive to the rancheria, a small ranch, close to Santiaguillo. While driving out of the city, she could see that Zacatecas City was a beautiful town; it looked ancient, with large Mexican-style buildings. She would have preferred to stay there in the city and explore the old narrow cobblestone streets, but they had no time; the family was waiting.

It was an uncomfortably long and bumpy drive. Once the family arrived at the rancheria, the smells were not as pleasant as she remembered. The smell of horse and cow manure was strong and offensive to her city-girl nose. Then the chickens ran around her and she became frightened, making everyone laugh. For some reason, on this visit, her family looked dirty. She noticed their teeth were yellow with black holes and many were missing..

She wasn't comfortable, so she stayed in her room, reading. During the family visits, everyone was chatting, laughing and seemingly having a great time, especially her dad. Manuel was so happy to see his family that he could not stop talking very fast in Spanish with his mom and siblings. But since Elizabeth didn't speak good Spanish, she couldn't follow the conversation. Elizabeth could see that her mom wasn't having a good time either, so it was easy for her to hate this visit. From that time on, every time she thought of Mexico, memories of bad smells, dirty streets, and chickens running around came to her mind.

Maria named her Elizabeth because she didn't want a Mexican name for her daughter. In many different ways Maria taught Elizabeth to conceal that she was Mexican and to assimilate. Elizabeth grew up in a stable home; Manuel and Maria had the same jobs until they retired. While neither side of the family had any member who received higher education, Maria had always been very impressed with the lawyers in the firm she worked for, and she told Elizabeth that her biggest dream was for her daughter to become a lawyer. With her mom and dad's hardworking habits, Elizabeth got scholarships and made her parents proud by graduating with a law degree from Arizona State University.

And then she met Lorenzo and her life and family grew.

CHAPTER FOUR

THE CANDIDATE

When school closed for summer, Katie enrolled in a math camp because she wanted to keep her 4.0 average, which she was barely able to make. Math was her hardest class, especially all of it in chemistry, and she was convinced she needed straight As.

On the other hand, Mark's grades were less than stellar, but he escaped math camp, or any scholastic summer camp, by telling Elizabeth that his football coach insisted that all varsity team members had to attend a summer football camp, which was starting late in the summer. Lorenzo did not agree with Mark wasting half of the summer playing sports with his friends all day, but Elizabeth overruled Lorenzo's opinion this time.

Mark was Elizabeth's favorite, and it showed in subtle and sometimes not-so-subtle ways. Her attention made Mark feel he was special and he developed a sense of entitlement. When Mark was born, everyone always said he was "such a pretty little boy." He had light skin like Elizabeth. Being the oldest, being a boy, and having looks similar to hers, Mark was always told by Elizabeth that he would grow up to do great things.

Mark and Katie fought, as siblings do. Mark liked to call her "Browny" because her skin was darker than his, and "nerd" because of her smarts. Mark enjoyed throwing objects at her when she studied. She would yell and accuse him, but when he wouldn't stop, and Katie was fed up, she would attack him and punch him with ferocity. Their wrestling matches wouldn't last long, because although Mark was much bigger, Katie was fierce and Mark would have to give up and let her win. Lorenzo's lessons on how to treat a woman were deep inside Mark, and he would never punch or hurt his sister. Tease her, yes, but never hurt her.

Mark rarely helped with chores at home, so when Katie was asked to do the dishes, she would complain that Mark was not helping and claiming it wasn't fair.

Elizabeth would just say, "Well, he is a boy."

Lorenzo, on the other hand, did not believe in parents who showed favoritism to their children and argued with Elizabeth when she showed preference to Mark.

Mark and Katie were fortunate to be born into a family of successful, loving parents, who loved their kids very much, maybe over-indulged them. Because Mark never had to work hard for anything, he assumed the rest of the world had it easy as well.

That evening they had a lovely dinner delivered by Enzzo's a local Italian restaurant. They all loved the delicious breadsticks and the chicken fettuccini Alfredo with extra Parmigiana cheese. The meal put everyone in a great mood, so the conversation at the dinner table was comfortable, light, and fun.

After dinner, they sat in front of the TV watching the presidential campaign, which was heating up. Lorenzo was very interested in it, but no one else wanted to hear about it. He convinced the family to watch the news with him by promising that after ten minutes, they would watch Game of Thrones together. It was June 2015. Donald Trump had declared as a candidate by identifying Mexicans as a national problem, contending that, "Mexicans… are bringing drugs, are bringing crime and some, I assume, are good people."

An awkward silence filled the room as the family watched. Lorenzo muted the TV and was ready to say something when Elizabeth burst out and said, "I agree. I have to deal with those dirty Mexican criminals. They need to do something about that border." After she said that, she turned to see Lorenzo's response, and noticed his eyes were full of indignation.

"Elizabeth, how can you say such a thing? I'm Mexican. Does that mean I'm a rapist? This man is humiliating an entire nation of people, and you and your children are Mexican as well."

Seeing how her husband felt humiliated by Trump's words, Elizabeth responded much more cautiously this time. "What I mean is that the newer Mexican immigrants, mostly illegal, are bringing crime, and some of them even have ties to the cartels. I'm sure Trump didn't mean all Mexicans." She looked at her kids and said, "And we are not Mexican. We are American."

"Sorry, Honey, but we are all Mexican-Americans. He is offending all of us. And you know as well as I do that the vast majority of Mexican immigrants are hardworking, honest people."

Katie jumped in. "Yes, Dad, but how can he dare say such a thing about the Mexican people on national TV? I'm sure he is going to get in a lot of trouble. Can you imagine if he said such a thing about other people, like Jews or African Americans?"

Mark rolled his eyes. "Dad, you're overreacting. Plus, I agree with Mom, we are not Mexican, we are American. And you are an American citizen too. He's just talking about the illegal Mexican immigrants."

"My son, I don't think you fully get the gravity of these statements," said Lorenzo. "First of all, we are Mexicans, and you are a Mexican-American, not just American. Like Americans of Jewish descent who call themselves Jewish, and Americans of Italian descent call themselves Italian, and Americans of Irish descent call themselves Irish. This is a nation of immigrants, we all have culture and traditions, which give us identity and give us pride and understanding of our heritage. We are Mexican, and we can't escape it.

"Trump is trying to make Mexicans responsible for many of the bad things America is suffering. He's making us scapegoats, and by encouraging dislike for Mexicans, he is destroying our reputation and making us feel ashamed of being Mexican. Statements labeling people like this cause irreversible damage in people's minds. It makes people who previously would not say racist things to now think and say racist things, assuming it is okay since Mr. Trump said them on national TV. The damage is greater on young minds, and it has the potential to damage a generation of young Mexican-Americans' self-worth, drastically decreasing their chances of future success."

While Lorenzo spoke, Elizabeth and Mark gave each other looks of disagreement, and then Elizabeth interjected, "Lorenzo, I agree with Mark. You're getting upset over nothing and making way too much out of this, and getting the children upset for nothing. Anyway, Trump will never win the election, and no one will ever take him seriously. Of course, he does not speak for the majority of people. I am sure there will be a good-sized outcry about his remarks tomorrow. He'll apologize, and it will be over with."

They sat in silence for a few moments, and then Katie said, "Should I start Game of Thrones?"

Tomorrow came, and the racist remarks were reported with mild denunciation. Few in the Mexican-American community reacted, and there was no unified outcry. Instead, the national news outlets pondered if this statement about Mexicans bringing more crime had any validity, sharing available research. The numbers showed that Mr. Trump's speech had no merit and Mexican's propensity to crime did not differ much from the general population. The figures also showed that Mexican immigrants had minimal effect on the economy, and, if any, it was a positive one.

Mr. Trump never received enough pressure to apologize for the grave offense shown to the millions of Mexican-Americans. Instead, he insisted his statements were correct, always refusing to show any proof. His direct attacks upon Mexicans continued, which finally pushed some Mexican groups to threaten to boycott the products endorsing Trump's brands, which led to many of Trump's brand vendors like Macy's to stop selling his products. Because the pressure was halfhearted, the boycott was very short- lived and had little effect. Trump continued his campaign vilifying Mexicans.

Lorenzo watched the news and observed more abusive talk about Mexicans from candidate Trump, and soon other politicians who originally denounced him were now joining in his rhetoric attacks. Lorenzo talked with his family with concern about this subject during dinner, and Katie echoed her dad's concern. Elizabeth and Mark stayed out of the discussion; they were convinced this had nothing to do with them, and it would not affect them.

CHAPTER FIVE

OPERATION ALAMO

Unbeknownst to the Suarez family, an event in Trump Tower had taken place almost a year prior that would profoundly affect their future, and the fate of millions. The most brilliant strategists from Trump Corporation had arrived at an important meeting. They were being escorted into two large private elevators decorated with floor-to-ceiling mirrors divided by gold frames, with classical music playing in the background.

The guests walked out of the elevator into a long hall with white Italian marble floors and a long, red silk carpet runner in the middle of the hallway. The walls had carved wood paneling, and on each panel hung fine examples of American and European paintings, ranging from French Impressionist to cubist and abstract. Spaced throughout the hallway were bronze sculptures on pedestals. Each piece had special lighting to accentuate its beauty. This very long hall was intentionally designed to intimidate and demand admiration and respect.

Two beautiful assistants welcomed each participant with their choice of cappuccino, coffee, or tea from around the world, all served in fine china with the Trump corporate seal.

The boardroom was unusually large, the carpet was red, and the entrance had the name "Trump" in gold letters. The board table was solid African blackwood with integrated monitors at each station, as well as connections for laptops, translation earphones, and other audio/visual needs. Each board chair was made from Napa leather. Donald Trump's chair was at the head of the board table and was specially designed with the Trump Enterprises logo in gold embroidery.

Trump surrounded himself with people who knew that to work for Trump Corporation meant getting results or getting fired in the most embarrassing way possible, just like the TV show. In this business, failure is not an option; "the end justifies the means." The methods used to make money or succeed on the deal were not of great importance; they never discuss collateral damage.

Machiavelli would be proud of this group.

The meeting took place early in the presidential campaign when the numbers were low, and the more qualified and experienced presidential candidates mocked and underestimated the viability of Mr. Trump. This was a time when Mr. Trump's closest advisors scrambled to find ways to make a multimillionaire from New York, who shared nothing in common with the American Republican base, be someone who people would identify with and want to vote for.

This was no small feat. With all the Trump Corporation might, public relations, and marketing research experience, they chose the old, tried and true tactics of finding a common enemy that Trump could identify, one which the base already feared and also disliked. Thus, his followers would see they had common enemies, concerns, and interests with Trump. The gathered team was now scrambling to identify one or multiple "common enemies" to center the campaign around.

Donald Trump was not present at the meeting. Warren Parker, one of Trump's most trusted employees and the guru of marketing and public relations for the Trump Corporation, was entirely in charge of the meeting and its strategies.

"Let me make this absolutely clear," Parker said. "You're here because you are the brightest business, marketing, public relations, and political minds in our company, and we're not leaving this room today until we fine tune this strategy. Also, let me remind you this is an ultra-private meeting. Each one of you has signed confidentiality agreements, which means if anything leaks out, there will be hell to pay for you.

"You all understand and have been briefed that at this point our polls show that to energize our base and build a bond between Mr. Trump and the average Republican voter, we must find hated common enemies. This is a tactic our research shows will work well. Our research points to some groups, which are already disliked by our target base. Our strategy is to have Mr. Trump share his intense dislike of these 'bad people' who are hurting America, and this will demonstrate to the voter how Mr. Trump shares common values.

"We must find a perfect villain or make them look really evil, because crowds really like to hate a nasty enemy," Parker continued, "Ideally, this enemy should be different from us, but be among us, someone who our political enemies have ignored and allowed to grow, and who are believed to be causing harm to society. Mr. Trump will become the only candidate who has the guts to identify and protect America from this enemy."

Using polling and focus groups, the team had developed a list of possible villains, with enemy nations at the top of the list: North Korea, Iran, and China. Those were easy but dangerous targets, and leaning too hard on them could cause an international crisis that at this early stage of the campaign could spell disaster. The decision was to use these foreign enemies for softer attacks, as they would do well as secondary targets, especially on defense and economic topics. They would come in handy any time some media attention might be needed for the Trump campaign. But all agreed these nations would not be their primary "common enemy."

The discussion started with the very vocal group, "Black Lives Matter," which had caused a lot of commotion and infuriated some pro-law enforcement groups, which were part of the target base. It was deemed that leaning hard on this group was extremely dangerous because, in this day and age, no one wanted to look like a racist against the African-Americans. Such accusations could lead to political disaster and an early exit from the race.

Muslim immigration was an intensely debated subject, and there is, undoubtedly, deep resentment held by Americans who thought their way of life had changed because of radical Muslims. But Muslim groups are influential and can be very vocal when threatened. This was a tinderbox, and Trump's advisors argued against leaning on the Muslims too hard—nevertheless they were deemed a great secondary target, and Michael Moon, an expert in Islamic studies, was placed in charge of developing a solid campaign.

Donald Trump himself couldn't care less who would become the common enemy or scapegoat. He felt far superior to the rest of the world, and apart from him and his family, everyone was inferior and disposable. Like his books, The Art of the Deal, Think Big and Kick Ass, and others showed, Trump doesn't really like or dislike anyone, it is more in terms of, are they useful.

Conveniently, he admired and praised people who could serve his purpose or serve him well, but once they were of no use to him, he gladly said, "You're fired." An important strategy shared in his books was that, if anyone got in his way, he liked to use a big show of force, a big lawsuit, and offensive language to put those losers in their place. Trump wanted people to fear him and know he held grudges.

In their methodic planning, his advisors went down the list of "common enemy" prospects and finally arrived at the Mexicans. They made no effort to make distinctions between "legal Mexican Immigrants" or "illegal Mexican immigrants." A shrewd Trump advisor was quick to point out the fact that there were a lot of Mexicans and Mexican-Americans in the US and the Hispanic vote was becoming increasingly important. Offending Hispanic voters might hinder their chances in some primaries and certainly in general.

Another advisor who was well-informed on the Mexican immigration problem told the group there was definite discontent amongst the suburban Republican base about Mexican immigration. Numerous research studies showed legal and illegal Mexican immigration had little to no real consequence on the economy or on crime. If they used the Mexicans as the "common enemy," opposing candidates could quickly point to the lack of evidence, and it could backfire.

The group agreed to use the Mexicans as another secondary soft target. Then a voice was heard—Jerry Valenti, one of Parker's newest protégés, eager to impress the boss, jumped into the conversation. Jerry was an impressive and handsome young man who always wore Italian designer suits. He was a young, Dean Martin lookalike. With an international business degree from Columbia University where he majored in Latin American studies, he spoke with excellent knowledge on the subject.

"Boss," Valenti said, "I think this might be the ideal target and the perfect common enemy we are looking for, and that we can safely make them the center of our attacks. First of all, while it's true the real numbers show unimportant consequences from Mexican immigration on crime and the economy, this is our advantage."

"How can that be an advantage?" asked Parker.

"Look, all of the other candidates always talk about the Mexican immigrants as a minor problem, and they are soft on them. It'll be our advantage if we identify them as a major problem. The others will have to scramble to agree or disagree and we will become the leaders on the issue. A lot of people see them as a problem and don't like them, especially in the South and Southwest states where there has been a lot of Mexican migration. And many of our target base states are in that area."

"Hmm," said Parker, "I'm afraid that we may alienate the Hispanic voters."

Valenti continued. "With the proper strategy and careful manipulation of the facts, they will be the perfect scapegoats. I'm sure it won't take too much to make the Mexicans responsible for the drug problem, increased crime, welfare abuse, unemployment, and every other vile thing happening to our country. You could use a symbol like "Let's build a wall to keep them out" because, as you know, symbolism is significant."

Jerry Valenti looked around and saw most people silently nodding in agreement. His conviction grew stronger, and he burst forth, "Hispanics are divided into Cubans, Puerto Ricans, Dominicans, and other Hispanics who have different concerns than Mexicans. Central and South American Hispanics who recently immigrated to America prefer not to be confused with Mexicans because of the negative historical connotation so Mexicans can be isolated easily."

"What do you mean, 'isolate'?" asked Parker.

Valenti looked at Parker for approval and said, "It's essential to isolate and vilify the Mexicans. We must be cautious to exclude the rest of the Hispanic community and only make references about the Mexicans. That way, the rest of the Hispanic population won't feel affected." Valenti was on a roll and could see his boss, Parker, smiling in approval at his pupil's machinations.

"Mexicans themselves are divided. The wealthy and successful Mexicans blend into the US quickly and prefer to not to be associated with the peasant Mexicans. The Mexicans born in the US and the mixed Mexicans distance themselves from the "newcomer Mexican immigrants" and don't want to be called Mexicans, because of the negative connotation, choosing to be called Chicanos, Latinos, or Hispanic, or just American. Many will feel that attacks on Mexicans do not affect them. They have no unified front, so they are weak."

Valenti knew this subject thoroughly and continued his explanation with a confident and sinister smile. "And one more thing. If you look at history, like after the Mexican-American War, when you attack Mexicans, they will double down. They were abused so badly by the Spaniards, it's in their nature to retreat and accept their fate. They're generally a peaceful people. Boss," he said with a smile, "you can lean as hard as you want. This is your best bet. Make them the common enemy. It will be very successful."

Parker and the team were satisfied. Jerry Valenti was placed in charge of this vital project. He was given one week to develop and start implementation of this strategy, which he code-named Operation Alamo in reference to the famous Texans' battle cry against the Mexicans. Valenti was determined to impress his boss, so he worked day and night and reread his schoolbooks and history books related to how Mexicans have been dealt with after the US took over Mexican land. He was diligent, smart, and thought of everything.

As the man in charge of Operation Alamo, Valenti supervised everything that could be even remotely related to the project, including any section of Mr. Trump's speeches which referenced Operation Alamo. He would research and scout parts of the country he deemed vulnerable and then deploy his propaganda. He would use friendly reporters to publish articles suggesting a dramatic increase in crime and drug abuse attributable to the Mexican immigrants. This started the spread of rumors and energized people against the Mexicans immigrants.

Valenti's ideal scenario was when a Mexican committed a crime around a target area. He disseminated this information to the press and over social media to show how "these bad people" were damaging the American way of life. Once he primed the towns, he had Mr. Trump go to the city and get people fired up. It worked so well that people started loving Trump because he understood the "problem."

The more Jerry Valenti and his team were able to get people to hate Mexicans, the more people started to believe in Mr. Trump because he had the correct values and was the man trying to save American from these evil people. Valenti also looked for like-minded, influential people, who had already shown animosity against Mexican immigrants, or people who used Mexicans as scapegoats to further their careers. When Jerry found Sheriff Arpaio in Arizona, he felt he had won the lottery. Operation Alamo was a huge success, and Parker was pleased with Jerry Valenti.

Valenti was relentless. Operation Alamo had to be spread all over the country, even in states where Mexican immigration was not a problem. Valenti had his team comb the news for excellent opportunities, and if they found a crime committed by a Mexican in any town, they would deploy Operation Alamo in that town. They leaked information to friendly reporters and became very good at stirring hate and distrust.

A few months into the Alamo project, one of Valenti's subordinates, Moses Stone, heard of an armed robbery committed by an illegal Mexican teenager, Ramiro Dorado, in Mississippi. Moses leaked damaging information acquired by the local police to the news and infiltrated the local neighborhood watch groups to make everyone aware of this and other crimes committed by

Mexicans. He was successful in getting the town up in arms.

Valenti then organized a rally for candidate Trump, which had massive attendance and emotional calls for action. Valenti called the local sheriff a hero and encouraged him to be more vigilant about removing the dangerous Mexican criminals from the streets. A few weeks later, Moses found out that Ramiro Dorado had been accidentally confused with someone else and wrongfully accused. Young Ramiro was, in fact, a good, churchgoing kid with an impeccable reputation and was college-bound. With a lot of hard work, his parents had helped his older sister Dolores get into college.

The sheriff had known this for quite a while, but the glare of the spotlight and adulation clouded his reason, and he decided to hold on to the information as long as possible. Unfortunately for Ramiro and his family, the sheriff waited until things calmed down to clear Ramiro of the crime due to lack of evidence and released him to ICE, who quickly deported him. This devastated Ramiro's family and split them in half. It forced Ramiro's mother to move back to Mexico with her son and leave the rest of the broken-hearted family behind.

Moses approached Valenti and confessed his feelings of guilt for his involvement. He'd started to realize that this clever Operation Alamo had collateral damage and destroyed people's lives. Jerry Valenti became a beast, and his eyes were red with fury. "You're just a pussy and a classless professional," he bellowed at Moses and fired him, but not before threatening to destroy Moses's career and life if he ever talked about Alamo to anyone. Moses was scared and could tell Valenti was serious about his threats.

CHAPTER SIX
LA PONDEROSA

Mallory Ochoa's mom, Soco, was twenty-one when Miguel, her husband of two years, said, "Let's move to the United States. My cousin Jacinto told me he has a job for me doing gardening, and I will make ten times more money than I make here as a teacher." Jacinto failed to mention to Miguel that the cost of living was eight times larger than in Tepatitlan. Jacinto and Miguel were cousins who grew up together. They loved each other like brothers, and they missed each other. Miguel recounted to Soco all the fantastic stories Jacinto, who had moved to the US five years before, had told him.

Miguel tried to convince Soco to move and spoke of the subject with great excitement. "Mi amor, Jacinto told me that he drives an almost brand-new Ford Thunderbird and you know how much I love that car. He has an apartment with a dishwasher and all the latest house appliances, and money to go to the movies every weekend. Doesn't that sound like a great life?"

"But Miguel, I just finished my school teaching program, and I was so looking forward to starting teaching. Plus, Miguel, Cindy is just a one-year-old baby. I think we are okay here."

Soco and Miguel lived in Tepatitlan, Jalisco, in central Mexico, and it was rural and beautiful. Cobblestone streets, green rolling hills, beautiful and colorful small homes; it was the quintessential Mexican small town. While most people were not wealthy there, they worked hard and made ends meet. The small-town people were kind and hospitable, the food delicious, and every Sunday the beautiful town square with its vast colonial church on one side and city hall on the other lit up with music, celebration, and dancing.

The young men strutted around wearing their cowboy hats, while the women wore their Sunday dresses and promenaded around the large colonial iron kiosk or pavilion. The town followed a tradition that went back centuries: if a young man likes a girl, he will buy a red rose from the flower lady and bring it to the young lady, and if she likes him, she will accept it. Life in Tepatitlan was simple but good.

Miguel was relentless in his effort to convince Soco. "But think about it, so many of our relatives have moved to the US. They all talk about how they are living the American Dream. Plus, we will have so much family there, we will not be alone."

Soco loved Miguel and trusted him. She knew he was a good man and he would protect her, so without fully considering it, she accepted. He moved first, with the plan to have everything prepared for the arrival of Soco and Cindy. Miguel's first attempt to cross the border failed, but the second time he made it. Miguel did not tell Soco the horrors of the border crossing with the help of the coyotes, the human smugglers, who treat their cargo like animals. That experience would haunt Miguel, and later the same experience would haunt Soco, for many years.

After a year apart, Soco was happy to be reunited with Miguel in Phoenix, where he had rented a tiny apartment in La Ponderosa. Soco was ready to enjoy the American dream Miguel and Jacinto had promised. Her dreams were soon shattered.

Life for people living in La Ponderosa was very different than life in Paradise Valley. The residents of La Ponderosa were ninety-eight percent Mexican, and Soco was surprised to see all the signs in Spanish. On her second day at La Ponderosa, she went grocery shopping and saw on the street several unusual looking men with crew cuts, wearing long white stockings, long black shorts, and bandanas. She thought it was some sort of funny costume for a party.

Naïve, she asked one of the men, "Para que es el disfras?" (What are you wearing a costume for?")

The man, a cholo, responded with an intense, menacing voice, saying in broken Spanish, "Estupida, callate o te va ha ir mal" ("Don't be stupid, shut up, or you will regret it.")

Soco was shocked and scared and went straight home. She did not buy groceries that day. When Miguel arrived back from work that night, she told him what had happened

"Oh my god, those men are very dangerous. They are gang members, cholos, and you must avoid them at all cost." That made Soco even more scared.

Soco would live scared at La Ponderosa for the rest of her life. La Ponderosa was a dangerous neighborhood, and neither the authorities nor the police seemed to care what happened there. Roads were rundown, traffic signals and most walls were covered with some sort of graffiti, and street cleaning trucks never went to La Ponderosa.

The following day, Soco struck up a conversation with Helen, a kind neighbor who spoke broken Spanish. She looked about seventy years old and said she was born in Phoenix. Knowing Helen was a local, and hoping she would have some experience, Soco asked Helen if she had some advice as to how to use her teaching credential to become a teacher.

"Honey, don't waste your time. Your credentials are useless here, and even if you have a credential, they'll never give you a job. If you have a Mexican accent, they won't give you a good job in Phoenix."

Soco's throat tightened when she heard that, and asked Helen, "Who are 'they'? Why they don't like us?" Soco was a smart and attractive young woman, and in Mexico, she would have had her pick of teaching jobs. Her two older sisters were excellent teachers, and she was confident that she would be a fantastic teacher. When Soco moved to the US, she assumed she would take a test and get a teaching credential.

Helen was a Mexican-American woman who was raised during times of severe segregation and repression against Mexicans in Arizona. Her life experiences had forged a second-class-citizen mentality, and she was pessimistic about the idea of life improving for Mexicans. The concept of moving up or improving was foreign in her mind. Helen was surprised Soco even asked, with such a pessimistic environment in Mexican-American neighborhoods, she was used to Mexican immigrants solely taking laborer jobs.

"Look, dear, it's better to not even try. You'll be disappointed. When I was young, I tried to apply to nursing school, but they wouldn't allow me to go, so I got a job in a soap factory and worked there for all my life. After the civil rights movement things were slowly getting better for Mexicans here, but then Arpaio showed up, and his campaign against Mexicans has been making things more difficult for us."

That night, tears streamed down Soco's face as she recounted to Miguel her conversation with the older lady. "Is it true that Americans don't want us here and I won't be able to become a teacher?"

Miguel was broken-hearted from what he had learned over the past few months living in Phoenix, and he did not want to tell Soco. "Mi amor, Americans really don't like it when we speak Spanish in front of them. Since I arrived here, I have been yelled at a couple of times for not being able to speak English clearly. Jacinto has learned English, so he talks to the clients, and I just smile. And we just don't talk when people are around, so they don't get upset with us."

Miguel's voice broke. "Look, mi amor, Jacinto said that as long as we stay in the Mexican neighborhoods like La Ponderosa, we are fine and no one will bother us."

"So, we cannot go anywhere else?" asked Soco.

By now, Miguel's spirit had started to break. He had been a spirited young man, attractive and prideful, but the moment he crossed the border, cramped like an animal into a truck, his self-worth diminished. Once he arrived, he was told by all of his Mexican acquaintances that Mexicans were unwanted in the country, and to stay away from the white neighborhoods, except for work.

On one occasion, he decided to go explore the other side of town and go shopping for new jeans he needed. He ventured to the Phoenix Fashion Mall. Walking around the mall, Miguel saw lovely, beautiful, clean shops and the smell of perfume was everywhere. It did not look like the stores at La Ponderosa. He wore his faded Mexican clothes and knew little English. At every place he stopped to ask a question, or tried to shop, he could see people looking down on him, ignoring him, impatient with his inability to speak clearly, and more than once he was rudely asked to move out of the way.

"So, we cannot go anywhere else?" Soco asked again,

"Mi amor, why would we want to go to the Anglo side anyway? We don't speak English, and they don't like us on that side. We have everything here in La Ponderosa, and there are many other Mexican neighborhoods we can visit."

Miguel could see the anguish on Soco's face and it reminded him of how he felt the first few months after he arrived. Then, to change the direction of the conversation, he said, "Mi amor, I have great news! My aunt Dolores is having a party this weekend and she invited us. There, we will reconnect with so many of our family and friends from Tepatitlan. It will be a beautiful reunion."

Soco's face showed a faint smile. "That sounds good, honey. Thank you for working so hard to give us a better life."

Miguel tried hard to paint their situation as rosy, but he started to question his decision of moving his family to this country. But it was too late. They had made this huge journey and sold everything—going back was not an option.

The party took place in another Mexican neighborhood, Buckeye, at Aunt Margarita's home. It felt like a party that would take place at Tepatitlan because of the mariachi music, the delicious Jalisco delicacies like carne en su jugo and birria, and the colorful table adorned with small piñatas and traditional fruits. Soco had a lovely time reconnecting with friends and family she had not seen in years.

Soco saw her cousin Lucero who she had not seen in ten years. Lucero was older than Soco and had moved to the US many years before. Lucero had been La Reyna de Tepatitlan, the beauty queen of her town. She had moved to Phoenix with her husband Eugenio, and Soco had not heard much about them in a long time, other than the usual lies Mexicans tell their relatives back home to not lose face, like, "We are doing great and we have so many things here."

Soco approached Lucero. "My god, Lucero, you look great. Still the beauty queen."

Lucero was flattered, as she had gained quite a bit of weight and did not feel attractive anymore. "Soco, wow, you have grown, and you are quite the looker yourself, just like your mom."

Lucero grabbed Soco's hands and raised them to expose Soco's lovely figure. "I'm so happy to see you here."

"Yes, I am happy to reunite with so many loved ones, but I have to tell you, there are so many things I'm finding out, which I didn't know before we moved here. I never knew Mexicans were so unwanted in Phoenix. Are you happy here?"

"Honey, you get used to it. We learn to live separate from them. I rarely go to the Anglo side."

While Lucero spoke, her nine-year-old son walked up and hugged her. Lucero hugged him back. "David, this is your Auntie Soco, from Tepatitlan. Say 'hello.'"

David was shy and only smiled. "Okay now, go play with your friends," Lucero said, and he walked away.

Soco was horrified when she saw David had a crew cut and white stockings with long shorts. She could not believe it. Without thinking, she whispered, "Lucero, aren't you afraid people will think David is a cholo?"

"This is how kids want to dress these days. I don't like it, but he really wants to dress like his older brother Eugenio Jr. He's his hero." Lucero's eyes filled with tears. "That Jr. is giving me such headaches—he is only fifteen and he has gotten in trouble with the law already. I don't know what to do."

"Pues que Eugenio le da sus riatasos. " (Then Eugenio should give him a whipping) like our parents used to do to us when we misbehaved," said Soco.

"No, you can't do that here. If you discipline them, even a little spanking, the neighbors will call the police on you."

Lucero's body got stiff, her eyes swelled. "Last week, I got distraught with Eugenio Jr., and I was trying to pull his stupid oversized flannel shirt off, and he told me, 'Mom, if you pull my shirt again, I will call the police on you, and they'll deport you.'"

"It breaks my heart that my son feels that being an American citizen gives him special powers over his own immigrant mother," Lucero cried.

Soco's mouth dropped open, and she didn't say any more about the subject out loud but thought that she would never allow this to happen to her kids. Only a few years later, David would be shot and killed by a gangster's bullet.

Soco saw Miguel from afar and caught up with him. "Hi, my love." Miguel was already drunk and hugged and kissed her. Soco had been looking forward to seeing her other cousin Camila, but she was not there. "Miguel, do you know why Camila and her husband, Benito, are not here?"

Miguel did not think before he answered and blurted out, "Benito got deported last week."

Soco's eye widened and Miguel knew he had made a big blunder. "Why didn't you tell me?"

"Mi amor, I just didn't want to stress you more. I knew you were having such a hard time with this transition, I didn't want to add one more thing."

"What happened?"

"This man, Sheriff Arpaio, has directed his police force to stop any person who looks Mexican and ask for their papers, especially if they are in the white neighborhoods. Benito was doing his gardening job and used the leaf blower in a white neighborhood. One of the neighbors got upset because of the noise and called the police. When the police arrived, they asked Benito for his papers, and he didn't have them, so they took him to jail. From there, they quickly deported him. But don't worry, honey, he will be back soon."

"Oh my god, this could happen to you any time." Soco was upset. "Take me home." Trying to make as little commotion as possible, Miguel and Soco left the party.

Once in the car, Miguel tried to calm Soco. "Mi amor, don't worry. Jacinto and I have it down. We use the broom in the morning so the neighbors won't be upset with us. Jacinto and I are very careful, we do our job, talk as little as possible, and as soon as we are done, we come back to La Ponderosa. It will be okay."

"Are we in prison? Why did you bring me here?" Soco stared out the window. "We sold everything we had in Tepatitlan to move here. What are we going to do? I don't want to live like this."

"Mi amor, there are lots of great things in this country, give it time."

Soon after, Soco became pregnant with Mallory, and the excitement of a new baby took away all the sour feelings. Life took its course, and both Miguel and Soco adapted to their environment. Miguel's spirit became increasingly more broken. While his clients smiled at him because of his good work, he could feel their disdain. Sometimes it was his imagination, but after feeling so unwanted for so long by his new country, he lost his self-worth, started drinking heavily, and became extremely reclusive.

Soco was very strong and she never saw herself less than anyone else. She worked hard to give her daughters a sense of self-worth and hope for a better future. Both Miguel and Soco realized that the American Dream was not for them to have, and in turn, they focused on the possibility that their daughters could achieve that dream.

A year after Mallory was born, Soco decided to temporarily give up her dream of being a teacher as she realized that with a growing family, she needed to work to complement Miguel's gardening income. Soco realized she had to learn English so she bought an English Language System on CD and would walk around the house repeating the words every day. Mariquita, Jacinto's girlfriend, was a nanny in an affluent neighborhood. She got wind that a family next to hers was in need of a good nanny. Mariquita got Soco an interview at the Mackintosh home by telling them she was a teacher in Mexico.

Up until her interview, Soco had barely ventured into the white side of Phoenix. Arpaio and his allies' efforts to segregate Mexicans and keep them in their neighborhoods by terrifying them had been very successful in Phoenix. In the almost two years since her arrival, Soco had not interacted with any people outside the Mexican neighborhoods, and she didn't look forward to doing so. She had only heard about how abusive, dismissive, and condescending they were to Mexicans, so she had no desire to get to know them.

On the day of her job interview, Soco dressed in her best dress; it was a yellow sundress, which showed her nice figure. Soco put makeup on as well to highlight her green eyes. She looked lovely. When Soco arrived at the Mackintosh mansion, she was overwhelmed. The house was huge and very intimidating. "Wow, this is how they live. I'm in trouble."

Anne opened the door with a kind smile. "Come in, Socorro. I hear your friends call you Soco. May I call you Soco too?"

Soco nodded.

"By the way, my name is Anne."

Soco made an effort to speak some English, although it was very broken. "Si, sorry, jes, Miss Anne."

"I hear you were a teacher in Mexico. Did you bring those credentials with you?"

"Jes, I hav been hir." With pride, she presented her teaching credential.

"Very nice," said Anne, "even though I can't read Spanish, but if you don't mind, I would like to make a copy of it, okay?"

"Jes, okay."

"So what classes did you teach in Mexico?"

"I di't got to teach. Wen I finisc school, me husband, Miguel, and I move hir."

"Oh, okay. Do you have children of your own?"

"Jes Miss Anne, two, Cindy and Mallory, I have piture." Soco pulled it out of her wallet and showed the picture of her family, the Ochoas—Miguel, Cindy, Mallory, and Soco, all dressed up for Mallory's baptism.

"Nice looking family! Your daughters are gorgeous!"

Soco smiled and felt good and proud. "T'ank you, Miss Anne."

Then, a four-year-old girl, holding the hand of a toddler, appeared, both with blonde hair and dressed in blue.

Anne said, "These are my kids, Jenny and Zachary. We call him Zack. Kids, say 'hello' to Soco, your new nanny." Jenny approached Soco and instead of shaking her hand, gave her a hug. Soco's heart melted for those beautiful children.

"Wow, they seem to like you, Soco."

"They are lovy," Soco said as she hugged them back. Little Zack hugged Soco, and the great bond started immediately. He did not want to let go of her.

"I want you to teach them Spanish. It'll serve them well to learn Spanish. Of course, I see your English needs practice, and I will help you."

When Soco left the Mackintosh home, her entire perspective of the scary Americans changed, and in one quick moment, she understood that people are people. When Anne offered her the job, she accepted without hesitation.

The Mackintosh family treated Soco like an equal, like family. Anne always sent her home with gifts, especially candy during Halloween, and ornaments for Christmas. One Christmas, Anne gifted the Ochoa family a new 52-inch flat screen TV, something most of the wealthy families didn't have. In turn, Soco used her teaching skills to be more than a nanny. She was a teacher to those children, and taught them math, science, and of course, Spanish, through the use of fun games. The children thrived, and Soco loved the Mackintosh family, and they loved Soco.

As soon as Cindy and Mallory were ready for school, Anne assured they would be accepted at Paradise Valley Elementary and did all the paperwork necessary because she wholeheartedly wanted the girls to have all the opportunities.

Over the years, Soco and Anne became friends. Anne saw Soco as one of her best friends, someone she could trust. Soco met other wonderfully kind American people who cared about her well-being, and she was grateful that teachers from Paradise Valley Elementary and other parents treated her and her daughters with equality, love, and fairness.

Soco realized that most Americans are kind and compassionate people. She also realized that like with any other culture, there are unkind, abusive people who do not like others because they are different, or because they stood in their way and wouldn't think twice to step on them. Soco kept hearing about such a man, Sheriff Arpaio, who promoted hatred in Arizona toward Mexicans for his own advancement and whose policies would affect her life in unexpected ways.

Chapter Seven

Closet Mexican

One block away from the Maricopa County Courthouse sits Manny's Pub, a New York-style deli restaurant, an institution in itself. For over fifty years, its dark wood-paneled walls, large mirrors, and white tile floors have seen and heard some of the most private and essential negotiations of lawyers and prosecutors in preparation for their court appearances.

On this particular day, Lorenzo was having lunch with some friends and colleagues, celebrating Malcolm Cumber's birthday. His friend was a senior partner at Cumber & Klein Accounting, a forensic accounting firm that did a lot of work with Lorenzo's firm. The people at the celebration, almost twenty in total, were well acquainted and generally liked each other. The group was going through a lot of liquor. They were loud, and they all were having animated legal and political conversations.

The night before the birthday lunch, Senator Patrick McMasters of Arizona decided to support Trump's campaign and his idea of a border wall to protect America from the dangerous Mexicans. Mary, one of the senior secretaries, decided to crack a joke related to the news: "So how did Trump convince McMasters to join his campaign? He promised to remove all the illegal Mexicans out of Arizona but let him keep his gardener and his maid."

Everyone laughed.

Everyone except Lorenzo. He could see how Trump's words and actions were polarizing people and creating a wave of prejudice against Mexicans and Mexican-Americans with unpredictable consequences. During the luncheon, he discussed the matter with Edgar Batali, whose father was Italian and whose mother was Mexican. Edgar was a closet Mexican, meaning he generally hid his Mexican ancestry, only acknowledging his Italian roots.

"Edgar, don't you think that we educated and somewhat influential Mexican-Americans should take some action to stop Trump's attacks on Mexican-Americans?"

Looking around to see who heard, Edgar was visibly uncomfortable.

"I think it damages our community and has great potential to harm the future of our youth," Lorenzo continued.

"What do you mean harm the future of our youth?" said Edgar, annoyed.

"You know how a bad a reputation can hurt you. With Trump's shocking character assassination of Mexicans, who is going to want to hire a Mexican-looking kid if they have other options? These kids will be destined to become the second option to others. And with their own self-esteem damaged, our kids are going to have a harder time."

"Trump's not speaking about Mexican-Americans, he's just talking about illegal Mexicans." Edgar became increasingly more uncomfortable as Lorenzo kept referring to him as a Mexican-American. Very few people knew about his Mexican mother. Lorenzo knew because when they first met, Edgar had mentioned it to Lorenzo, in an effort to gain his trust and his business. "And look, Lorenzo, illegal immigration is a problem, and they need to stop it."

"I agree, we need to have better border protection and stronger laws to discourage illegal immigration, at the same time fair immigration reform, protecting the unity of American families. People who have been here for thirty years and made an honest life, paid taxes, and created an American family have to be treated humanely. The American-born children of illegal immigrants, they need their parents. If they get deported, those kid's futures will be irreversibly damaged." And Lorenzo eyes welled. "The people who will pay for this anti-Mexican Border Wall campaign are the next generation. They are who I worry about the most, the millions of children and teenage American-born kids, children of Mexican immigrants. The damage caused when important people on national TV say, 'Mexicans are rapists and criminals, and we have to build a wall to keep them out.' How will that hurt their future and their self-worth?"

"I get you. You're Mexican and feel more offended, but our kids are no longer Mexican, they are American. They need to forget their Mexican background and assimilate."

"Do you think that if Trump was to say, 'All Armenians are rapists,' Armenian-Americans would be happy? Or would they say, 'It's okay, as long as he means only the ones born in Armenia?'" Lorenzo looked Edgar straight in the eye and said, "Edgar, you often talk about your Italian background. Would you or your fellow Italian-Americans be happy if Trump said, 'All Italians are mafia criminals, thugs, and assassins'?"

"Wow, Lorenzo, chill out, you're taking this way too personally." Edgar's face got red and his voice became deeper; clearly offended.

Maggie Fisher, who was listening to their conversation, chimed in. "Edgar, I do see a problem with Trump, Arpaio, and other politicians jumping on the anti-Mexican bandwagon. They are creating and encouraging a generation of prejudice and fear against Mexicans. People who have steered away from those prejudicial thoughts and language may now feel more inclined, or even permitted, to feel and say similar things."

"Look," Edgar responded, "it's clearly a political stunt, and it'll soon pass. You guys know as well as I do that the chances of Trump being selected as the Republican candidate are zero. His offensive statement will soon disappear from the news."

"But the poisonous words he has put out there and the feeling and thoughts he's planted in people's minds and hearts have already created irreparable damage. It will stay on people's minds for many years to come," said Lorenzo.

And then, as if seeing a ghost, Lorenzo said, "And can you imagine if he wins?"

That evening, at the Suarez home, Elizabeth finished work early and had time to cook dinner. She made the dish she knew was her best—green chicken enchiladas. The family was happy to enjoy a home-cooked meal for a change. As usual, the dinner conversation started by Lorenzo questioning the kids about their day. Mark was moody and didn't want to chat; he acted like he didn't hear Lorenzo's question and stared at his plate silently, not wanting to be part of the conversation.

Lorenzo decided to share his experience at the birthday lunch, mentioning the damaging effects Trump's language was starting to have on people, and how the talk of a border wall to keep Mexicans out would hurt young Mexican-Americans.

Mark had heard his dad complain about this before, and he was annoyed at this conversation. He emulated his mom's indifference about her Mexican roots; he felt American, not Mexican-American.

"Not to be mean, Dad, but you keep repeating that young Mexicans are going to lose their pride. But honestly, what do they have to be proud of anyway? Mexico is just a crappy Third World country, and without American money, people there would starve. That is why they come here." The second those words came out of his mouth, Mark realized he may have insulted his dad, and expected a reprimand.

Instead, Lorenzo calmly responded, "My son, what you think is based on a lot of misrepresentations. Of course, America is the richest nation in the world, and Mexico, next to America, is much poorer, but Mexico is not a poor country and Mexicans don't starve. In fact, Mexico has been a rich and highly cultured nation even before the Spanish conquistadors arrived. The Aztec empire was the largest and most powerful nation in the Americas and only the Inca, in South America, could rival it. The Aztecs built large, beautiful cities with great edifices and pyramids, organized commerce, had arts and sciences, and had formidable armies. Among the Spanish colonies, Mexico, then called 'New Spain,' was the wealthiest colony on the continent.

"Today, Mexico is the richest Spanish-speaking nation in the hemisphere, and Mexico's economy is amongst the fifteen largest in the world. The media is filled with terrible misrepresentations about Mexico."

"Really?" Mark responded sarcastically. "Are you exaggerating again, Dad?" Mark did not believe what his dad said.

"Most importantly, there is a lot for Mexicans in America to be proud of," said Lorenzo, "because the Mexican culture has influenced American culture deeper than people understand. Americans have pride and brag about their cowboy culture. But the boots, hats, colorful shirts, corrida-style country music, and the rodeos are directly inherited and a copy of the Mexican vaquero culture. And Mexican food, some of the best food in the world, influences American cuisine every day. The beautiful Mexican architecture and art plastered all over America are also uniquely Mexican. Sadly, instead of properly acknowledging it as Mexican, Americans choose to call it 'Spanish style' or 'Southwest style.'"

"Dad, why would anyone want to hide the contribution of the Mexican culture? You're silly," said Mark.

"You may not know this, but there's a historical reason why there was an effort to minimize the contribution of the Mexican culture in America and damage its reputation, and it's part of a dark, almost forgotten part of American history."

Mark, Katie, and Elizabeth could see Lorenzo's passion as he spoke; it was as if he were talking to a jury. He loved history, and they would not dare interrupt.

"Before 1840, California, Nevada, Texas, New Mexico, Colorado, Utah, and Arizona, about one-third of what is today's United States, was Mexico. These lands were sparsely populated, but the Mexicans owned large and small cattle ranches and grew crops of all types all over these lands. Mexico City was far away, and the ranchers and landowners felt ignored by the distant government. Some Mexican ranchers wished for independence.

"Americans moved west and started to settle on Mexican land. The Americans who settled were slave owners from the South and wanted to bring slavery to Mexico. Mexico had abolished slavery and did not allow slave selling or trading. The settlers were upset with these rules and the disorganized Mexican government. Many Mexicans and the Americans living on the lands decided to unite and fight for independence from Mexico. They were supported by the United States, which had plans for westward expansion."

"So, both Mexicans and Americans fought for independence?" asked Katie.

"Yes. After the Mexican-American War, Arizona and all the other regions became part of the US. At first, the Mexicans, who fought alongside the American settlers, were happy to become part of America and free themselves from Mexico. The peace treaty of Guadalupe required that the Mexican landowners, big and small, would be allowed to keep ownership of their homes, lands, and ranches.

"But soon, greed got the best of some unscrupulous, powerful Anglo-Americans and they found legal and illegal loopholes to take lands and possessions away from the Mexicans who were now Americans. These bad people wanted to appropriate the lands and property from their rightful Mexican owners, so they used the old strategy of creating fear; they spread rumors that Mexicans were plotting against America. This incited suspicion and hatred toward Mexicans. They were successful in manipulating the American opinion by way of scare tactics and natural human prejudice to reach their goals. "

Elizabeth had never heard this part of history told this way and rolled her eyes. "Really?"

Lorenzo nodded his head. "These actions were carefully orchestrated to manipulate the American people's minds, by the few powerful perpetrators looking to benefit from these atrocities. In the end, the Americans who conquered the Mexican lands did what the Spaniards had done to Mexicans 300 years earlier, although with less brutality."

Katie listened in rapt attention, as she loved history like her dad. "What did the Spaniards do to subjugate Mexico?"

Lorenzo was happy to see Katie was listening and wanted his daughter to understand how history explains the present, and many times, the future.

"Honey, the Spaniards were brutal conquerors. When they first arrived in Mexico, they recorded in their diaries how the Aztecs were highly civilized and had a well-organized government, education system, and were even more advanced than Europeans in some areas of science. They also found they had a pagan religion, which encouraged human sacrifice.

"Once the Aztecs were conquered, the Spaniards destroyed any vestiges of civilization the Aztecs ever had, killing and torturing anyone who made Aztec art, spoke the Aztec language, or even farmed using Aztec techniques. They were forced into slavery, forced to convert to Catholicism, or be tortured or burned. Under this brutal strategy for almost 300 years, Mexicans were forced to believe that the Aztec ancestors had no cultural value, they were savages and the only enlightenment came from Spain. By destroying the Aztec's reputation, the Spaniards made it clear that the only source of pride should come from being Spanish.

"Americans were kinder conquerors. Nevertheless, some of the people in charge of those new lands used techniques that conquering nations have used throughout history to subjugate and control conquered people. They embarked on an intentional effort to vilify and humiliate the conquered people. 'Remember the Alamo; was a fighting call used to united Anglo-Americans against Mexicans, to malign, repress, and destroy their reputation, thus making it acceptable to perform such atrocities." Lorenzo looked up to the ceiling, as if thinking deeply, and said, "I see this happening again today."

He looked at Katie, who listened with deep interest. "Imagine being a Mexican in America after the Mexican-American War. You would have faced the terrible injustice of having your home, your land, and your possessions removed. Then you may have been forced into a camp, and only allowed to do menial jobs."

Katie shook her head in disbelief.

"Soon after, pushed by the injustices, many Mexican ex-landowners and their kids became famous bandits or 'bandidos,' like the mythical 'Zorro,' and started to fight against this system of injustice. This, of course, was followed by harsh repression. Mexicans were forced to segregate, were not given equal rights, were treated almost like slaves, were only allowed to do labor and servile work, and were not allowed in schools. They were forced to become second-class citizens. This action has caused severe emotional damage to Mexican-Americans who have lived in America for several generations, who have been imprinted with a second-class-citizen mentality. This is the historical reason Mexicans are considered to be the servant class in America, even today."

This explains that, the current poor economic condition of the Mexican-American community is not related to their lack of ability, but to the forced repression and denied opportunities it suffered for over 150 years.

Katie's mouth was wide open, and she said, "Dad, I had no clue about this. Why don't they teach this in school?"

"Honey, this is almost hidden history, but it is there to be found. First, the powerful architects of this strategy were careful to hide and disguise their true intentions, and their human rights violations. And now, all these years later, because it's not a pleasant history, it's not something to look back and be proud of. It's easier to ignore the atrocities committed by past generations."

"You're twisting history and are hurting our children," Elizabeth said. "Just because you came from Mexico, you can't make up your own facts. They feel like an offense toward American goodness."

"Yeah, Dad, I don't ever feel any of this 'second-class' mentality," said Mark.

Elizabeth grew visibly upset. "Lorenzo, you may need to check your facts. Mexicans wanted to join the US and actually fought against Mexico, and America paid Mexico for the lands they took."

Mark jumped in. "And Dad, that was a long time ago. This is the twenty-first century. There's no more oppression against Mexicans."

"Look at Sheriff Arpaio," said Katie.

"Oh, he's just a nut case," replied her mom.

Lorenzo looked at his irate wife and son and exhaled deeply. He was saddened by them. "Well, this is the problem. I see a new wave of oppression against Mexicans, just like the 1840s, when Mexicans joined America and had no clue what was to be of them. Today things could change very quickly."

Lorenzo had no clue how prophetic his words would be....

CHAPTER EIGHT

PROFILING

As he did most Saturdays, Zack was preparing to go out to wash his car, which he liked to do very early in the morning before the hot Arizona sun made it a painful task.

Suddenly the phone rang, and Zack picked up as fast as possible, hoping this unusually early call would not wake his parents. It was Socorro, and her voice sounded in severe distress.

Zack, who loved Soco, was panicked. "Soco, what are you saying? I can't understand, what is happening?"

His father heard the commotion and asked, "Zack, what is going on?"

Zack put the phone under his arm and told Tom, "It sounds like Soco is in jail, or something like that. She is speaking so fast, I can barely understand."

"Give me the phone," Tom said and calmly spoke into the phone. "Soco, calm down, you know we are here for you. Slowly tell me what happened."

Anne, half asleep, came down to see what all the commotion was and her heart stopped when she realized something terrible may have happened to her beloved Soco. Anne and Zack were on pins and needles trying to discern what was happening from listening to Tom's responses.

"Miguel was going to the store to pick up milk and who took him?" Tom listened for a while and then said, "Just like that? The police stopped the car for no reason?"

Anne said to Tom, "What is she saying?" Tom waved at them to be silent; he was trying hard to listen.

"They asked him for his immigration papers?" Tom was astonished that the police would randomly ask a driver on the street for immigration papers.

"Can they do that?" asked Anne. "Just ask people on the street for immigration papers? Isn't it racial profiling?"

Tom waved his hand again for silence.

Anne was unaware that for years in Arizona under Sheriff Arpaio's leadership and that of other likeminded people, the police had intentionally created an atmosphere of fear amongst Mexicans, legal and illegal. They racially profiled Mexican and Hispanic-looking people.

The justice department had sued Arpaio and his department multiple times for these unconstitutional and unlawful arrests, but he laughed and ignored the documents. His behavior continued with impunity for decades, as he knew nobody cared enough to make him stop.

Tom now had more understanding of the situation. "So now they are holding him until he proves his status, or they will deport him? Okay, then bring his papers to the police. Do you need me to go to your home and help retrieve the papers?"

As he listened, Tom's eyes opened, and his voice got thin. "Oh my god!" He stopped to take a breath. "Okay, I will go there and see what I can find out."

Tom hung up the phone and explained the situation to Anne and Zack. "…and neither one of them have green cards."

Anne was mortified. "How come Soco never told us? She must have given me a fake Social Security card."

Tom and Anne got dressed as fast as they could and got in the car to go to the police station. On the way, they called their friend and lawyer Benjamin Smalls, who specialized in immigration law, and asked him to meet them there.

Soco and Miguel Ochoa had both lived in the US for over twenty years, worked hard, paid taxes, and bought a small home. They had one child born in the US, Mallory, and another child, Cindy, that they brought in when she was one year old. The Ochoas had visited lawyers multiple times, paid large amounts of money to find out that it is almost impossible for Mexicans to get legal immigration. The Ochoas had several relatives who were American citizens and were willing to sponsor them but learned that the waiting period for Mexican immigration is extremely long, decades, considerably longer than for anyone else in the world. All immigration lawyers know that.

Since Miguel got caught on his first attempt to cross the border and was booked with a misdemeanor, he had a police record. That made him eligible for immediate deportation.

When Tom and Anne arrived at the police station, Soco, Mallory, and Cindy were all in tears. They were a united family, and the idea of having to live without Miguel for the rest of their lives was too much to fathom. Since Miguel was a gardener, and Soco a nanny and housekeeper, they both had low incomes and lived paycheck to paycheck. They did not have much in savings and now they would have to hire a lawyer?

Miguel and Soco lived a life of isolation from the Anglo world, in hiding. Their only meaningful connection to the mainstream American world was the Mackintoshes. And that is why Soco, who was fiercely proud, had to call and ask for help.

When Soco asked them for help, Anne looked at Tom and said, "Absolutely! You know you are like family. We had no idea about your situation.

"Soco, why you didn't ask for our help sooner? Honey, you have kids born in the US. That should resolve the problem."

Soco explained that they had gone to a lawyer to try to get papers, but the lawyer explained that the rule is that parents who have US-born children and enter the US illegally have to apply outside of the US and have a ten-year penalty period. Once they are eligible, they will have to wait their turn for a green card. And with current immigration laws, other nationalities get preference over Mexicans. Knowing all of this, Miguel and Soco chose to wait, hoping they would be lucky and not get caught, a new immigration law would come into effect, or they would receive amnesty.

Anne and Tom hired an expensive immigration lawyer, imagining that a better lawyer would do the trick, but they received a similar response. They were told that nothing could be done and that Miguel would be deported. A few days later, he shipped out of the country.

The Ochoa family was devastated. Soco was inconsolable, and she was now a woman without a husband. She could never go see her husband in Mexico because if she left the US, she could not get back. Being the good mother that she was, her first priority was the girls. Miguel could not visit her in the US because his chances of getting a visa were zero.

With the help of Tom's lawyer, they immediately filed papers for Miguel because he had a US-born daughter, but they waited to file for Soco because she could not leave the country and leave the girls. Soco and the girls panicked that Soco could get caught as well. The deportation had put the Ochoa girls in a perilous place.

CHAPTER NINE
THE PRACTICE

Summer was coming to an end and the Suarez kids were happy to be back in school. Katie, as usual, rushed through the hallways with a determined look, organizing her study materials. She strategized ways to reach her goal of being first in class and prepared for any extra projects offered, which would take her to the above-4.0 grade-point average she needed to have any real chance to be accepted into Harvard, her life's dream.

Mark, on the other hand, walked the school hallways basking in the idea that he was now a cool senior varsity football player. "This is going to be a year to remember," he thought. Mark had not forgotten the look in Savannah's blue eyes at the end of last year and had been reeling over it all summer, hoping to run into her somewhere around Paradise Valley. Sadly for him, it never happened.

Being a good wide receiver with dreams of getting a football scholarship to a major university enabled Mark to neglect his studies. On the other hand, Zack Mackintosh was NFL material. He had a natural talent, the ability to rally people around him, and excellent leadership skills. Zack and Mark met as young children and played soccer together for a couple of years, but when the teams changed, they lost contact.

As sophomores at Washington High, they reconnected and immediately liked each other because they were both good guys and loved football. They both had competitive natures and wanted to try to outdo each other, occasionally getting into trouble for good-natured pranks toward each other, their teachers, or fellow students. They never put people down or bullied them—just pranks.

On the other hand, fellow varsity player Cole Jones was a troubled kid. When Cole was ten, his dad, a DEA detective, was killed in the line of duty by a small-time Mexican gangster high on PCP. The man had ties to the Juarez Cartel. Cole's mom, Coleen, was devastated and for a long time could not get out of bed. She received her late husband's pension, and a fund put together by fellow police officers helped her and Cole.

With this money, Coleen, who was very shrewd, made a good investment and bought a fixer-upper in Paradise Valley. She went back to teaching and worked hard to give Cole a good life. Up until his father's death, Cole's childhood was idyllic, but afterward, he felt his world had shattered to pieces. Reasonably, he carried a deep resentment against Mexican gangsters, and his mom often talked about her hatred toward "those damn Mexican criminals." Trump and Arpaio's character assassination campaign of Mexicans found the perfect target in Cole.

A polite and loving son to Coleen, in front of others he was awkward, antisocial, and displayed a dark side. Occasionally, he would torture lizards with a magnifying glass in the sun. Seeing the lizards and other small animals squirm gave him pleasure and allowed his rage to vent.

Cole was a good-looking teenage boy with a handsome face, framed by light-brown hair that in the sun looked red and complemented his hazel eyes. But he had terrible skin, marked by heavy acne. Average height, with a thin runner's build, Cole had speed and endurance. Because of his awkwardness, he was not popular at school, or with the girls, which made him resentful.

Cole hung out with David Witmeyer, a skinny kid whose nickname was Bones, and Anthony Collezi. Both kids were outcasts, had dark outlooks on life, and liked to think of themselves as anarchists. They hated authority and anyone who got in their way. Cole, David, and especially Anthony were bullies; they enjoyed terrorizing the freshmen and anyone who exuded weakness. Anthony was 6'2", overweight, and looked huge and menacing, especially to the young freshmen who had not had their growth spurts. Washington High was a school with no tolerance for bullying or abusive behaviors, so David and Anthony were often in and out of the principal's office. Cole, on the other hand, was the smart ringleader who always found ways to go unnoticed.

It was an unusually hot late summer afternoon in Paradise Valley, just over 120 degrees. The beautifully maintained artificial turf of Washington

High had to be constantly sprayed with cold water to keep it cool for practice. The varsity team practiced without their full gear and took constant water breaks. The coach considered canceling practice due to the extreme heat, but they had to be ready for the big game, which was the following week. The heat made everyone testy and inpatient, especially Coach Murphy.

On the shaded side of the field, the cheerleading team practiced by dancing and singing their cheers. A commotion happened when the team mascot almost passed out from sunstroke.

"Eleven, Twenty-two, hike, hike." Zack took four steps backward. The starting defensive line was protecting him. Mark ran a perfect route. Zack threw a beautiful spiral, but it was slightly behind Mark and Mark dropped the pass.

"What the hell, Mark? This is the third time today you've dropped a perfect pass," said Zack.

"Hey, it wasn't perfect. It was behind me, and I had to really turn to try to grab it," said Mark.

"Bullshit," said Zack. "I can see it in your eyes. You're distracted because the cheerleaders are practicing behind us."

Zack was right. Mark had noticed Savannah kicking and jumping in her cheerleader outfit, and he had lost concentration.

Cole, wanting to humiliate Mark, screamed, "I think Markie is in love with Savannah."

"Cole, don't be an asshole," said Mark.

"Mark, don't get any ideas," said Zack. "Savannah and I have been talking all summer. She likes me, so hands off."

Cole jumped in and said, "Haha, yes Markie, hands off. Plus, why would she choose a wetback Mexican over Zack?"

Mark's brain started buzzing with rage and words could not come out of his mouth. He was tired of Cole's attacks and lunged at Cole, who was agile and dodged him. Mark slipped and fell to the ground.

Cole looked at Mark. "Haven't you heard, Trump is going to build a wall so you fucking Mexicans can't get in anymore."

Zack could not believe Cole had said such racist words. He defended

Mark. "Cole, you're really an asshole. That's pretty offensive. What the heck has gotten into you?"

Mark got up and was ready to charge at Cole again when Coach Murphy stomped toward them and yelled, "What the hell is going on over there?" Coach looked at Mario Garcia, who watched the entire thing. "Who started this?"

Mario was afraid to say anything, but his eyes pointed at Cole.

Coach Murphy was not amused and said, "I'm not going to deal with childish behavior. Mark and Cole, next time, one of you will be off the team."

As Murphy walked away, Cole turned to Mario and said, "Fuck you, Mario, you had to be a chicken shit tattle-tail Mexican."

"Screw you, Cole. I am not Mexican. I'm Venezuelan, it is very different."

"Same shit," said Cole.

Mark's head was spinning. He had never been a victim of racist remarks and never thought of himself as a Mexican. Then he remembered his dad's words: "When people hear Trump offend Mexicans on national TV, that makes it okay for them to think that way and say those things."

Later that day, Mark and Zack were at their lockers talking about the practice. They had almost forgotten about the fight when Savannah approached Mark and asked, "What happened? I saw the commotion. Did you guys get into a fight?"

Mark felt excited that Savannah was interested in what happened to him and said, "Not really. Cole was just being an asshole."

Zack, wanting to show off as the big man in front of Savannah, said, "Cole almost kicked the shit out of Mark. I had to step in to protect him."

"Come on, Zack, I can defend myself, and it really was nothing."

"Zack, why do you always have to be the hero?" asked Savannah.

"What? You're taking Mark's side?" asked Zack.

"Whatever, Zack," Savannah said. She turned toward Mark and said, "You looked really good at practice. I look forward to seeing you at the game." She said "Bye" to the two testosterone-filled boys and walked away.

Mark grinned like the cat that ate the mouse, while jealousy raged in

Zack's heart.

On the other side of campus, Katie sat in the front row of her history class. She had made a special request to be in Mrs. Smith's class again because she liked her so much. Mrs. Smith loved Katie back, as did most of her other teachers. Katie was determined to get good grades, interested in all subject matter, smart, polite, and helpful, which was refreshing for her teachers.

On this particular day, Mrs. Smith instructed her students to choose a relevant and current news story, with historical implications, and write an essay. Because this essay was critical to their final grade, Mrs. Smith's approval was required for each essay's subject. The students had to justify their topic to her and to the class in one minute or less and explain the historical relevance of the current news piece. Katie chose one of Trump's speeches about Mexicans, and it was Katie's turn to justify her choice.

"Mrs. Smith, I've chosen Mr. Trump's June sixteenth speech because I believe it has far-reaching consequences." Echoing her dad's words, Katie continued, "The type of hate speech Trump is using against Mexicans has the potential to encourage and promote racism. The idea that a wall has to be built to keep Mexicans out gives the wrong message—that Mexicans are undesirable."

Katie ended her presentation, almost choking with a combination of courage and embarrassment and said, "I am a Mexican-American, and this specifically affects me." It took courage because, at school, most students never considered Katie to be a Mexican.

Mrs. Smith was in disbelief. Katie was so smart and one of her favorite students, and she didn't see her as Mexican.

Mrs. Smith was very confused. She abruptly said, "Okay, that's fine." Mrs. Smith's quick response made Katie think that Mrs. Smith did not like her subject or her presentation, but unbeknownst to Katie, Mrs. Smith was conflicted, and Katie's subject matter and words made an impact on her.

Traditionally, when Mrs. Smith thought of Mexicans, she thought about the nice but smelly gardeners, the cleaning ladies, the Mexican selling flowers outside the cemetery, or the woman selling fruit in the park. She thought of Mexicans as docile servants and was never scared of them. Mrs. Smith had always been an Arpaio admirer. She felt he was tough on crime, which was good. Over time, Arpaio's consistent character assassination of Mexicans had made her see them differently—as criminals. Arpaio had been using Mexicans as scapegoats to promote his campaigns against crime. All of those fear tactics had an effect on Mrs. Smith. Sometimes she worried that cartel criminals were ready to cross the border and destroy America's peaceful streets.

As Mrs. Smith listened to Katie's speech, she realized she was surrounded by Mexican-Americans, people like Katie, her dental hygienist Lupe, and her chatty hair stylist Mary, who never said they were Mexican. She thought of two co-workers, Jane and Bernice, who looked Mexican and always brought homemade tamales to special events but were offended if anyone asked them if they spoke Spanish. They clearly resented if anyone saw them as anything else other than American, and Mrs. Smith felt that was the way all Mexicans in America should feel. She felt that Mexicans should integrate and not show pride in being Mexican. "What do they have to be proud of anyway?" she thought.

In fact, she had rarely seen any second-generation Mexican be outspoken about their ancestry. Katie's disclosure was strange and unexpected. Mrs. Smith was shocked when Katie showed her pride in her Mexican heritage. From that point forward, Mrs. Smith was confused. She realized it bothered her to see Mexican-Americans showing pride in their Mexican heritage. She was unaware that outside influences were turning her from a sweet, caring woman into a person filled with prejudiced attitudes.

Chapter Ten

The Game

It was Friday night—time for the big game. Washington High was playing against its cross-town rivals, Rio Lobo High. The excitement was palpable, and the rivalry ran deep. In reality, neither school had a good team. The players on both sides were mostly rich kids for whom football was just a pastime; their real future lay in the stock market, medicine, law, or engineering.

Nevertheless, the game was as important as the Super Bowl to the town. Both teams were pumped. Washington High's cheerleaders looked lovely in their sky-blue outfits.

The small stadium was full—not one more soul could fit in. Katie was, as usual, looking determined and a little stressed out, trying to find her family good seats. She looked lovely in a fitted floral summer dress that showed off her shapelyl figure. Several of her male classmates waved, trying to attract Katie's attention, but she was oblivious—on a mission to find the best seats for her family.

Seeing all the attention his daughter was getting from the boys, Lorenzo said with a mischievous smile, "Katie, I see lots of boys looking this way. Do you want to introduce us?"

Elizabeth gave Lorenzo a dirty look. "Lorenzo, leave your daughter alone. Don't embarrass her."

Katie barely noticed her dad's comment because her mind was still focused on finding seats, and ultimately, she found some on the 50-yard line.

During halftime, Katie offered to go buy her parents some refreshments. Lorenzo asked for a hot dog and a coke, while Elizabeth wanted a pretzel. As

Katie walked toward the concessions, she saw Brandon Schwartz, and she froze. Brandon was the only boy Katie had ever thought was smarter than she was. They had some classes together. Katie had seen Brandon grab first place in math class and write the loveliest short story she had ever heard for English class. Ever since she heard the short story, she developed a crush on Brandon, but never told anyone, so he had no clue.

Brandon was attractive and tall with red hair, very polite and well-mannered. Both his mom and dad were physicians, and he had always shown an interest in being a doctor. Katie got in the soft drink/hotdog line and was trying to be inconspicuous and turn her head away from Brandon to avoid being seen.

But Brandon spotted her and said, "Hi Katie, didn't expect to see you here. I didn't think you liked football."

"Yeah, you're right. Football isn't my thing, but my brother is playing, and my family wanted to see the big game."

"Well, I'm here with some friends, and I'm so happy I didn't miss it. This is a good game," said Brandon with excitement. Brandon liked sports, especially football, even though he was not very athletic. "I saw your brother make a great catch. You must be proud of him."

"I'm not so interested in football, but I'm proud of my brother. He is a good guy, but I worry so much that he could get injured. I close my eyes whenever it looks like he's going to get hit."

Brandon laughed. "You sound like my mom. She hates to see the hard tackles. Whenever my dad and I watch the Cardinals, she always says, 'Football is like the Roman Coliseum,' and it makes us laugh."

Katie finally received her order. "Okay, Brandon, it was nice seeing you." Katie was ready to walk away when Blaire showed up. Katie cringed because she knew her friend was trouble.

"Hey Brandon," Blaire said. "What are you guys chatting about?" As Blaire said this, she looked at Katie's eyes and smiled with her eyes. Katie felt like hiding under a rock.

Blaire, with a mischievous smile, said, "So Brandon, what are you guys doing after the game?"

"I think we're going to Rocky Cola. Maybe you guys can join us later?"

"Let me see if I can convince my antisocial friend Katie here to go with me."

Katie did not find this amusing at all.

As soon as Brandon left, Katie turned to Blaire and said sternly, "Blaire, I can't believe you did that! I was so embarrassed."

Blaire, still smiling, said, "Katie, if I don't help you, you'll never make out with Brandon. Don't pretend you don't like him. I know you too well."

The game was exciting and Zack was especially good that night. He tossed three touchdown passes, one of them to Mark. The game was tight 21 to 21, and there were only two minutes left on the clock. Washington had the ball on its own 20-yard line. The team marched forward. By the time the clock had thirty seconds, Washington was on the 20-yard line of Rio Lobo. Both sides of the crowd were on their feet cheering. There was time for one, or maybe two, plays.

The ball was snapped and Zack had the ball. Rio Lobo chose to rush the passer. Zack felt the breath of the pass rushers; they were coming fast as the receivers were trying to open up. Mark followed his route, but he could not get separation, so he changed direction quickly.

There was an opening and Zack saw Mark from the corner of his eye, but one of the pass rushers had grabbed his jersey and started pulling him down. Zack made a last-chance throw, but the ball was thrown behind Mark's back. Mark's body contorted as much as a human could; he was able to touch the ball with one hand but was unable to make the catch. The ball tumbled to the ground.

The play had taken too long. As the team made an effort to line up again for a second play, the clock registered :00 and the ref's whistle signaled the end of the game. It was a tie, so no one had won the rights to brag that night. On the field, the Washington players had almost tasted victory, and they were visibly disappointed

Zack ran to Mark and said, "Sorry! I tried to send you a better pass, but they were pulling me down."

"Brother, you had an amazing game, and I wish I had been able to grab that ball." They were walking off the field when Cole came running toward Mark and pushed him hard to the ground.

"God dam beaner, you cost us the game," Cole shouted, and threw a punch at him.

Mark deflected the punch, and before any more punches were thrown, the entire team stopped Cole. People in the stands were horrified. The team walked toward the lockers, with a couple of guys restraining Cole, who was behaving like a madman. Mark was very upset, sensing that trouble was inevitable.

Mark was not a violent person, and all this hatred against him was a new experience.

"Dude, I don't know what is with Cole," Zack said. "He really has it out for you."

Finally, the coach caught up to them and in a stern tone said to Cole, "Your behavior is unacceptable. I want you to leave immediately. You're not allowed in the locker room tonight and tomorrow we'll talk about your future on the team."

Mark felt uneasy, as he could sense the problem was not over; it was just starting,

Not far from the stadium, Rocky Cola's, a '50s style hamburger joint and a favorite destination of the local Paradise Valley teenagers, was buzzing. Most people were wearing Washington High colors and were in an upbeat mood. Overall, people felt it was a good evening, as Rio Lobo had won the last three encounters, had a better team, and was the favorite that night.

Ending with a draw was not bad. Brandon and three other buddies were sitting in a large booth, talking loudly—almost screaming—as groups of teenagers often do. They were having a good time recounting the details of the game and arguing over who was at fault that the final touchdown pass was dropped.

People had utterly differing opinions, depending on where they sat in the stadium and what perspective they had on the game. Brandon said that Zack's pass was thrown too far back to be catchable, while his friend, John, felt that it was definitely catchable and Mark cost them the game. As that discussion raged, Katie and Blaire walked in.

Brandon had been glancing at the door every thirty seconds and spotted them immediately. "Hey! Over here. I saved you a spot."

Katie blushed, hating that everyone turned to look at them. Blaire, on the other hand, smiled with great pleasure; she loved to be the center of attention.

"Hi guys," Blaire said, "what a game, right?" Blaire didn't really care who won because football was not her thing. She wanted to socialize and meet boys.

Brandon looked at Katie. "I was just telling the guys that for sure Mark had no chance of catching that ball, but John here doesn't agree."

John stuttered. "Well, from my perspective, it looked like it may have been catchable, but it was definitely a hard catch." He changed his statement, hoping Katie would like him.

"It's just a game," said Katie. "I know Mark tried as hard as he could, so what happened, happened." Katie was still shaken by the fight after the game between her brother and Cole. Even though she had a hard time seeing or hearing anything from where she was in the stands, people who were closer to the action filled in the details.

Blaire didn't want to let the conversation go sour and said jokingly, "Okay guys, move over, I'm going to order the cheese fries. Who wants to share with me? I definitely can't eat the huge portion they serve here by myself."

Blaire's bright blue eyes sparkled when she smiled, and while Katie was the prettier of the two, the guys at the table were fighting to sit next to either one; they were just excited to have two hot girls at their table for a change. The only boy who was not acting like a hormone-filled wild teenager was Brandon. He didn't have a clue Katie had a crush on him. Not knowing was good for him because it allowed him to be his usual self—smart, kind, and polite, which were the reasons Katie liked him so much. While John and the other guys shared an order of cheese fries with Blaire, Brandon and Katie enjoyed a conversation about math, science, and current events.

"You guys are such nerds," said Blaire.

Brandon decided to bring up the subject of Trump's candidacy. "I can't imagine anyone taking Trump seriously; he's a celebrity with a bad reputation. The ridiculous things he says are dividing the nation. Such offensive, negative talk about women, Hispanic people…"

Katie interrupted, "Mexican people. For some reason, he's chosen to directly attack Mexicans, not Hispanic people."

"Aren't they the same?" asked Brandon.

"Come on, Brandon, you know better. If you say Asian, it could be Chinese, Korean, or Pilipino, and they're not the same." Katie continued, "But you haven't heard him say, Cubans this or that, or Colombian this or that. He's been very specific about Mexicans."

"I guess you're right. I wonder why. Well, the good news is that there's no chance Trump will win. That would be a terrible thing for our country."

Blaire joined the conversation. "I think you're wrong. My dad thinks Trump is going to win, and he's kind of happy." Then, with a frown on her face, she continued. "He said, 'Finally we're going to build a wall and keep those Mexican criminals out,' and I got mad with him for saying that."

John chose to side with Blaire's dad and said, "Absolutely. Build a dam wall and keep them out."

John was unaware that Katie was Mexican, as were most other people at the table, so they spoke without filters. There was a definite disagreement on the table, while most people at the table nodded.

Blaire looked at John with her eyes wide open in disbelief. "John, you know Katie's Mexican, don't you?

John looked at Katie and said, "Are you from Mexi...Meeexican... Hispanic?" In John's eyes, calling someone Mexican was almost an insult, so he was afraid and unsure how to say the word "Mexican" and have it not been seen as an offense.

"Yes, I am Mexican-American."

John tried to correct his statement and said, "Well, what I mean is that those Mexican criminals from the drug cartels are hurting the country. I didn't mean nice Mexican-Americans like you, Katie."

Up until that point in her life, Katie had never had to explain or defend her Mexican background. Katie was surprised by how many people at the table agreed with Trump and wanted to build a wall to keep Mexicans out. Katie realized how correct her dad's prediction was and that when people hear abusive language from a national figure on TV, they figure it is okay to think and say those things out loud.

Brandon, on the other hand, was offended. "John, what you're saying is pretty offensive to me, and it's bullshit. My nanny, Esperanza, is Mexican and she is the finest human being I know. Miss Ramirez, my fourth-grade math teacher, is Mexican-American. I could give you a list of all the Mexican people I know, and they are just as good and worthy as you and me. Trump is just focusing on the bad people, ignoring that every group of people has good and bad members.

John felt the need to argue his point. "Look, there are a lot of good Mexicans, and we all know that, but they're bringing crime and stealing our jobs."

"Look dude, there's good and bad in any group of people. You always say you're Italian. Well, look at the mafia and all of the deaths and terrible things they caused in this country. Should we expel Italians, or say 'Those Italians are all criminals'?"

John could tell he was outnumbered and decided to raise the white flag. "This conversation is going nowhere. I agree there is good and bad in any group of people, end of story."

Blaire changed the conversation and everyone talked about the game again.

Katie continued to be impressed with Brandon's knowledge and ability to argue his point. Listening to Brandon speak made her forget about the actual conversation. Katie felt that the feelings she had for Brandon were founded on solid reasons.

Katie was so interested in everything Brandon said that she even lost track of time until Blaire said, "My god, it's late. My mom is going to kill me."

Katie looked at her watch and froze. "Blaire, let's go!"

Brandon was a gentleman and walked them to their car. Opening the door for Katie, he held her hand firmly and said, "It was so nice to spend time with you. You're so smart and funny, and I enjoyed our conversation."

Katie smiled and said, "Brandon, I had a great time." She wanted to say so much more, but the words wouldn't come out. Her heart beat fast, and she felt a type of affection for Brandon that she had never felt before.

Blaire yelled from inside the car and interrupted their gaze. "Katie, let's go!"

Brandon watched the car drive away. His mind was fixated on Katie's soft hands and her deep, distinctive voice. He could not get himself to go back in and join the group, so he decided to walk around the block to clear his mind.

A few blocks away, a post-game party had been raging at the kicker's home, a Tudor Revival mansion with dark brick walls and rich wood paneling and a front lawn with large, manicured shrubbery. In the interior, marble floors led to a beautiful double-stair entrance.

All the fine art and most of the furniture had been removed for the party, so this house was made for entertaining. Most of Washington's varsity team was there, as were the popular kids in school. They were drinking, and the atmosphere was becoming wild.

By now, the game was out of most people's minds, and partygoers were now focused on dancing to the loud music, trash talking, and making out in dark corners. Groups of girls and boys were going in and out of a bathroom doing coke. Mark did not want to go to the party after the game. It had left him with a bad taste. He felt guilty for dropping the ball, and worried people would give him grief about it, but Zack insisted he go.

"Mark, it wasn't your fault, dude, and if anyone gives you shit, I'll kick their ass."

Mark wanted to say that he could defend himself, but he didn't. He appreciated Zack's support.

When Mark and Zack arrived at the party, it was in full swing. Zack, the star quarterback, was a celebrity. Like any teenage football hero, many girls liked Zack and wanted to be with him. Mark was popular as well, but that night he felt like he would rather hide. Zack enjoyed the attention and being pulled in multiple directions, while Mark, across the room, chatted with some of the guys. Savannah came over and talked to Mark and they quickly engaged in a fun conversation. Zack noticed how their discussion continued for over thirty minutes. Once in a while they would look in Zack's direction and laugh.

Zack started to feel jealous, and while starstruck girls were trying to get his attention, he could only focus on Savannah and Mark, all the while not noticing he was drinking too fast. Zack had felt it was only a matter of time until Savannah would end up being his girlfriend, but all the female attention had distracted him from declaring his interest. In Zack's mind, he felt Mark invaded his space, and he thought to himself, "Who the hell does Mark think he is?"

Zack walked up to the chatty couple a little drunk. "Hi, Savannah, did you see the game? Not too bad, three touchdown passes."

Savannah, annoyed to see a drunk and arrogant Zack, turned. "Yeah, nice game, Zack, but your last pass wasn't catchable, and we didn't win the game."

Savannah did not realize her words wounded Zack. His face got red and he barked, "So, this is what this freaking loser's telling you? The pass was catchable; he just dropped it." Zack had assumed that Mark and Savannah had been talking about the game.

Mark was shocked and tried to say that he had not said anything about the pass. "But I didn't…"

Zack cut Mark off with a hand wave.

"Wow, Zack, nobody told me anything. I saw it, but who cares, you're an asshole."

Zack looked at Mark and said, "Fuck you, amigo."

Savannah stared at Zack. "You arrogant asshole. I want nothing to do with you. Please don't call me anymore," she snapped, and stormed away toward the back of the house.

Zack was furious with Mark and thought he had put a wedge between him and Savannah. He pushed Mark hard into the wall, then ran toward Savannah trying to explain and patch things up.

Mark was dazed. This was not his day, so he decided it would be better for him to let them talk. Mark grabbed a beer from the cooler and walked to the front yard to get some air. He crossed the huge front lawn and sat behind one of the large old trees surrounded by shrubbery on the side of the house. It was an isolated area, and he needed space.

What a day! His best friend sarcastically called him "amigo"; he felt like his best friend suddenly saw him as a foreigner. He wondered what Savannah and Zack were talking about.

Megan Clark saw Mark from afar, walked toward him. "You see, Mark, bitches like Savannah are trouble, and what you need is a real woman."

Megan was average looking but had a voluptuous body, which she usually accentuated with scanty clothing. Tonight, she was wearing a skin-tight mini skirt. Megan had liked Mark since middle school. Mark was aware of this and usually avoided her. Being drunk, with her inhibitions very low, Megan stumbled toward Mark. She fell on top of him, making him lose his balance, and then kissed him by sticking her tongue down his throat.

Mark grabbed her by the waist and pushed her forcefully away from him. "You're stinking drunk, get off me."

With Mark's push and her drunken lack of balance, Megan fell face first to the ground, scraping her forehead. It started bleeding. In physical and emotional pain at that moment, she cried with a loud, ear-piercing pitch, Mark stared at her in shock and didn't know what to do. People with scared looks on their faces started to rush toward her, think something horrific had happened.

Megan was embarrassed and humiliated. The crowd was stunned and silent. One of the girls tried to stop the bleeding from Megan's forehead with a napkin, but it wouldn't stop. Someone asked, "What the hell is happening here?"

"Mark was being a jerk," Megan said, "and tried to fondle me. When I tried to stop him, he got mad and pushed me to the ground." Everyone looked at Mark incredulously.

Cole stuck his head out from the crowd and said, "Yeah, I was watching through the window and saw Mark push his hand under Megan's skirt and try to grab her, and then push her to the ground."

Megan, feeling reassured said, "You see?"

In reality, Cole had not seen anything, but he could not pass up an opportunity to hurt Mark, having acquired a hatred for him. The crowd looked at Mark, Megan, and Cole and tried to make sense of what happened. Mark, who was also a little drunk, tried to argue his point and said, "Come on, guys, Megan's drunk."

Cole was emboldened by Mark's weak response. "You fucking coward, I saw you! You're like all your beaner buddies — a coward and a rapist."

David, Cole's friend, seconded his words and yelled, "Yeah, what's up with you fucking rapists?"

The sentiment turned against Mark, and the crowd took Cole's side. Zack arrived to see what the commotion was about.

"Your beaner friend here just assaulted Megan," Cole told Zack

Mark felt that if Zack backed his character, things would turn out good. "Zack, you know me. I've always been respectful to women, and I would never do such a thing."

Zack had not been able to patch things up with Savannah. He was still hurt and upset with Mark. "I don't know, amigo." Zack would regret turning his back on his friend at that crucial moment for the rest of his life.

Someone called the paramedics and cops, and before anyone knew it, Mark was handcuffed and booked on assault and suspicion of sexual assault.

CHAPTER ELEVEN
PARIAHS

The following morning the sky was gray from clouds that blocked the sun. The Suarez home was somber when Elizabeth, Lorenzo, and Mark arrived home. Katie made coffee to help them regain some energy because no one had slept the night before. A heartbreaking phone call from the police woke up Lorenzo and Elizabeth. They were informed that Mark had been arrested on charges of assault and suspicion of sexual assault.

During the drive to the police station where Mark was being detained, a huge fight started between Lorenzo and Elizabeth. Elizabeth found reasons to blame Lorenzo for Mark becoming a criminal. She told Lorenzo he had been too lenient with Mark. Then she told Lorenzo he had been too strict with him and made him a rebel.

Unfortunately for Mark, he had just turned eighteen and could now be held at the central facility, a place much worse than the facility for minors. When they arrived, Elizabeth took charge because the police station was a place she knew well. With her usual authority, she asked for the detective in charge. When Detective Summers arrived, he was dismissive and rude. He did not care about Elizabeth's power.

"Look, I'm just asking for some information. He's my son."

Detective Summers looked at her. "I'm just going by the book, and I can't provide you with any information. You'll find out soon enough."

Lorenzo identified himself as Mark's attorney and was walked into the room where Mark was being interrogated.

When Lorenzo walked into the room, he saw Mark, hands on his face, clearly distraught, saying, "No sir, that's not what happened."

Immediately Lorenzo demanded that the interrogation stop, and said, "My client has nothing else to say today. You can schedule an interrogation with me, or with subsequent representation present."

Once alone, Lorenzo asked Mark if he had admitted to any crime. Mark said, "No, and I didn't do anything wrong." Lorenzo was satisfied to hear this.

Elizabeth felt helpless and could not handle that her baby boy was in jail. She tried to use her influence to accelerate Mark's release. Elizabeth did not want Mark to wait for Initial Appearance court and asked the duty judge to quickly establish bail, which the Suarezes paid. Mark was released.

Back at home, they sat silently in the kitchen, with Mark, Katie, and Elizabeth at the kitchen table and Lorenzo at the high bar table sipping coffee.

Finally, Elizabeth looked at Mark and said, "Okay, Mark, tell us exactly what happened."

Mark's voice was low and sad. He didn't have any fight left in him. "I told you, Mom, Megan is lying. I didn't attack her, she jumped on me, I pushed her away, and she fell. Then that jerk Cole, who has it in for me. I can't believe my luck," Mark sobbed. "I can't even imagine how I am going to go to school and what everyone is going to say about me."

Katie eyes turned red and she said, "Don't worry, Mark, everyone knows you're a great guy. I'm sure it will be okay." Katie's voice got deeper and she said, "When I see that bitch Megan, I'm going to…"

Lorenzo stopped her and said, "You will do nothing to her. Don't even talk to her. Anything you say or do can be used against your brother."

"Mark, so who is this kid Cole? First, he looks for a fight with you at the game, and then witnesses you attacking Megan?" asked Elizabeth.

"Yeah, Mom, I have no idea what I did to him, but he hates me, and he has been trying to pick a fight with me since last year. Recently he started calling me 'beaner' and 'fucking Mexican.'"

"Be very careful with people like that, my son," said Lorenzo. "I have also noticed that since Trump started his campaign against Mexican immigrants, more and more beaner and Mexican jokes are being passed around work. It seems to me like people are becoming more polarized than ever toward Mexicans."

"Look, we are not Mexicans," said Elizabeth. "We're Americans. We are strong, and we will beat this."

"Mom, why should we have to hide who we are?" asked Katie. "We're Mexican-American, and as long as we act embarrassed about it, people are going to continue to use it against us."

Lorenzo saw that Elizabeth did not like Katie's observation, and tried to move forward. "You guys just need to go back to school and try to forget all about this. Let your mom and me deal with the legal stuff. Our goal is to either have this dismissed or make it a misdemeanor and make sure Mark's name does not go onto the sex offender registry."

When Mark heard those words, his heart felt like it had been squeezed. Lorenzo saw the look on his son's face and realized he should not have said that out loud.

"I'm sorry, Mark, I should not have said that. I am sure that your mom and I can make this go away." Of course, Lorenzo knew better than to assume anything when it came to legal matters. Deep inside, he knew the outcome of this legal matter would impact the future of his son.

The next day Elizabeth met with her boss, who was very clear with her.

"Don't get involved in Mark's case and don't question the prosecutor in charge. Any involvement, or apparent involvement, could be considered obstruction of justice and will make this case a hell of a lot worse."

Lorenzo was not a criminal lawyer but a family lawyer, so they decided to hire a reputable criminal attorney. Nevertheless, this did not stop them from getting involved. Elizabeth and Lorenzo constantly argued about the right direction of the case, and a terrible wedge started to form between them.

Going places together became torture, for they found it increasingly more difficult to answer all the questions their friends and family had. Often Elizabeth would find Lorenzo's responses inappropriate one way or another, and they would end up in heated arguments.

Their fights went on and on. Katie, in the beginning, tried to bring reason but discovered it was of no use. Both she and Mark learned to go to their rooms and put in their earphones.

Back at school, Mark went from one of the most popular students at Washington to an exile; he no longer felt welcome. When he arrived at school, he felt all eyes on him. Walking the hallways, he heard murmuring all around him.

He walked into the locker room to present himself for football practice. "I need this workout so badly to clear my mind."

Coach Murphy stopped him and asked him to his office. "Son, I have no choice but to suspended you from the football team."

"But coach, I didn't do anything wrong. Megan has been trying to hook up with me for a long time. I don't even find her attractive. It's not fair."

"Don't worry, son, I'm sure all of that will be resolved soon, and then you can rejoin the team."

Walking out of the gym, he saw Zack. Mark walked toward him to say hi, but Zack turned his head as if he had not seen him and ran toward the field. Things only got worse for Mark. Everyone he knew avoided him. Savannah, in particular, did not know how to take the news; she did everything in her power to not be anywhere she thought Mark might be.

From that point on, Mark could only count on being seen and talked to by Cole and his friends. They found tremendous enjoyment in ridiculing him by saying words in Spanish with distorted accents, pushing him in the halls, and taunting him.

"Hi eseee," Cole started. "Did you see some of your raza in jail?"

Mark tried to walk away, but Cole's friend David stepped in front of him. "Look, man, I don't want trouble, just leave me alone. I don't know what I did to you, but please leave me alone." Mark turned his head down in defeat and walked away, and that time they let him walk away; other times they were crueler and pushed him harder.

Walking away, he realized that for the first time in his life he felt like a "Mexican" and remembered the story his dad told him about the Mexican ranchers in the 1840s. From one day to the next, they were no longer welcome on their own lands and were vilified and oppressed by the new conquerors.

Katie found out that she, too, was going to have to pay a high price at school for the accusations against Mark. She heard murmuring all around her, which sometimes turned into flat-out offensive speech.

Patricia was in Katie's history class and resented Katie because she got a lot of attention from her teachers. "So, is your rapist brother out of jail?"

Patricia's friend Natalie said, "I guess Trump may be right about you Mexicans."

"Look," said Katie, "Mark didn't do anything. Those are false accusations."

Blaire looked at Patricia with fire coming out of her blue eyes. "Listen bitches, you better keep walking." They could tell Blaire was serious, and they turned away.

Blaire, although thin, could be aggressive and fearless. As Katie's most stalwart defender and supporter, she was always ready to fight against people who attacked Katie; she assumed Katie wasn't feisty,

"Blaire, don't get into a fight for me. I can defend myself."

"No way! What they do to you or Mark, they do to me."

Mallory, on the other hand, had disappeared. She was also Mexican-American and wanted nothing to do with Katie or Mark, as they had now become the infamous Mexicans on campus. Mallory did not want to become a target as well, mainly because she never felt like she really belonged, as she was the daughter of a housemaid. Soco, her mother, worked for the Mackintoshes inside the Paradise Valley school district, which qualified her daughters to attend Washington High. Anne Mackintosh had encouraged Soco to send her daughters to Washington, and Soco agreed, knowing they would be safer away from gangs and would get a better education.

The following months were tough for the Suarez kids: Mark's confidence started to falter, and his self-esteem deteriorated rapidly; in Katie's case the opposite occurred, her timid and insecure personality became more self-confident, forged by adversity.

CHAPTER TWELVE
BBQ

Paradise Valley was a beautiful, small community in the middle of a large metropolis, where everyone knew each other. When people went to the supermarket they had to dress up because chances were they would see the parent of one of their kids' friends, or maybe someone who was in the same Eagle Scouts group years prior.

Late in the afternoon at Sprouts, an organic whole-food grocery store, Elizabeth Suarez walked the aisles and looked for a new brand of coconut chips. Her mind was spinning out of control, thinking about her son, when she came across Anne Mackintosh. They hadn't seen each other in years. They liked each other and used to be closer when Lorenzo coached soccer for Zack and Mark when they were seven and eight years old.

"Anne, how are you? I haven't seen you in a long time. Is Jenny still in Zimbabwe?"

"Yes, and I'm so worried about her, but she insists that she has to do everything she can to help those poor children. She loves them."

While Anne talked, Elizabeth wondered if she knew about Mark.

"Jenny has the kindest heart. Please tell her I send my love."

"Yes, I will… Hey, by the way, it has been too long, and tomorrow we're having some of the neighbors over for a barbecue. You may know them, the Schorers and the Carters. Why don't you, Lorenzo, and the kids come over. It will be fun."

"Wow, that's so nice of you. Let me look, but I don't think we have plans. I'll confirm with Lorenzo. It would be fun."

Elizabeth was unaware that Anne knew about what happened at the party; in fact, all of Paradise Valley knew about it. But Anne had a big heart and imagined the heartache Elizabeth and her family were going through. Anne was convinced Mark was innocent because she had known him for so long, and knew he was a good kid. Anne wanted to say something in support, but she just didn't want to make Elizabeth feel bad, so she acted like she knew nothing.

When Elizabeth arrived home, she mentioned her encounter to Lorenzo and dismissed the idea of going to the barbecue. She didn't feel like socializing and worried that the neighbors might know something. On the other hand, Lorenzo thought it would be good for the family to go visit the Mackintoshes. They were good people, good friends with the kids, and Mark and Katie needed a distraction.

The Mackintosh home was beautiful. A salmon-colored, five-thousand-square-foot Spanish-style home with a red-tile roof, it had rounded windows, smooth stucco siding, and a large central courtyard with traditional pillars. The interior was traditional and impeccably designed, with a balanced combination of polished Saltillo red tile and hardwood floors that spread throughout. The floors were covered by exquisite Mexican-design carpets. Rough iron detail, wooden beams, stucco walls, beautiful tile accents, and large planters with palms and other large-leaf plants decorated the house.

When the Suarez family arrived, the other two families invited were already there. The Schorers and the Carters were both neighbors with teenage children. Allison and Jason Schorer had one son, Andrew, who was nineteen and already at Arizona State. June and Luke Carter had two children, Blaire, who was sixteen, and Charlie, her younger brother, who was thirteen. The young people were in the pool, so Anne told Katie and Mark to go to the guest room and use the guest bathroom if they needed to change into their swimwear.

Anne pointed to the backyard and looked at Lorenzo. "Tom and the guys are back there, next to the barbecue and the bar. Beers are there as well." Anne turned and started talking to Elizabeth. They both walked toward Allison and June, who chatted in the Mackintoshes' beautiful kitchen, which was made with traditional Mexican heavy carved wood, and finished with Miele and Sub-Zero kitchen appliances.

Lorenzo arrived at a roaring barbecue with flames coming out. Tom ignited it at full blast to burn off old remnants and start the traditional barbecue cleaning. Tom and Lorenzo were not friends, but they liked each other. They had spent time together at soccer practice, and both felt each had good values and loved their families. Tom knew about the Mark incident but had agreed with Anne to not mention it, unless the Suarez family brought it up.

Luke, who was in real estate, admired Tom's home and all the beautiful details. "Man, you have one of the best Spanish-style homes I've seen, and trust me, I know Spanish style. Phoenix is filled with Spanish homes and buildings. All the beautiful details… whoever designed this home thought about everything."

Jason, a plastic surgeon, added, "Yes, beautiful. I've seen way too many places built in this style made with cheap Mexican shit, and they look tacky, but your home is tasteful and classy. Who is your designer?"

Tom laughed. "Well, Jason, I believe just about all the furniture and details you see here were imported from Mexico by my designers, Samuels & Sons, and I think they're the best firm in town."

"In Mexico, we call this style of home Mexican Style." He turned to Tom. "Your home looks like one of the finest haciendas in Mexico."

Tom looked at Lorenzo and gave him a half smile. The statement sounded silly to him.

"Well, Lorenzo, here we call it Spanish style," said Jason.

"I know, Jason, but what we have here is not Spanish style. Mexican and Spanish styles are different, and you won't see homes like this in Spain. Of course, Mexican architecture has a lot of influence from Spanish architecture, but it has unique features. No different than Roman and Greek or English and American; there are clear differences."

Tom did not like confrontation, and he quickly moved the conversation to sports. They all agreed that the Diamondbacks looked very good so far, and they continued to talk about sports while they drank beer and cooked steaks.

The Mackintoshes' backyard had a large, kidney-shaped salt-water pool, and at one end it had an eight-foot-tall waterfall with large natural river rocks and plants, with the periphery in slate. To the right of the pool was a large lawn where several pool chairs were lined up. The smell of the barbecue permeated the air. Everyone was having a fun time, and Katie walked out of the bathroom wearing a big t-shirt.

Mark knew the pool and felt relaxed that day, so he ran to the pool and screamed, "Cannonball," and splashed everyone around him.

Blaire faked being upset. "You're an asshole, Mark." Blaire had a crush on Mark and had told Katie that she liked her brother, but Katie told Blaire not to waste her time because Mark had a big crush on Savannah.

"Yuck," Blaire said.

Zack had been playing some form of football-water polo with Andrew and Charlie, neither of whom was athletic, so he was bored. When Mark showed up, Zack was visibly annoyed because his mother had informed him only that morning that the Suarezes were also invited.

Mark immediately asked, "Hey, can I join the game?"

Zack shrugged his shoulders and said, "Whatever."

Zack, who was a better athlete, took Charlie. Mark and Andrew made the other team. As usual, Mark and Zack were very competitive, but this time it was not friendly. Zack threw the ball into Mark's face, and Mark responded in kind; they pushed and shoved each other and forgot the other two players were there. Mark smiled a couple of times in hopes they would have a breakthrough and become friendly again, but Zack had none of that.

One of the passes thrown by Charlie was too high for Zack to catch and it hit Katie in the head.

"You jerks, be careful!" Katie looked at Blaire, who she had been chatting with in the pool chairs. "Let's go in and disturb those jerks' game." Katie was not to be messed with.

After Charlie retrieved the ball, the boys continued to play and splash like crazy, when Katie and Blaire got into the pool. Zack turned his head toward them and saw Katie who had removed her t-shirt and showed off a stylish one-piece swimsuit and her gorgeous curves.

Zack froze. Katie had always been Mark's little sister, but now he realized she was all grown up, she was beautiful. At that moment he felt his heart melt for her. When Charlie threw a pass toward Zack, who was distracted, it hit him in the head.

Mark laughed; he did not notice that Zack's attention had shifted. When Katie got into the pool, she pushed Zack, took the ball, and threw it onto the lawn. Mark screamed and complained, but Zack didn't say anything. Katie and Blaire started doing laps to disrupt the rest of their game.

After dinner, the grownups sat together, had drinks, and conversed about their kids, talking about where they hoped the kids would go to college, and what careers they hoped they chose. Each took a turn talking about their job. Lorenzo was not shy but did not like chitchat and preferred to listen. Allison asked Elizabeth, "Your job seems so exciting. What are the most common crimes you have to prosecute?" Elizabeth said, "Sadly, lots of drug charges."

"Aren't you afraid to prosecute some of those men from the cartels?" Allison said.

"Well, most of the charges are for drug possession; usually users and some small-time dealers."

Jason said, "You know, it makes me so upset how those damn Mexican cartels keep pushing drugs onto our children, and they get away with it. That's why I hope Trump will win and build the wall. I think he's going to be tough against those damn people."

Anne had always been vigilant with her kids about drugs. "Jason, I don't see any Mexican cartel people ever pushing the drugs in school. The biggest enemies are peer pressure, TV and movies because they glorify drug use and make it fun, like that movie 'The Pineapple Express.' When we went to see it together, I forced my family to walk out of the theater."

Allison joined in. "Yeah, when I was in school, peer pressure was the biggest reason people tried drugs and got hooked on them."

"Well if those damn Mexicans didn't sell it, then the problem would be less."

Lorenzo decided to jump in. "Jason, those cartel people are despicable, and I wish there were a way to eradicate them from this earth. But they are just the suppliers, and the problem didn't start in Mexico, the problem is the insatiable appetite for drugs this country has. Movies, TV, peer pressure, and bad parenting are all responsible. Before, it was the Colombians. Then the Mexican criminals realized what a good business it was, so they took it from the Colombians. Unfortunately, when that happened, the price Mexicans in Mexico have paid is unimaginable and the spike in heinous crime increased in a way the country had never seen, similar to what the 1920s Prohibition did to crime in the US."

"Yes, those poor people," Anne said. "I remember going to Acapulco as a child, and my parents did not have a care in the world. Now, I hear it's very dangerous because of the cartels."

"The price Mexicans have paid for the addiction in this country is very high," added Lorenzo. "And trust me, if the Mexican suppliers disappeared, new suppliers would appear, from all over the world."

Tom, wanting to stop any confrontational conversations, asked everyone if they wanted another drink. He got up and took orders, Lorenzo offered to help, and the partygoers dispersed into smaller groups.

On the drive home, Elizabeth fumed at Lorenzo and could not wait to get home. "I am so tired of your stupid comments about Mexicans being the martyrs and how Mexico this and Mexicans that. Just shut up about it. No one cares, and you just found a way to embarrass me again. And it makes you sound like you love Mexico and hate America. It's going to make our neighbors hate us."

Lorenzo was caught off guard. "Honey, I didn't realize I did anything wrong. I thought I was merely explaining to our friends how the blame may be with the wrong people and, ultimately, I think they know it's my opinion. I've said it millions of times to everyone: America is the best country in the world. But that doesn't stop me from loving the beautiful Mexican culture or the people."

Unlike Elizabeth, Lorenzo was Mexican-born in Mexico City. He was not embarrassed to say he was Mexican, to talk about Mexico in positive terms, or to defend his culture. He saw a clear difference between his cultural pride and his love of the United States. When Elizabeth first met Lorenzo, she found his love for his culture refreshing, as she had not been raised to be proud of her culture. During their courtship, she found it endearing, but now she found it repulsive.

Lorenzo was a highly educated man, born into an educated upper-middle-class family, not from a family of corrupt politicians who often turned mega-rich in Mexico, but from a well-to-do family who for generations had valued education. In fact, Lorenzo's family traced their ancestry to one of Mexico's greatest heroes of the independence, also an educated man. Lorenzo had attended the Universidad National Autonoma de Mexico, or UNAM, the most prestigious university in Mexico, and the oldest higher education institution on the American continent. His father, grandfather, and other ancestors had graduated as lawyers from that same university.

As a young man, after finishing law school, he was sent for a postgraduate degree in the US, as many wealthy Mexicans do, and it was there, at Arizona State University, where Lorenzo first met and fell in love with Elizabeth. Lorenzo learned English in the private schools he attended during childhood, but when he realized he was going to marry Elizabeth and stay in the US, he decided to work on his English and learned to speak it almost perfectly.

At Arizona State, Lorenzo was happy and was treated well by teachers and fellow students. He was a solid student—not a straight A student, but a solid B+—and was courteous and committed to learning. He lived on campus in a close-knit community of learners and mentors with open minds and dreams of creating a better world.

Occasionally he heard derogatory comments about the Mexican laborers and cleaning workers. One time he was chatting at the cafeteria with a fellow master's student when a couple of undergraduates of Indian background chatted with each other in front of him and said, "These freaking Mexicans are so stinky, what do they eat?" while looking at the cleaning lady who was picking up the trash from all the cafeteria trash bins.

Lorenzo turned to them. "Excuse me, but you are speaking of a hard-working woman who has to do a dirty and thankless job."

This behavior was not totally surprising to Lorenzo, as Mexico was a classist society, where the rich and educated felt great superiority over the less wealthy and uneducated. Lorenzo didn't like it but understood it.

Lorenzo loved America, especially the American charitable spirit. Unlike Mexico's rich who look down and trample over the poor, the wealthy Americans usually establish charities and find ways to help the less fortunate. He was impressed to no end with the American respect toward order and the law—people actually pay attention to traffic laws and the police give tickets for infractions, instead of asking for a bribe. And he absolutely loved

American fairness and the generally accepted attitude of equality.

Unlike Mexico, where the wealthy and educated usually treat the poor laborers as inferior, almost like a different species, to him it was clear that Americans believed in the saying that all men are created equal. During most dealings, he would see how a cleaning person and a lawyer were treated with the same respect, and the well-being of all parties during any transaction was considered. It only made sense to him.

When he decided to stay in the US, he discovered that fairness would not be extended to everyone. Lorenzo needed to find an internship to apply for an H1 visa, which would allow him to work. He felt it was obvious for him to apply to the top law firms first, as he knew he had excellent experience and education, which would be attractive to any firm. During the application period and interviews, things went very well.

The interviewers looked interested, were very polite, and he would leave thinking, "That was a great interview," and then nothing—no calls, no offers. This continued for some time, and he started to lose his confidence. Was he was doing something wrong? Things became clear during an interview at one of the top family law firms in Phoenix, Callis, Judichic & Fong, where he was interviewed by one of the partners, Stan Judichic, who started with a friendly smile and said, "Nice resume. I see you have a master's degree in family law from ASU. I'm also an ASU alumnus."

"Yes, Mr. Judichic, I just finished my master's, but I do have quite a bit of legal experience. I come from a family of lawyers, and I'm confident I can be of value to your firm."

"I notice an accent. Where's it from?"

"I'm from Mexico City," Lorenzo said.

An almost imperceptible flinch was evident on Judichic when he said, "Nice. You seem very talented, and I wish we could use someone like you. Our firm used to have a Spanish-speaking department, but it was closed because we decided to focus on our more affluent clients." He took a big breath as he said, "But I hear that Perez & Gonzales in downtown is hiring. I wish you the best of luck, Loreenzoo."

Lorenzo felt that Judichic intentionally distorted his name and he could smell the condescension a mile away. He was furious.

In fact, Perez & Gonzales did hire him and agreed to sponsor his H1 visa. The firm was owned by a very nice, but average lawyer, John Perez, an Arizona native of Mexican background who could trace his ancestry in Arizona back several generations. He was the first in his family to ever have an education beyond high school. John was an honest man, who wanted to help his people. Unfortunately for his clients, he had a self-imposed glass ceiling, and every time a client had to fight against a large reputable Anglo law firm, Perez would be intimidated and lose his client's case.

Mr. Perez was born in Arizona, a state with a hundred and fifty-year history of oppressive attitudes toward Mexicans, and grew up with the usual second-class-citizen mentality. Even after finishing law school, Mr. Perez's second-class-citizen mentality and glass ceiling were firmly in place after generations of being told, "Your people are worthless," which left him feeling unwanted, disrespected, and oppressed.

While small progress had occurred over the years, there is a palpable feeling that Mexicans and Mexican-Americans are not welcome foreigners in Arizona. It is clear that the really good jobs were rarely offered to Mexican-Americans and racial profiling of Mexican-American-looking people was acceptable and even encouraged by politicians, permitting their arrest and detention until they show proof of citizenship.

Mexicans in Arizona have learned to keep a low profile, stay in their own community, and not venture to the other side of town. The Mexican-Americans who blend in well with the American society feel the need to become closet Mexicans and find ways to conceal their Mexican ancestry by using other generic terms like Hispanic and Latino when referring to their heritage.

Lorenzo was fortunate to not have a glass ceiling because he had not been born in Arizona or the US. Being born in Mexico City made him feel special because Mexico City is not just the largest and wealthiest city in Mexico, it is the largest and most prosperous city in the Spanish-speaking Americas. At his university, UNAM, Lorenzo enjoyed seeing affluent students from central and South America who went to Mexico to get their master's, in the same way wealthy Mexicans would go to the US. In Mexico. Lorenzo befriended many actors and musicians from Central and South America who wanted to make it in the "Big Apple" of Latin America, Mexico City.

Lorenzo was not arrogant even though his father was from a very wealthy family. Lorenzo's mother, on the other hand, was a self-made woman from a poor but hard-working family in Monterrey, one of Mexico's most affluent industrial cities. Lorenzo's mother taught him to hate Mexico's class system, and to dislike people who robbed the dignity of others less fortunate. While in law school in Mexico City, Lorenzo interned at a reputable law firm where the senior partner, Lic. Mario Rebollado, was a friend of his father. In this law firm, he saw all its ugliness, the pervasive arrogance of the wealthy in Mexico.

While Lic. Rebollado charged large amounts of money for his services and made millions, the fifty people he employed, from secretaries to the parking attendant, made barely enough to live. Lic. Rebollado treated his employees like servants, spoke arrogantly to them, yelled, and reprimanded them like children. Lorenzo hated Lic. Rebollado. He hated to think how tough his co-workers' lives must have been with those miserable salaries. True to the easygoing Mexican mentality, all fifty employees appeared to have very happy lives.

A few months after Lorenzo joined Perez & Gonzales, a young and beautiful Mexican-born woman hired the firm to represent her against Harrison Lombar, a wealthy man she was divorcing who was twenty-five years her senior. Her name was Claudia Islas, and she was from Sinaloa, a state in Mexico where some of the most beautiful women in the world are born. Harrison was forty-five when he met Claudia on a trip to Las Brisas, a posh resort near Manzanillo. She was twenty and stunning. Claudia was smitten with Harrison's blue eyes and his apparent power and success. He quickly proposed marriage and took her with him to Phoenix, where they had two beautiful children, both with sandy blond hair.

He was abusive from the start. He did not allow her to speak Spanish to their children. "My children are American, I don't want anyone to treat them like damn Mexicans," he said.

She argued that she was Mexican and she wanted them to appreciate their culture.

He yelled at her, "Fuck your culture. Mexicans have nothing to appreciate, other than good tacos and beer."

She had signed a prenuptial agreement agreeing that she would not receive any alimony if she divorced him before their tenth anniversary. Six months before the ten-year mark, Harrison presented Claudia with divorce papers, giving her zero alimony, and requesting full custody of the children. He claimed she had no income, no education, and that she was abusive toward their children because she spanked the kids once in a while. When Mr. Perez realized that Harrison was represented by Callis, Judichic & Fong, he panicked and was about to refer Claudia to a different firm. But Lorenzo interceded and said he would take the case.

At the first court meeting, Judichic recognized Lorenzo. Judichic smiled and pleasantly said, "Hi Loreenzoo, I see you got a job in downtown, good. Not a good idea to go against the big boys. You're going to learn more on this case than all you learned in law school."

Lorenzo recognized Judichic immediately and clenched his teeth hard, but responded pleasantly, "Yes Mr. Judichic, I recognize you, and I have the feeling your firm may also learn a thing or two."

The court case lasted over a year, and it was a hard-fought case. Callis, Judichic & Fong made him work hard. They asked for court date extensions at the last minute to delay and frustrate Lorenzo, requested the production of every imaginable document, demanded forensic accounting even though Claudia had no real finances of her own, and requested unnecessary background information about Claudia from both the US and Mexico.

They wanted to bury Lorenzo with interrogatories and used every trick in the lawyer's book, but Lorenzo was not intimidated because he also knew the tricks and was a great lawyer. Lorenzo worked long hours, and during court time he barely slept because he was busy preparing for any trial contingencies, witnesses, and cross-examinations. He honestly cared for the well-being of his client, Claudia.

He also wanted to prove something to Judichic, and he did. Claudia was awarded fifty percent of Harrison's fortune, and fifty percent custody of the children. Harrison was devastated and furious with Judichic, and soon after the trial, he sued Callis, Judichic & Fong for malpractice.

With time, Lorenzo learned to accept the fact that in the US, Mexicans were seen as second-class citizens. New immigrants from other countries soon learn to look down on Mexicans, and Lorenzo struggled to figure out how this happened.

After a year and a half of working at Perez & Gonzales and winning all his cases, he decided it was time to open his own firm. He invested way more than he had in order to establish an elegant office that was not very large but had a first-class feel. Opening a new law firm in downtown Phoenix was tough because there was so much competition. At first, only Mexicans and Hispanics were eager to be his clients, but the firm grew fast. With time, Lorenzo's excellent results and ability to win cases, even against the most reputable and expensive law firms, gave him an excellent reputation.

Soon, Lorenzo Suarez, JD, Law Firm became a top law firm, and the entire Phoenix community wanted to be represented by him.

CHAPTER THIRTEEN
THE ESSAY

The day Katie was to present her essay had arrived, and it was important because it would be one-third of her grade. Mrs. Smith gave each student ten minutes to present their essay orally, and five minutes for the class to counter-argue. Good counter-arguments were also graded and were necessary for the class. Katie Suarez meant she was an "S," and close to being the last person in class for everything unless her teacher flipped the order, which was not the case this time. This gave Katie extra time to prepare her oral presentation.

She asked for her dad's help, and they both treated the project like she was preparing for a day in court.

The student essays showed an interesting trend. Even though Washington High was in the middle of Paradise Valley, a mostly Republican area, the young members of the wealthy Republican families were fiscally and socially progressive, as millennials usually are.

Students did oral presentations of their essays on a variety of current subjects. One suggested the US government space agency NASA, not SpaceX, a private company, should be spending money on the development of rockets to visit Mars, and how that could have a positive effect on society. Another student presented an essay on a news story showing how artificial intelligence was accelerating too fast and how computers may become too smart, creating unforeseen problems.

Molly Sverstky, a pretty redhead with a socially progressive mind, took on a Washington Post article claiming Sheriff Joe Arpaio had a long history of promoting racial profiling of Mexicans and his actions cost the Maricopa

County one hundred and forty-six million dollars to settle lawsuits for his various acts of misconduct. He had been tried and convicted and should have been removed from office.

Molly argued that Sheriff Arpaio had been in office for over twenty years, was an active spokesperson against Mexican immigrants, and may have sparked anti-immigrant sentiment in Arizona. Out of all of the subjects discussed up to that point, this had been the most heated. Some students argued that Arpaio's firm hand on crime was right for Phoenix.

The presidential race was a popular subject in the classroom. At the time, both Republican and Democratic candidates fought with each other. Many assumed Hillary Clinton was a sure thing for the Democratic ticket and a couple of students made strong arguments for the first woman president. There were many Republican candidates.

One of the students argued that it would be inappropriate for one family, the Bush family, to have three of its members be president because it could be considered nepotism. Every time Donald Trump came up in the conversation, students quickly dismissed him and said, "There's no chance he will ever be chosen by the Republicans." He was not taken seriously by anyone, except Katie.

Katie started her presentation by boldly acknowledging something most Mexican-Americans preferred not to talk about. "For some time now, speeches by Donald Trump and Sheriff Joe Arpaio have been targeting Mexicans as bad people, criminals, and rapists. The language used in their speeches is polarizing people against Mexicans and Mexican-Americans. Mexicans, in turn, are feeling attacked and being made to feel ashamed, which is causing unimaginable damage.

"Well, I am a Mexican-American, and I am aware that being Mexican has a negative stigma attached to it. Even other Hispanics in America don't want to be called Mexican; they take it as an offense.

"I know many of you have Irish, English, or German ancestry and feel attachment and pride in your culture, while at the same time you are proud Americans. America is a land of immigrants. But for example if you're of Irish ancestry, how would you feel if someone started attacking the Irish, generalizing and falsely saying you are all criminals and rapists? Would that make it more difficult to say, 'Kiss me, I'm Irish' on Saint Patrick's Day?" She smiled, and the entire room chuckled.

"People with English, Italian, Jewish, German, Russian, Cuban, Indian, or any ancestry, acknowledge their background with a sense of identity and pride. Mexicans feel they have to hide it." She paused and allowed the room to take that in.

"Successful Mexicans usually hide their Mexican background because they fear it may hinder their success or lower their perceived value. There are countless celebrities and powerful people who are partial or full Mexican-Americans, but because they blend well, people barely consider them Mexican and generally ignore their ancestry. I feel their behavior is cowardly but understandable. They rob Mexican-American youth of positive role models."

Once more, she paused.

"Now think of how Jennifer Lopez or Ricky Martin flaunt their Puerto Rican ancestry, and how proud Gloria Estefan is when she talks about her Cuban culture, and Jerry Seinfeld cherishes his Jewish idiosyncrasies." Again she paused, then asked, "Why? Why do Mexicans not have a culture to be proud of?" This time Katie looked around the room and imagined people thinking, "Of course, Mexicans have nothing to be proud of." But Katie's courage was unstoppable; she drew strength and conviction from current events, especially the way her brother was being treated.

Katie could tell she had her audience's attention and recounted her dad's story. "The rich Mexican culture has contributed greatly and is an indispensable part of American culture. Did you know that the beautiful and rich cowboy culture of boots, hats, colorful shirts, the way cattle are lassoed, and rodeos are all inherited from the Mexican culture?"

She stopped for a second and then said, "The beautiful Mexican architecture and art, incorrectly called Spanish or Southwest, are also widespread. And don't forget that the amazing cuisine, which is one of the best in the world, has influenced American cooking in endless ways." She used much of what she had learned from her dad.

Katie moved on to the harder point to accept. "So why has so much of the rich and influential Mexican culture been devalued or ignored? This goes way back to a long and dark historical context, which is hard to accept."

She recounted her dad's story about the Mexican-American War. "Mexicans had their lands and possessions illegally removed and were forced to become laborers by bad and greedy people, using fear tactics to vilify and distort perceptions of Mexicans and their culture to justify the harsh subjugation. Most Americans did not know they were being manipulated by greedy people.

"And just like some of our ancestors who were slave owners did unimaginable harm to African-Americans, some of our ancestors did some bad things to the Mexican-Americans, and the effects of it are still felt today. The most dangerous part is that those strategies of using fear and misinformation are being repeated by people like Arpaio, and now Trump.

"You may ask, why should anyone care about the past or acknowledge the terrible abuses of the past? Why should anyone care about the ignored contributions of the Mexican culture or pay respect to a people and culture that have given so much to America? Two important reasons: First, fairness. Mexican-Americans were oppressed for so long, it has scared them and placed them at a considerable disadvantage, and now again they are being attacked mercilessly and unfairly for political reasons.

"The second, and the most important reason, is Mexican-American youth. They have always felt marginalized, have fewer opportunities, and feel hopeless, which will often lead to aggressive and destructive behavior. Unless we do something, the future of this youth, as well as our collective future, will be compromised.

"Americans are good and fair people, and it is time to recognize the injustices of the past and fight against perpetuating this unfairness. Millions of impressionable Mexican-American children are now feeling unworthy and unwelcome in their own land because of people like Donald Trump and Joe Arpaio. These men are like their predecessors one hundred and fifty years ago. They are willing to sacrifice Mexicans and use them as scapegoats for economic and political gain."

Finally, she stopped, and fellow students waited to see if there was more but realized she was finished. They applauded. And even Mrs. Smith, who did not like some of her arguments, applauded.

Her speech was powerful, and the response was positive. Most found Katie's argument compelling, and during the five-minute debate said things like, "Wow, Katie, I didn't know," or "Katie, that was an amazing history lesson." Mallory got involved and talked about some of the stories of her ancestors.

Nevertheless, some students countered Katie's findings. "Katie, you're oversimplifying the situation. Illegal Mexican immigrants continue coming at large rates and are harming the American economy."

Katie was prepared for this question. "I don't think anyone disagrees that illegal immigration should be stopped. It's been going on too long. Comprehensive immigration law is needed and respecting people's human rights and protecting family unity and stability is a must. I don't know if you're aware that legal Mexican immigration has almost stopped because current laws favor immigrants from other nations. Mexicans seeking legal immigration, some who want to unite with very close relatives, have to do it illegally."

Another boy said, "The problem you're forgetting is that Mexicans are bringing crime."

Katie was again prepared and said, "Well, in fact, there are many studies which clearly show that Mexican immigrants are not committing more crime than American natives. A recent article by the Wall Street Journal shows that Mexican immigrant don't commit crime at a higher rate than American citizens. Of course it's not difficult to show some anecdotal cases and point fingers. But the bigger problem is that young Mexican-Americans feel disenfranchised by the terrible comments from Trump and others, and my fear is, as I said before, people who are marginalized feel unwelcomed, become bitter, and may find crime their only option."

Marlon, another student, said, "Katie, you're unfairly attributing the cowboy culture and architecture to Mexicans. Isn't it the Spanish who did this?"

"Marlon, there is a good amount of Spanish influence on the Mexican vaqueros and architecture, but after over three hundred years of that Spanish influence mixed with Aztec culture and evolution in Mexico with different weather, terrain, local materials and influence, the Mexican vaquero and the Mexican architecture are far different from what you see in Spain.

"The American cowboy closely resembles the unique Mexican vaquero, in many ways. The way they rope livestock, use their lasso, the rodeos, and chaparreras. Let's remember, nothing is absolutely new. American institutions resemble English institutions, Roman architecture and institutions closely resemble the Greek, and Greece copied a lot from the Persians, and on and on."

Finally, Mrs. Smith could not stop herself from sharing her opinion and said, "Katie, you're almost asking us to rewrite history, and your findings are a little extreme." She was impressed with her student's presentation but felt that Katie had gone too far.

"Mrs. Smith, history has always been written by the victor, but there is plenty of evidence of what really happened, and sometimes wrongs, which have harmed others and continue to cause harm, should be corrected."

Katie had done excellent historical research and shared facts Mrs. Smith did not know. She did a good job connecting her findings with current events. Mrs. Smith was a proud Arizonan and felt conflicted again by her once-favorite student because she thought Katie overreached and was trying to rewrite history to the benefit of Mexicans, making them look like martyrs and Americans as abusive conquerors.

Mrs. Smith heard in her head the voice of Trump saying, "They're bringing drugs. They're bringing crime. They're rapists." Mrs. Smith had learned at a rally that there may be a conspiracy by Mexicans to attack America, and maybe Katie was part of it. After all, her brother was a rapist.

CHAPTER FOURTEEN
THE RALLY

When Katie received her history class results, her eyes swelled up with tears, and she felt betrayed by her beloved teacher. Mrs. Smith's comments to Katie about trying to rewrite history stuck in Katie's mind, but she was confident that Mrs. Smith was a fair teacher. Mrs. Smith had been Katie's favorite teacher all throughout her sophomore year and now as a junior. But since her oral presentation, Mrs. Smith had changed, becoming dismissive and cold toward Katie.

Mrs. Constance Smith was one of the best and most-liked teachers at Washington High. She was a tall, thin, average-looking woman, who liked to keep her hair short because it was practical. She had been born and raised in Phoenix and lived in the middle-class suburb of Gilbert with her husband of fifteen years, Mike, and her two young teenage children. She got her teaching credential at Chandler-Gilbert Community College, following in the footsteps of her mom, who had also been a teacher.

She and her husband Mike had done very little traveling. They had gotten married young because of an unexpected pregnancy. Mike was a roofing contractor who often complained of the unfair competition due to "damn Mexican roofers, who offered dirt-cheap prices." Mike had four workers; two were Mexican immigrants who did all the very hard labor, both extremely hard-working and reliable, and he paid them half of what he paid his other employees. He saw absolutely nothing wrong with paying them less.

Constance Smith was a hard-working, dedicated teacher who read and graded papers instead of watching TV because she wanted to influence her students and have them appreciate the importance of history. Unfortunately, she did not make good money as a teacher, and her husband's inability to make good money made their finances tight, and sometimes unmanageable.

Mike blamed "the damn government" for not stopping illegals who stole his jobs. Constance blamed the government for not paying teachers better salaries and assumed the government spent too much money on stupid social services, so that not enough money was left to help hard-working Americans. Both were devoted Republicans, and both had voted for McCain for president. During Obama's presidency, both were terribly frustrated with the government.

Initially, Mrs. Smith was impressed with Jeb Bush and planned to vote for him because she thought Trump was a joke. Her entire perspective changed the day her friend Gertrude invited her to go to a Trump rally. She only went to support her friend and because she was curious.

At the Phoenix Convention Center, Trump used his sophisticated showmanship skills to promise he would "destroy ISIS, bring more jobs, and stop the press, who were terrible liars." In front of a Republican crowd, he claimed the Democrats, under their chosen candidate, would give America four more years of Obama's values, which ignored and dissolved America's values. He reminded the crowd of how the Democrats allowed foreign nations to rob Americans from under their noses. Trump made a point to say that only he had identified these problems, and only he could resolve them. He said, "We, the silent majority, are going to make America great again."

Gertrude and Mrs. Smith were impressed; they liked what Trump said.

To launch the most critical part of his rally, Trump and his team used their fine-tuned TV show-making skills. They presented a clip of the father of a young man killed by a Mexican illegal. He recounted his unfortunate and sad story, and the grief-stricken man said, "We need to fix the border; we don't need them people."

Tears came down Mrs. Smith's face as she listened to the story and felt the pain of the man. She felt irate about the Mexican criminal behavior and was terribly scared by the idea of these people coming to hurt and kill Americans.

The identification of a scapegoat and creation of a "common enemy" are tactics that have been used by leaders and politicians for centuries. The Nazis used powerful propaganda to make the Jews look like they were the cause of every evil in German society. Candidate Trump used these techniques against his chosen group, the Mexicans. Somehow, Mrs. Smith had missed that part in her history lessons.

Trump used the audience's emotions, stirred up by the video and the story, to increase his fear-building rhetoric and suggested a conspiracy about the Mexican government: "They're killing us at the border, and they're killing us in trade," he said of Mexico. "They're killing us."

Trump took advantage of some minor scuffling amongst protestors outside the rally, and built on that to create more fear. "I wonder if the Mexican government sent them over here," he said. "I think so. We'll take our country back."

Cole Jones and his friends had decided to attend this rally, and at this point, they started to yell, "Build the wall! Build the wall!" The entire arena broke into a chant, "Build the wall! Build the wall!" Cole chanted so hard he felt as if his vocal cords were on fire and his heart would beat out of his chest—it was magical! After the rally, Cole was ready for battle.

Sheriff Arpaio was there to support Trump, and his presence alone represented decades of civil rights violations against Mexicans. Trump called him a great man.

The end of the rally had manipulated ordinary Americans to fear and dislike Mexicans, and to support the man who promised to build the wall to keep them out.

Once more, unbeknownst to the Suarezes, this rally had stirred up emotions in some people, which would have devastating consequences for their family, and millions of other scapegoats.

CHAPTER FIFTEEN

DETENTION

Before the Trump rally, Mrs. Smith may have been confused as to how to grade Katie, but after the rally, things became clear for her. She wrote a lengthy explanation and stapled it on top of Katie's essay to justify why she had given Katie a failing grade on this project.

It read, "Miss Suarez, you clearly worked hard on this project, and your oral presentation was organized. It had an effect on your audience, but the way you presented your argument was deceitful and manipulative. It leads to the oversimplification of a big problem, and an inappropriate conclusion of almost suggesting a history re-write.

"As you are well aware, one of my clearly stated instructions was to present a defendable premise and defendable conclusions. I find that your conclusions are not defendable, bordering on anti-American, and for this reason, I must disapprove the premise of your essay and fail your conclusion."

She wanted to write, "Your oral presentation almost wants to justify the presence of Mexicans in this country and wants to make Mexicans look like victims of mistreatment, which is ridiculous," but decided against it.

She added, as to soften the blow, "As you know, the essay counts for 30% of your final grade. Study hard for your final test and you can still pass my class."

Katie was heartbroken; she had worked so hard. And now her chances to get straight As were gone during this crucial junior year—the year that college admissions officers look at the most. And passing the class would now be very difficult, as she would have to get a perfect score on the final.

Even if she passed, it would not be anything better than a C grade. At this point, she doubted her decision to address the Mexican issues. Maybe she underestimated the strong feelings people have toward this Mexican issue and sticking her head out for her beliefs was a mistake.

Katie knew her chances to get into an Ivy League college would vanish into thin air if she failed this important history class and her head buzzed thinking about the consequences of this. Katie resolved to find an opportunity to speak with Mrs. Smith.

The next day, right after history class was over, Katie approached Mrs. Smith's desk. Katie was so nervous she was sweating. She had admired and liked Mrs. Smith for so long that she felt if she could have a heart-to-heart with her, they could find a resolution.

"What can I do for you, Katie?"

"Mrs. Smith, I was so sad to see my grade. I'm not here to challenge you, I am here just to ask if there is anything I can do to change my grade. As you know, my dream is to go to Harvard, and it won't happen with a failing grade."

"Well, Katie, you should have considered the consequences of offering such an inflammatory essay. In life, sometimes we make irreversible mistakes."

"My intention wasn't to be inflammatory but to bring out a social problem, with historical implications, which is playing out on the news on a regular basis. I thought this is what you asked for."

"Well, I was offended with your intention to rewrite history for your people's benefit."

"I never said such a thing, but I did research this problem very thoroughly."

"It looked like your research was very one-sided. Anyway, the grades are final."

"Mrs. Smith, this is so important for me. Could you possibly consider giving me an extra assignment or a redo?"

"Look, Katie, it is inappropriate for you to ask for special privileges. If I give it to you, I would have to do it for all, so please stop asking."

Katie left that short meeting heartbroken. It was clear Mrs. Smith would not change her mind, and the grade would be very low and possibly cause Katie to fail the class.

The following day, Mrs. Smith started her class with an unexpected speech.

"I am very disappointed with some of you because you think that you can use this class to present inflammatory and unpatriotic premises and then push your way back to getting good grades."

Everyone knew she was talking about Katie.

Without even thinking, Katie said, "But I did what you asked for, present and defend a premise based on important current events."

Mrs. Smith became enraged when Katie responded and questioned her in front of the entire class. "Katie, you're out of line, and you failed because your premises and conclusions were wrong and offensive. Please go to the principal's office. You will be suspended, I hope for a long time, for your behavior, which is clearly confrontational and out of line."

Brandon stood up and said, "Mrs. Smith, I think this is unfair. You say her premise is wrong and offensive, but that's your opinion, almost a political statement. It looks like Katie did some good research, she shared her interpretation, and just because you don't agree doesn't mean it's wrong."

"Well, when a statement is suggesting changing American history, I think I can say it's wrong and offensive. And I can also say you're out of line, so go with Miss Suarez to the principal's office to be suspended as well."

She looked around and said, "Anyone else want to argue with me?"

No one else said anything, although it was clear that many students disagreed with Mrs. Smith.

For a good student like Katie, the principal's office was the scariest room in the school. It was situated in the very back of the office building, behind the secretaries' cubicles and other school administrators' offices. It had a big window so everyone could see who was in trouble. Katie had never been to the principal's office, and when she heard the words "Go to the principal's office," she imagined her academic career coming to an end. Astonishingly, she was now smiling and happy. Seeing Brandon defend her made her feel like a knight in shining armor had defended her against an ogre.

"You're crazy, why did you do that? Now you're in so much trouble," Katie said.

"Hey, I was not about to let Mrs. Smith abuse you like that. She was very unfair with you." He had been thinking about Katie ever since the night at Rocky Cola's, and he felt Katie could do no wrong.

"That is so nice of you," said Katie with a sweet smile. She felt such affection for Brandon.

They talked the entire time until Principal Stevens, a tall, fifty-something man with a kind face, asked them to walk into his office. Principal Stevens was surprised to see how giddy they looked, and while in the principal's room they both argued that they felt Mrs. Smith had been unfair. Mrs. Smith had requested a two-week suspension for Katie and one week for Brandon. While Principal Stevens supported Mrs. Smith, he only gave them detention for three days.

When Katie and Brandon left the principal's office, Brandon got the courage to ask Katie out on a date, and at this magical moment, she said yes. They agreed to go out for dinner the following Thursday night.

That afternoon Katie called Blaire after school.

"What happened? Did you get detention?" asked Blaire in a panic.

Katie sounding giddy, "Yeah, I got three days detention, but…"

Blaire interrupted, "What's wrong with you? You almost sound happy about it."

"Brandon asked me out!"

"What? He did? That's awesome…wait, so is that why he got so protective over you with Mrs. Smith? That was a good move!"

"No, that was not a move," Katie said. "He honestly believes she was unfair and narrow-minded."

"I agree, and I think most kids in class agreed with you, but there is no arguing with Mrs. Smith." Blaire continued, "But now the difficult part, how are you going to tell your dad?"

"Oh, my dad is going to be proud of me when he finds out I got suspended for supporting my beliefs."

"No, I mean how are you going to tell your dad about Brandon taking you out?"

"Ooooh, uhm, I hadn't thought that far…what should I do?"

"Mexican parents are way too strict. You're seventeen, for god's sake! Just tell them."

"I have a plan… I'll tell them you and I are going to study together. Will you cover for me?"

"Okay, but I don't like the idea of lying. I wish you could just tell them."

"Thank you, thank you!" said Katie.

"Okay, okay, what are you going to wear?"

"Oh my god, how will I be able to change if I'm telling them I'll be studying?!"

Blaire laughed hard, "You see, lying just makes everything so much more difficult."

They both laughed and planned the entire evening together.

That Thursday, Brandon and Katie met at Rocky Cola again and talked about school. Katie told Brandon she was very disappointed with Mrs. Smith, and furthermore, she felt that students should have the ability to question grades and that grades should not be so subjective, especially if political opinions were discussed.

Brandon was impressed with Katie's eloquence and bravery. "I agree with you, and in fact, I think you should run for class president next year and use that as one of your campaign slogans."

Katie was so happy with Brandon's suggestions, as she had considered doing just that, but never spoke about it out loud, or thought it could be possible. Having Brandon in her corner boosted her confidence.

"You think? I've thought about it, but do you think I could win?"

"For sure. I'll help you. He extended his hand and took Katie's. The room went silent. They both stopped talking and looked into each other's eyes. Brandon smiled, and Katie smiled back; no words.

After several minutes Brandon said, "I've been dreaming about this moment for weeks."

"Really?"

Brandon moved closer and kissed her lips, and once more the room became silent.

CHAPTER SIXTEEN
ZACK'S PAIN

The following Monday, after Miguel got deported, Soco, a very strong woman, sent her kids to school and went to work. She figured she could not afford to lose her job or income now that she was a single mom. After the Mackintosh children grew up, Soco had become the housekeeper and cook. She was treated like family, and they promised they would never let her go. Being from Jalisco, a land of great food, Soco was a great cook. Tom loved Mexican food, and so did the rest of the family. That same morning, Anne decided to leave late for work to talk to Soco and see how else they could help her.

"Soco, how are you? And the girls?"

"Miss Anne, we are okay, very sad, but we are strong people. Last night we talked with Miguel for two hours. He finally arrived at his home town of Tepatitlan. His family was shocked to see him after so many years."

"How is he doing?" asked Anne.

"Miguel is very resourceful, and he is already looking for a job. Tepatitlan has grown, it is now a pretty big city with lots of jobs, but he is worried he doesn't have many skills. He's determined to get a job and send us money."

"I know Miguel is a good man," said Anne, who looked Soco in the eye, touched her shoulder. "Soco, we are here for you, and we are worried about your finances since now you only have one income and two young ladies to take care of."

"We will be okay, Miss. We have a little saved, and the girls said they are going to get part-time jobs to help me." Soco was too proud to tell Anne the entire truth. She was anxious and had only a few dollars in savings, and without Miguel's income, they could not afford the house, and soon the girls would have to get jobs.

The next several weeks were devastating for the Ochoas. They were three women suddenly by themselves and scared. Cindy was also frightened she might be stopped and deported, as she did not have a green card. She signed up for the Dreamers protection but did not know the future of that program and became severely depressed.

Money was very tight, and the girls started to look for jobs. When Miguel was around, he and Soco wanted the girls to focus on school. Mallory was still in high school, and Cindy was going to Mesa Community College. Now that luxury was over. Cindy got a job at Starbucks and Mallory a job at Jamba Juice. They both worked many hours and tried to help their mom as much as possible, but unfortunately, with all the work, their grades started to slip.

Soco became reclusive and would only go out to work at the Mackintosh home. She stayed home as much as possible because she wanted to avoid being seen. Her fear of being caught caused her to become paranoid.

Even with the girls working, there was not enough money to cover all of their costs. Miguel had been a hard-working gardener. He would wake up at four-thirty in the morning, pick up his assistant Leopoldo, and do his landscaping route all over Paradise Valley and other surrounding communities, until six or seven in the evening. He made good money for a gardener.

After two months, Soco found she could not afford the house anymore and stopped paying the mortgage. A few weeks later, threatening eviction letters appeared.

It was Friday at the Mackintosh home, and Zack came back from school, parked his black Jeep Cherokee in the driveway, and entered the house. As usual, he left his backpack near the door and walked on the shiny tiles toward the kitchen to find Soco with her eyes red and swollen. Zack immediately felt that something was terribly wrong.

"Soco, what happened?"

"Nada, mi hijito." Soco often spoke to Zack in Spanish and liked to use the term of endearment, mi hijito, my son. "I just finished cooking your favorite dish, carne en su jugo, and the onion got to my eyes."

The thought of Soco making this special dish for him made Zack's heart feel more tenderness toward the woman who for most of his life had tried to make his life more enjoyable.

Knowing how proud and tough Soco was, as he had only seen Soco cry one other time, convinced him something was wrong, so he insisted, "Come on, Soco, I can tell you are sad. I am worried." Zack looked away like remembering something, "and now that I'm thinking about it, I haven't seen Mallory for a few days in school. I thought she was sick. What's going on?"

Zack was not aware that Mallory and her mom had had a huge fight and Mallory had moved out to live with her friend and her family, because of what Soco was about to say.

Soco fixed her apron, raised her head and stood tall, cleared her throat and said, "The girls and I have decided to move back to Mexico. It is too hard to live here without my husband and their dad. Now we are scared, and we feel people don't want us here. I don't know what has happened, but now everywhere I go, it seems like people are giving me bad looks, and every time I drive home, I am scared the police will stop me and deport me. And then what will happen to my girls?" She started to sob. "We have to move, but Mallory refuses. This is destroying our family!"

"But Soco, what are we going to do without you?" He choked as he spoke. "I think you're overthinking this. The police aren't going to take you."

"Mi hijito, you don't get it. You live in this beautiful home, in a beautiful neighborhood, and the police, when they see your blond hair and a nice car, they smile at you. We live in the Ponderosa, we have a ten-year-old red Accord with a large dent, which we have not had money to fix, and when the police see us, they see possible illegals, and people don't like Mexicans here in Phoenix."

Zack had never heard Soco sound so bitter or unhappy living in his hometown. He was confused. He didn't understand the feeling Soco had buried in her heart of living in a place where she didn't feel wanted.

The feeling of not being wanted was what made Mexican families stay in Mexican neighborhoods. The Ochoas never felt welcomed in the US, and things only got a lot worse with Sheriff Arpaio's and Trump's attacks on

TV about Mexicans being criminals and bad people. It made Soco and her daughters feel like people watched them all the time."

Not fully understanding how life looked from Soco's perspective, Zack said, "Soco, I think you're exaggerating. It's not that bad, plus, what are you going to do in Mexico, starve?" The moment he said those words, he saw Soco's eyes turn red, and her face become solemn.

"I'm leaving now. I have already said goodbye to your mom, and I waited to say goodbye to you because I have loved you like my child."

"Soco, wait, I'm sorry, I didn't mean..."

Soco did not look back. She had all her belongings ready at the door, and she walked out.

Zack chased after her. She would not stop or look back. His heart was beating so hard—he loved Soco like a second mother. He could not believe or understand why she would want to abandon him. Until that moment he did not realize the pain Soco and the Ochoa girls felt when they lost a loved one.

That day Zack would learn the pain of losing a loved one.

CHAPTER SEVENTEEN

INTERROGATION

Unfortunately for Mark, the detective in charge of the investigation was John Summers who, after twelve years of an honest but uneventful career, decided it was time to move up the ranks and was looking for a way to make a name for himself. Summers was thirty-seven, but he looked more like a hard-lived forty-seven-year-old man who had a receding blond hairline already showing a lot of gray and leathery skin with deep grooves—a sign of excessive sun exposure.

Summers was sound asleep next to Joan, his wife, when he received the call of a party disturbance at the posh Paradise Valley neighborhood, with possible sexual battery or assault allegations. Some uniformed officers made the arrest. Sweet Joan, used to this routine whenever John was on call, got up to make him some coffee while he dressed to go to the crime scene.

By the time Detective Summers arrived, the partygoers were almost all gone except for the eye witnesses and parties involved. The others had been asked to leave their contact information in case they were needed. Mark was convinced this was a silly accusation, and he was very combative during the arrest. He kept repeating that his mom was a district attorney and they better be careful. Summers did not like Mark from the moment he laid eyes on him. Summers informed his chief about the claims, and after looking into it, they found out that in fact his mom, Elizabeth, was a prosecutor for Maricopa.

This was bad for Mark because from that point on, Elizabeth was told by her boss that she had to stay out of the case or else. Summers was annoyed by Mark's attitude, but he was not convinced that there was a crime. He was used to these rich kids getting into fights after drinking too much, and later having their parents fix everything with money and influential lawyers.

A couple of days later, Detective Summers and his partner called all the students who were at the party to tell their side of the story. The police precinct, usually a quiet and scary place, looked more like a principal's office, filled with pimple-faced rich kids with big attitudes, who were unhappy to be there. Most interviews were quick. Summers would ask, "Were you present at the party at 12 Olive Road?" The youngsters would respond to the detective the same way they would respond to their parents when asked about their day, with a one-syllable response, "Yes."

Summers asked, "Did you hear any loud screams?"

Students with attitude rolled their eyes and said, "No." This scene repeated itself over and over with most of the students.

"Did you see anything strange that night?" "…No."

"Did you hear screams?" "…Yes."

By the tenth witness, Summers was pulling the few hairs he had left. "Ok, so did you see Megan crying?"

"Yes."

"Do you know why?"

"Not really."

"Did you see Mark Suarez touch Megan Clark?"

"No…"

"This day is going nowhere," thought Summers. To make matters worse, some of the witnesses came with their dads' lawyers, who made all sorts of demands.

Finally, Summers interviewed Cole, and it was a refreshing change because Cole was polite and cooperative. With a fresh haircut, he looked like the perfect student. "So everyone keeps saying that you are the only real eyewitness. What did you see?"

"Sir, I was inside the house, and I had nothing to drink that night. We had just had a grueling game, and my body was sore, so I didn't want to drink."

"Okay, and then?"

"Well, around eleven o'clock, I was chatting with David, Steve, and a couple of girls about the game, and I just happened to be standing in front of a small window facing the side of the house, when I heard some yelling, and I looked out. That is when I saw Mark, also a varsity player, try to put his hand up Megan's skirt. Megan fought him, but Mark pushed her hard to the ground."

"Did anyone else see what you saw?"

"I don't think so. Everyone else was sitting down, and I was the only one standing in front of the window."

"I spoke to David and Steve, and they confirm they saw nothing, but heard awful cries from Megan."

"Yes, I am happy she screamed that loud. If we hadn't stopped Mark, who knows?"

"Do you think Mark would have raped her if no one had responded to the cries?"

"I think so, sir."

Megan was interviewed by Summers the night of the incident but was found to be too hysterical and intoxicated to provide a good interview. The next day, still at the hospital, Summers interviewed her. By then, Megan was sober but had little recollection of the events. She did remember that Mark had humiliated her and, afraid to go back on her claims, she confirmed that Mark had grabbed her private parts and then pushed her hard to the ground when she resisted.

Finally, Detective Summers looked Megan straight in the eye. "Do you think Mark would have raped you if people hadn't heard you scream?"

"I don't know," she said.

Megan Clark was an average student who craved people's approval. While Megan was average-looking, her mom had been Miss Phoenix, got pregnant by a wealthy lawyer who turned politician, and was getting hefty child support checks from him. Her dad lived in Paradise Valley, so she was allowed to attend the coveted school district. Megan's mom, June Clark, was a woman to be afraid of and when Megan told her what happened, her mom when into a rage.

All the time these rich people had called her a gold digger, all the veiled discriminatory actions against her, and feeling like an outsider at PTA meetings all came boiling out in a rage against the entitled rich people, who thought they could do anything. When she found out Mark was of Mexican blood, it gave her more ammunition. She started to curse, "Those goddamn Mexicans, they are all a bunch of rapists, like Mr. Trump says."

When June talked to Detective Summers, she told him how devastated and humiliated her beautiful daughter was. She told how she worked hard so Megan would be able to attend an excellent school and get a better education. "Now this damn Mexican boy has ruined my daughter's chances at a great future. Megan was thinking of quitting school because of Mark."

June's effort to create an emotion in Summers worked. He felt her pain and hatred toward Mark and thought to himself, "I'm going to screw over this entitled, rich Mexican kid."

It wasn't long until word of this case came to Jerry Valenti, and he salivated when he heard there was a sexual assault by a Mexican teenager in a mostly white neighborhood. When he found out the perpetrator was an American citizen of rich Mexican parents, he was disappointed because this was not the type of case he looked for, but then Jerry thought, "We have another rally next week in Phoenix. This case has the perfect timing and location to activate Operation Alamo, so what the hell, I'll take a look."

Jerry Valenti was on one of Trump Enterprises' private jets within minutes. While on the plane, he called his contact in the Maricopa precinct and shrewdly said he had been asked by the candidate to visit the precinct and observe some of the excellent police work they are doing to protect the citizens. Valenti expected to arrive at a dilapidated Old West police precinct; he did not have high expectations of Phoenix.

Instead, he found a highly organized, modern, and clean police building. The commander in charge, Sergeant Adams, offered him an official tour of the facility. Valenti then asked who was in charge of the attempted rape case in Paradise Valley.

Sergeant Adams responded, "It was not attempted rape, but the more minor offense of possible sexual battery and the one in charge of that case is detective John Summers, an excellent detective." Valenti asked if he could meet Detective Summers. Adams was happy to oblige and made a call for Summers.

Sergeant Adams walked Valenti to Summers' cubicle. Summers wondered why the sergeant was there to see him and got a little worried.

"John, meet Jerry Valenti. He's a senior advisor for presidential candidate Trump,. He's here to observe our fine work, and he specifically asked for you."

"Nice to meet you, Mr. Valenti," Summers said.

Adams left them to chat. Summers was surprised that he had asked for him but was excited because this could be the break he had been waiting for. Jerry Valenti was clearly a polished, well-spoken, and influential man who intimidated Detective Summers. From a small town, Summers liked to wear old, worn-out cowboy boots and a white straw Stetson, which had yellowed from use. He was an uneducated man who spoke purposely with a drawl and liked to think of himself as a real cowboy.

Jerry Valenti spoke to Summers like he was a man who cared about justice and the preservation of the American values. "I work for the candidate because he is a man who cares about law enforcement and maintaining justice."

Valenti was adroit, and he knew how to manipulate people. He said he was there just to observe for a short while and then report the police work being done at the precinct to his boss. Depending on what he saw, he may suggest to the candidate that he mention outstanding police officers by name in the upcoming rally.

"So, Detective Summers, I hear you're working on an interesting case, the Suarez case."

Summers knew that giving details about active cases was against regulation but took a gamble and volunteered to talk about the case, and, to impress Valenti, he embellished the case's details.

"Mr. Valenti, we're currently working on a very serious case, and a young man stands accused of violent sexual assault." And just like that, Summers decided to increase the severity of the case from possible assault to violent sexual assault, just to impress the presidential candidate's senior advisor. "This young man is the son of two Mexicans and is a real piece of work. He appears to have a violent and predatory nature, and because his mom is a district attorney, he acts like he has carte blanche to do his abusive behavior toward nice girls. I care to protect the people."

After the interview with Summers, Valenti decided to talk to his contacts on the news and leak information about the investigation. One of Valenti's connections, a reporter who never verified the facts, wrote a piece and posted it on e-Newswire: "A son of wealthy Mexican parents, Mark Suarez, 18, has been booked on violent sexual assault charges in the affluent Phoenix neighborhood of Paradise Valley, Arizona.

It is said that this young man has a history of violence and predatory behavior, and because his mother is a district attorney, he walks around behaving like this with impunity." Once the article was posted on e-Newswire, it caught like wildfire. All stations picked up the news, and the community outrage was palpable.

The following week, Trump held a rally at the Phoenix Civic Space. He took full advantage of the current news and congratulated Phoenix police for their exceptional job catching all of the illegal Mexican criminals. He promised to build a wall to keep them out, and the crowds cheered with passion. Valenti stood on one side of the stage.

CHAPTER EIGHTEEN
MARK'S CHANGE OF HEART

It was Saturday morning at the Suarez home and, after a tumultuous week, the entire family hoped to have a nice, relaxing weekend. The smell of freshly made waffles was in the air—they were Lorenzo's favorite and he would usually cook breakfast on weekends. He always talked about his special "secret" recipe for waffles, which in fact was just mixing two different boxes of premade pancake mix and salt, but he always talked it up, like it was a big deal, and the waffles were in fact delicious. With happy and full bellies, they were all ready for conversation. Katie recounted what happened to her in class with Mrs. Smith and told them about the possibility of a failing grade, and how she felt it was so unfair.

Lorenzo said, "Honey, I am proud of you and your social courage. Remember, if it must be said, you have to say it, but don't think that everyone will agree with you! And I can also tell you it will not be the last time you will have to fight for justice."

Lorenzo continued, "I think I'm going to pay a visit to your school and have a chat with the principal and Mrs. Smith."

Katie said, "No, Dad, I don't want you to get involved. This is my fight and I want to do it alone."

Elizabeth jumped in. "Lorenzo, I told you to stop with your Mexican stories. It's your fault Katie decided to do an essay on Trump's unfair treatment of Mexicans, and now she may lose the chance to go to an Ivy League law school." And then Elizabeth, with unusual disdain in her voice, said, "And quit it already with the stories. I don't want to think what kind of shithole, pardon my French, Phoenix would be if the US had not taken over Arizona.

119

It would be another ugly, Third World pueblo, like the rest of Mexico."

Lorenzo was surprised when Mark, who had been very solemn and quiet during most of the week, jumped in the conversation and said, "Mom, that is unfair to say. Do you remember when Dad took us to Hermosillo, Sonora? It was not an ugly pueblo, it was such a pretty city, and that is only a few hours from here. And of course, the beautiful Mexico City. Why do you always talk so bad about Mexico? Aren't we Mexican? You shouldn't hate so much."

Elizabeth responded, "Honey, what's gotten into you? I'm American with Mexican ancestry, like you and Katie. Americans need to forget their background and just be Americans. We must integrate. Otherwise, other Americans will always see us as foreigners."

Katie said, "Mom, we all love America and we know it's the best place in the world, and I think Dad appreciates and loves America more than we do. But like Dad says, Italians are proud of their background, and so are Jewish people, and Cubans and Armenians, so why do we Mexicans have to forget who we are and not defend our culture, especially if we're being attacked?"

Mark said, "Yeah, Mom, I agree with Katie and I'm starting to realize how selfish we are by turning our backs to what is happening. We're letting so many people get hurt and we're even hurting ourselves."

"Okay, I'm done," said Elizabeth. "I don't want to talk about this anymore. I'm going to watch the news."

Elizabeth walked to the living room and turned on the TV. No more than ten minutes went by before the newscaster stated reading, "A son of wealthy Mexican parents, Mark Suarez, eighteen, has been booked for violent sexual assault charges in the affluent Paradise Valley neighborhood. It is said that this young man has a history of violence and predatory behavior...and his mother is a district attorney." Elizabeth's head spun and she had no clue how this information had been leaked to the media, nor how it had been distorted in such a horrible way. She screamed to Lorenzo to come and see, but by the time he and the kids got to the TV, the piece was over. In a way, Elizabeth was happy Mark did not see the news report.

Elizabeth said, "Lorenzo, we need to talk. Can we go to our room?"

Katie asked, "What happened? What did you see?" She was suspicious and could see panic in her mom's face.

Elizabeth said, "Nothing, honey, your dad and I need to talk about important grownup stuff."

Lorenzo and Elizabeth walked to their bedroom and as soon as the door closed, Elizabeth started to sob; she could not hold it any more.

Lorenzo asked, "What happened? What did you see?"

"Lorenzo, I just saw on the news a story where they mentioned Mark by name and said he was accused of a violent sexual assault and he has rich Mexican parents and his mother is a district prosecutor."

"How did they get such information? Who leaked it?" asked Lorenzo.

Elizabeth said, "I don't know, but we are screwed: your career, mine, our family."

Lorenzo said, "Don't rush to conclusions. We are smart people, we will overcome this."

Elizabeth said, "But how could this happen?"

"I don't know, my love, but I feel that since Trump started with his attacks against Mexicans, life has become more complicated."

Elizabeth was visibly irritated and said, "Lorenzo, don't start with that. Trump has nothing to do with this and if anyone is to blame, it's you. You're making us crazy with your conspiracy talk."

The fighting between Elizabeth and Lorenzo severely intensified from that point on.

The night of the party and the incident with Megan, Detective Summers interrogated Mark for three hours until Elizabeth and Lorenzo arrived and Lorenzo presented himself as Mark's lawyer. During those three hours, Summers was aggressive with his interrogation and Mark started very standoffish, knowing he was guilty of nothing, but as Summers kept repeating the questions over and over in different forms, Mark found himself tired and confused.

Summers said to Mark, "Son, I have witnesses confirming they saw you attack the girl, and touch her inappropriately and then throw her to the ground. Look, you both had drinks, it happens. Just tell me the truth, it's no major crime, you didn't kill anyone. Confess and I'll make this very easy for you. You will probably not have any jail time, and you'll get a slap on the hand." Of course, he lied.

Mark said, "I didn't do anything. She stuck her tongue in my mouth and I pushed her off."

Summers said, "So you agree you guys had physical contact?"

Mark said, "Well…yes."

Summers asked, "Why are you so sure she stuck her tongue in first? Maybe it was you? You guys had been drinking."

Mark said, "I know what happened."

"But you did push her to the ground."

"Well…I pushed her, but I think she tripped and fell."

"So what was it? You pushed her? Or she tripped?"

"Well…I'm…not sure if I pushed her."

"You see, you're not sure what happened. Maybe you're not sure if you were the one who tried to grab her genitals and she fought you?"

"No, that I'm sure about. She attacked me. I didn't start this."

"So now you are saying she attacked you?"

As time went on, Summers twisted everything Mark said, to the point where Mark was and sounded more confused. This conversation was recorded on camera.

During the next few weeks, Summers kept asking Mark to appear for further questioning, claiming each time that new evidence had to be discussed. Each time Mark came in with Marcus Brazile, a very astute African-American criminal defense attorney and a friend of Lorenzo's. Detective Summers used the specific strategy to ask conflicting questions so Mark would contradict himself and cause people to doubt his credibility.

Detective Summers was convinced of Mark's guilt, and was affected by June's account of the suffering Mark's actions had caused poor Megan. Summers also despised rich people, and in this case, it was a spoiled Mexican kid. On top of this, Summers had not forgotten the glistening idea that a good conviction would ingratiate him with Valenti, and might help him get the promotion and recognition he deserved.

Detective Summers convinced the senior prosecutor, Aaron Johans, to upgrade the charges to sexual assault.

CHAPTER NINETEEN

SAVANNAH

A few weeks had gone by since the game and the party incident. It was twelve noon, lunchtime at Washington High, the sun was burning, and the temperature was already 115 degrees. Many of the students tried to stay indoors during recess. Others crowded beneath the stylish canopies the school placed all over the outdoor areas to protect them against the harmful UV rays.

Mark tried to keep a low profile since the party, and since he was suspended from the varsity team, he did not have his usual group of friends and found himself alone. Zack continued to avoid him since the party and blamed him for Savannah's refusal to talk to him. He was convinced Mark had intentionally poisoned Savannah's thoughts of him and talked trash about him, including the infamous final game.

Zack sat at the cafeteria with his teammates at the designated varsity table and talked about the temperature and how tough the practice was going to be. "What I don't get, is why freaking Coach Murphy has zero mercy with us, even on one hundred and fifteen-degree days." The other players all agreed.

Cole and his friend David saw Zack across the cafeteria and headed in his direction.

"Hey Zack, I hear that beaner friend of yours has been talking trash about your passes at the game. What's up with that?" Cole talked loudly so everyone would hear him put Zack on the spot.

Zack considered backing Mark, but at the last second said, "Yeah, I haven't talked to him for a while, but that's really a scumbag move—talking shit to cover his own mistake."

"Yeah, those beaners just can't take responsibility for the shit they do. Like I saw with my own eyes. Mark attacked Megan, and then the fucking weasel had the guts to say he didn't do it. They are all criminals."

"Yeah, Trump keeps saying that they are all fucking rapists," said David. "Maybe some are good… but we can see which one your buddy Mark is."

"Dude, you sound way too racist for my taste. I know a bunch of Mexicans who are great people, and yes, Mark is acting like a dam asshole, but that's on him."

"Whatever, dude," said Cole. "We'd be better off without fucking Mexicans, especially the obnoxious type like Mark."

David and a couple of the other guys in the team all said, "Yeah, that's true."

Zack decided to walk away from that conversation. He was shocked at the terribly racist tones Cole used when he spoke about Mexicans and the fact that some agreed with him. He'd never seen that at Washington. He was raised in a family that made an effort to see everyone as equal, but being so mad at Mark made him susceptible.

Mark sat close by on a bench under the canopy and looked over his papers in preparation for his next class. Like many other students, he fanned himself with a paper folder, trying to keep cool, when his usual tormentor and his posse found him.

"Be careful, guys," said Cole, "Senor Mark is hot and may become more aggressive."

With a clearly forced laugh, David spoke, adding a Mexican accent to his English, "Si, Senor Mark is hiding from the heat."

"Listen, Marky," Cole said, "this canopy is too crowded to have a dirty Mexican here. Go to the sunny area. You already have dark skin."

Mark was bigger and stronger than Cole and could have easily shoved him, but he wanted to avoid further confrontation, so instead, he calmly said to Cole, "Just leave me the heck alone. Don't you have better things to do?"

"What are you going to do, beat me up like you beat up girls?"

Mark got upset "Look, Cole, just leave me the hell alone. I don't want trouble."

A girl's voice spoke up. "Mark, leave this asshole alone. He's just trying to get you to do something stupid. He's not worth it."

Mark and Cole turned, and there was Savannah, glaring at Cole.

Cole was shocked that the most popular girl in school was yelling about him. Cole laughed nervously, looked at Savannah and said, "Why are you defending this fucking beaner? Don't you know what he did?"

Hearing this made Savannah really mad. "Cole, you're an asshole and a liar. I know Mark." She grabbed Mark by the arm and marched away.

Mark was surprised and unsure what to do. Savannah had not talked to him since the party, and he thought she was mad at him. He opted to follow Savannah in silence since it looked like a better option than staying with Cole.

Finally, closer to the cafeteria, they found an empty bench.

"Mark, I'm sorry you're going through all of this. I feel a little responsible for this mess, and I feel pretty bad that I may have damaged your friendship with Zack."

Her blue eyes gazed at Mark with warmth and sincerity. "Look, I know Megan, and she's a liar. I was in a class with her and had to do a team project with her. I saw firsthand how manipulative she is, and how she lied to the teacher to get her way. I know you wouldn't do the things they say you did. I've debated how to talk to you for days because I feel guilty that my overreaction at the party had a snowball effect and led to so much grief."

Savannah's sincere words and kind gesture melted Mark's heart. At his absolute lowest point, when Mark felt the entire world hated him, this angel came to his rescue.

Savannah Birkeland had had a crush on Mark for months, soon after Mark joined the varsity team. She noticed him immediately and liked his confidence, his dark hair, and especially his full straight eyebrows, which hid his dark eyes and made him look dangerous. Savannah saw that Mark was always in Zack's shadow because Zack was the most popular guy in school. To her, Mark was kind and innocent compared to Zack. Savannah knew Zack liked her, but she didn't like that Zack had girls around him all the time. It reminded her of her dad.

Savannah was not the spoiled rich girl her outer appearance showed. She was of modest means compared to most of the kids at Washington High. Her parents were hard-working, middle-class people. Her father was the number one sales manager at the downtown Phoenix Audi dealer. Her mom was a grammar school teacher at one of the poorest schools in the Phoenix Central School District. Married in Wisconsin, they moved to Phoenix to run away from the cold.

Looking for a good investment in a great school district, Savannah's parents bought the smallest house in Paradise Valley when the real estate was at the lowest level. Savannah's dad, Jon, was a very handsome and domineering man, and everyone suspected he was a womanizer. Her mom was the most caring and compassionate teacher in the district, and an equally good mother.

Mark and Savannah talked through the entire recess, and she told him about her abusive and womanizing father, and how she wanted to move away, work hard to get accepted to the USC School of Cinema, become a movie director, and tell stories that would help women. She told Mark she did not want to be an actress because she didn't like all the attention on her. Since she was a child, Savannah and her mom would evaluate movies for the quality of the acting, story, special effects, and editing. She was sure she knew what it took to make a good movie.

Mark's experience had made him very vulnerable, and he told Savannah how he now realized he had to be humble and more helpful to his family.

"Savannah, I look at myself, and I don't like myself. I realize I've been so selfish."

"Why? I see what a good friend you are to Zack, and you haven't said anything bad about him, even though he has treated you poorly."

"All of this has made me realize that I only thought of myself and that's going to change." He looked into her eyes. "I am going to be a better man. I'm going to study hard and become a doctor so I can heal others, and I'm going to get more involved in social causes and help my fellow Mexican-Americans. I've been blessed with a lot, and I must give some back."

"I like that, Mark."

"Savannah, I've had feelings for you for so long, and now that I know how amazing you are, I want to be a good person for you too. I will never take you for granted." A tear rolled down his cheek.

Savannah was touched by his raw emotion and selfless talk. This was the type of man she wanted to be with. Savannah grabbed Mark's hand and said softly, "You're a good man," and leaned forward and tenderly kissed him.

From that point forward they were inseparable as they developed a deep connection. The fact that Mark was so disliked by some made their love more intense; they both felt it was the two of them against the world.

A few weeks later Mark and Savannah were walking together in the school holding hands when they saw Zack walking in their direction, surrounded by an entourage of football players. Zack laughed loudly at someone's comment, but when he saw them, his jaw clenched. One of the guys noticed that Mark and Savannah were holding hands and said to Zack, "Looks like your friend just stole your girlfriend." Zack was enraged.

The group continued to walk in the direction of Mark and Savannah, and Mark felt that the polite thing to do was to acknowledge Zack.

"Hi Zack, how's it going?" Mark smiled and tried to be as friendly as possible.

Zack acted like Mark did not exist, turned around, and told his group, "Let's go this other way, the air stinks like Mexico around here," and they walked away.

Savannah noticed the sadness that Mark felt from Zack's cold shoulder and mean words. "Ignore him, he's such an asshole."

"He's mad at me because he feels I stole you from him."

"That's such bullshit. I was never his, and you didn't steal me. And he's upset with me because he keeps calling me and I won't respond to his calls. I can't stand him anymore."

"He's calling you?"

"The other day I told Paige that Zack won't stop calling me, and she said, 'Why aren't you with Zack? He is the captain of the football team.'"

Savannah looked at Mark and realized she opened a can of worms with that comment. Immediately Mark asked, "So what do your friends say about us?"

Savannah considered telling him the truth or sugarcoating it. She went for the truth.

"Babe, Paige is an idiot, and it turns out she's been talking to Zack and trying to get him to ask me out, somehow deceiving him that I may still be interested in him."

"Oh my god, no wonder he's so upset with me. Why would Paige do that?"

"Paige doesn't like you. She likes Zack."

"And what do you think?"

"Look, babe, I know you're a good man, and I'll deal with this. I'll explain things to Zack, and I'll stop talking to Paige since she is nothing but trouble. You are who I want. Not anyone else."

Next time Zack called, Savannah picked up and explained everything. She also talked to Zack about Mark not being guilty, explained that Megan was a pathological liar and she reminded Zack that he knew, better than anyone, that Mark had always been respectful to women. Savannah told Zack that Mark had never, to that day, said anything other than kind things about him. She hoped they would reconcile, but Zack was still too hurt to want to talk to Mark.

CHAPTER TWENTY

COURTHOUSE

Marcus Brazile was a veteran trial attorney who had the reputation of being a pit bull who rarely lost a case. He was a close friend of Lorenzo's, and he had no intention of losing this one. Everyone was surprised the prosecution chose to go for the more significant and more difficult-to-prove- charge of sexual assault, instead of simple assault. During preparation, Marcus reached out to some of Mark's closest friends and people who knew him the longest to be character witnesses. Mark was heartbroken when he heard that Zack refused to testify on his behalf.

The day of Mark's trial had finally arrived. There were reporters at the entrance of the Maricopa County Courthouse with news vans blocking the street and a great deal of commotion. Ever since the news broke, there was heightened interest in the outcome of this trial. Emotions ran high, as many folks wanted justice served and felt that because Mark was from a family of successful lawyers, he would get away with his actions.

When the Suarez family walked out of their car and into the courthouse, cameras were flashing everywhere. Mark wore slacks, a light blue, long-sleeved shirt, and tie, Elizabeth wore a black business skirt suit with a light gray shirt, Lorenzo wore a conservative, dark gray suit, and Katie wore a dark skirt with a white silk blouse.

Some screams were coming from the crowds. Support for Mark came from people who knew him, and some demanded justice. A couple of people yelled, "Go back to your fucking country, rapist." Elizabeth's eyes watered, and she made a gesture like she was about to say something, when she felt Lorenzo's arm around her, reminding her how important it was at this time to be strong and not allow any outside noise.

The judge had agreed with the prosecution to withhold Megan's name from the press to protect her identity until the trial. Although Marcus reassured the Suarez family that it would be tough for the prosecution to prove the intent to commit a sexual assault under the circumstances, they had not slept in two days, and their puffy red eyes were visible from a distance.

At the front of the courtroom was the American flag, and the seal of the State of Arizona was carved in the wood-paneled wall behind the judge's chair. The room was at full capacity, and the hall outside was crowded with the many witnesses who expected to be called. June Clark and her family, which had claimed the back bench, were the most vociferous.

The bailiff rose and called the court to order. "All rise, this session of the Maricopa Superior Court, the Honorable Marvin D. Defourt presiding, is now in session."

The judge sat down, organized his files, and appeared to review some documents. The bailiff told the people to be seated.

Jury selection had been heavily contested. The excessive news coverage of the case appeared to have polarized the people in general. Marcus attempted to find jurors who had male sons, as well as a more diverse group. The prosecution looked for older jurors who showed a clear preference for strict punishment. The jury sat to the right of the courtroom and was made up of an equal number of males and females, three Hispanic, one African American, one Asian and seven Caucasians. Their blank stares and nervousness showed how overwhelmed they felt about their responsibility. They all avoided eye contact with Mark.

Judge Defourt began, "Mr. Suarez, the state has charged you with sexual assault. What is your plea?"

Marcus Brazile said, "Your honor, my client pleads not guilty."

After Judge Defourt gave the preliminary jury instructions, he ran the proceedings following protocol.

He instructed the prosecutor, Aaron Johans, to start his initial opening statement.

Johans looked at the jury and said, "Ladies and gentleman, this case is about the right of young women to move freely in our community without fear of molestation or brutal attack. The victim is an honor student at Washington High School, who, like many of her friends, likes to attend the school's football games and after-game parties.

"We have an eyewitness who saw her being attacked and have identified Mr. Suarez as the perpetrator. Additionally, we have many who heard the victim scream in terror. They rushed to the scene of the crime and found her on the ground, bleeding and crying inconsolably, and in that crucial moment, heard the victim accuse Mr. Suarez of attacking her. We will present the victim, and you will listen to the emotional damage this violent act has caused her.

"Finally, the state will present recordings of Mark making contradictory statements during interrogation, which is evidence of his attempt to obscure his intent and actions. Ladies and gentleman, we ask you to be fair, and not to allow the media attention or the fact that the defendant is a rich and entitled young man with access to the best legal representation to affect your decision. Please focus on the evidence, which will show the defendant is guilty beyond a reasonable doubt of sexual assault."

The defense attorney, Marcus Brazile, was next to present his opening statement.

"Ladies and gentleman, Mr. Suarez has committed no wrong. In fact, he was more the victim than the aggressor in this encounter. The young woman is known to have pursued this attractive young man throughout their years at Washington High School. Her romantic overtures continued into the night in question when she followed him after a post-game gathering of fellow students.

"She accosted Mark Suarez as he was sitting alone on the front lawn outside the party. When he rebuffed her advances by pulling away, the girl fell over her own feet and scraped her forehead. Suarez, being a compassionate young man, reached down to help her up. She suffered no damage except a small scrape.

"The state will attempt to substantiate these ludicrous charges of assault with conspiratorial, hearsay testimony from biased fellow students who are likely jealous of Mark's status as an honor student and athletic hero. I would like to remind the jury that the state and Mr. Johans have the burden of proving my client guilty beyond a reasonable doubt.

"My client is a good student, a star athlete, and a well-respected member of the Paradise Valley community, who is held in high esteem by his teachers, coaches, and peers. The evidence will prove that he is an innocent victim of adolescent jealousy and malicious gossip."

The prosecution started with a big bang, calling Megan, the victim, as the first witness. Megan was dressed in a plain blue dress, which almost looked like a school uniform. Wearing no makeup, she looked fourteen years old, even though she was seventeen.

Mr. Johans began. "Megan, please tell us what happened on the night of…"

Megan fought back the tears as she recounted her side of her story. After all that she had gone through, she believed she was telling the truth, and she was persuasive.

"Do you believe that if people had not shown up, Mark would have forced himself on you at that moment?"

"I don't know," Megan said, as the words were coming out of her mouth Megan felt her facial blood vessels flush, realizing she knew the answer, but it was too late now to tell the truth.

The defense followed with its cross-examination.

"Miss Clark, isn't it true that you had been telling multiple people that you had a crush on Mr. Suarez?"

"Yes, but…," and then she started to cry.

"Would it be possible that in fact you were attempting to seduce Mr. Suarez and when he rejected you, you decided to accuse him of this act?"

Megan's crying got louder.

Mr. Johans said, "Your honor, I object to the defense's argumentative questioning."

Judge Defort said, "Objection sustained." Marcus made a note of "judicial error," in case there would be cause to appeal.

Although Marcus's questioning was good at creating minor doubt of Megan's testimony, Marcus was an experienced litigator, who knew not to be too harsh to the victim, as it could cause the jury to feel empathy for the victim. Megan was an attractive and sympathetic figure.

The prosecution's star witness was Cole Jones. Cole wore khaki pants, a white dress shirt, and a blue blazer, which made him look like an Ivy League student. Johans was methodic in his interrogation. He wanted to ensure Cole would be perceived as a good student and a caring citizen who had no bias against Mark.

"Mr. Jones, from your perspective behind the window, after you saw the accused push Megan to the ground, what happened?"

"After he violently pushed her to the ground, I saw him grope her, pushing his hand inside her skirt, while she screamed and tried to stop him."

"So, what you saw was a person who was violent and sexually attacked Megan?"

"Yes."

Johans ended his interrogation.

Brazile stood up and slowly walked to the front. "Mr. Jones, were you one of the first people to arrive at the scene and stop the actions of the defendant?

"No."

"If, from your perspective, what was a happening was a violent attack, why didn't you run to the scene of the crime? Why did you wait to get there?

"I don't know, it all happened so fast," said Cole.

"It all happened so fast. Tell me, Mr. Jones, could this have happened so quickly in front of your eyes that maybe you misinterpreted the defendant's intentions?

"No, I don't think so."

"Is it true that on the same evening of the incident, you started a fight with the defendant and threw a punch at him?"

"Yes, but he started it."

"Could it be that you dislike the defendant and that colored your opinion of what happened?"

Before Cole could answer, Brazile said, "You don't have to answer, I think it's obvious." He turned to the judge and said, "That is all."

Johans then called David Witmeyer.

"Mr. Witmeyer, you attend Washington High where you see and interact with the defendant on a regular basis. Is that correct?"

"Yes, sir."

"From your experience with the defendant, would you say he has a short temper, is irritable, and is capable of attacking other students if he doesn't get his way?"

"Objection, Your Honor, leading the witness."

Judge Defourt, Objection sustained."

Johans looked at Brazil with disdain. "Okay, David tell us how Mr. Suarez treats you in school.

"He acts like he is hot stuff in school, and he shoves and threatens me if I disagree with him during friendly banters we have at school."

"Are you suggesting he can be violent?"

"Yes, sir, for sure."

Johans turned to Brazile and said, "Your witness."

"Mr. Witmeyer, isn't it true you, Mr. Jones, and Mr. Callezi like to tease and harass the defendant in school about the fact that he is a Mexican-American?"

"It's all for fun. Mark likes to dish it as well. He's called me 'spaghetti arms.' He likes to dish it out, but then he gets angry and aggressive when anyone teases him."

Johans then called Anthony Callezi, who confirmed that Mark had a short fuse and that when he didn't get what he wanted, he could be violent. A couple more students were called by the prosecution to confirm Cole's whereabouts at the time of the incident, as well as character witnesses for Megan and Cole, to corroborate their credibility.

Johans and the prosecutor's team felt good about what they had done, and when Johans turned to see the jury, he noticed most of them looked him in the eye, which experienced lawyers know means a connection and agreement with what they presented.

Then it was the defense's turn.

Brazile's strategy was to discredit both Megan and Cole, as well as paint a picture of Mark as an exemplary citizen who would never do such a thing.

Savannah was the first called to the stand.

"Miss Birkeland, could you please tell us what you personally heard Megan say to a group of students a few weeks before the incident?"

"Megan and I are in the same English Lit class, and a few months before the incident, a few of the girls were talking about who they found hot in school, and Megan said something like, 'I would definitely fuck—pardon my language—Mark if I got the chance.'"

"Based on what you know of Miss Jones, is she a credible witness?"

"No. In English class, we had a project together, and she would lie all the time to teachers and to the rest of our group to get away with not working. It was very upsetting."

In his excitement, Brazile forgot to bring up the fact that Savannah was dating Mark. He turned the interrogation to Johans and said, "Your turn."

Johans said, "Miss Birkeland, you know you are under oath?"

Savannah said, "Yes."

Johans walked toward Savannah and said, "Is it true that you and the defendant are romantically involved?"

"Yes."

Johans said, "Would it be possible that you are protecting your boyfriend?" Johans did not wait for her response. He smiled and turned to look at the jury.

Savannah tried to respond, but Johans said, "That is all, Miss Birkeland."

Brazile called a few more witnesses who corroborated Savannah's story, as well as character witnesses who confirmed Mark's good nature, and who said he was never abusive to anyone. The rest of the trial went smoothly and was finished by noon on the second day. That afternoon, the judge issued his final instructions, then sent the jury out for deliberation. When they did not have a verdict by four p.m., the judge sent the jurors home.

While exiting the courthouse, Brazile approached Mark. "My boy, tomorrow you will likely be free and cleared from all of this."

The family went home for dinner in a good mood. They all agreed with Brazile and his assessment that the prosecution had not proven its charge; the evidence was all so flimsy.

The next morning, at nine a.m., the jury announced a verdict, and all parties were called to be in court at ten a.m.

Judge Defourt said, "In the matter of the State of Arizona vs. Mark Suarez, has the jury has reached a verdict?"

The presiding juror said, "Yes, Your Honor."

"What say you?"

"We find the defendant, Mark Suarez, guilty of sexual assault." A huge gasp was heard in the courtroom.

Megan's family cheered loudly, feeling vindicated. One of Megan's cousins screamed, "Rot in jail, you Mexican rapist!"

Katie started crying. Elizabeth was stoic, thinking, "We will appeal." Lorenzo's eyes turned red as he looked at his son, whose head was down with his hands on his face, openly crying. Lorenzo's fragile heart was broken at that moment.

Judge Defourt said, "With regard to the sentence, I will have to consider the matter carefully. The jury has spoken, but I want a thorough pre-sentencing investigation and report from the Probation Department. Let us have that within two weeks from today. I will pass sentence the following week. You all will be notified when this court will reconvene. In the interval, the defendant will be held without bond."

The sheriff's deputy moved forward to put Mark in handcuffs to be placed in custody. Savannah was crying as she tried to approach Mark. When the deputy stopped her, she cried, "Please, I just have to say something to him." The uniformed deputies refused to allow her to get close to Mark. She cried out and tried to push her way through, but a man grabbed her hand, saying, "No."

Savannah screamed once more, and at that moment Mark turned around to see her fighting the deputies. He tried to speak, but words did not come out. His lips moved, saying, "It's okay. I love you."

On his way out of the courthouse, a very happy Detective Summers called Valenti to give him the great news. He was salivating over the possibility of moving up in rank and hoped for the promised recognition by Mr. Trump, which Valenti had suggested.

Valenti didn't answer or return his call, or any of his many subsequent calls. Two months later, Valenti finally left a voice message for Summers saying, "Hi John, good job with your conviction. Sorry for the delayed response, but we have many more important issues going on now. Wish you the best." In the end, Summers did not get any recognition from Trump or promotion in rank.

Shortly after Mark's conviction, Anne received a call from a neighbor who told her the news. She was mortified. Anne liked Mark and knew he had always been a good young man. She was worried about Zack's state of mind when he received the news, knowing they had been best friends for years. She arrived home from work early and prepared a snack for her and Zack since he would be back from school soon. Anne knew little about the fight between Mark and Zack and did not know of Zack's refusal to testify on his behalf.

Around two-thirty, the door opened. Zack dropped his backpack by the door, and heard his mom say, "Zack, I'm in the kitchen."

He walked on the shiny polished red clay Saltillo tile he had stepped on so many times, said, "HI, Mom," and gave Anne a kiss. Zack then sat on a bar stool in the kitchen while Anne brought him fresh-cut jicama and cucumbers with salt and red powdered chili pepper, the same way Soco often prepared it.

They were silent while they ate, and Anne thought of how to bring up the subject.

Finally, Anne asked, "Zack, did you hear about the verdict?"

"Yes, Mom, the news spread in school like wildfire."

Anne was astonished that Zack did not look more bewildered.

"Zack, how could this happen? Do you believe Mark could do something like this?"

"I don't know, Mom, he's changed."

"You think your friend could have done that? Was he ever abusive with girls?" Anne's tone became very serious when she imagined her son might have known something. "Did you ever see anything? Why didn't you say something?"

"Noooo, Mom, that isn't what I said. I don't think he would do something like that. He's actually pretty respectful and pretty innocent, definitely not abusive."

"What do you mean by 'he changed'?"

"He's become very defensive, withdrawn, and he is always defending his

Mexican-ness. He walks around alone and has become very selfish and even aggressive."

"What do you mean defending 'Mexican-ness?' Is that even a word?"

"I don't know. Mark acts differently. He and Cole have been fighting a lot. Cole calls him Mexican and beaner, and now Mark and even his sister Katie are walking the campus with a Mexican chip on their shoulder."

"It sounds like he was defending himself from Cole's attacks. He is of Mexican ancestry, so what would you expect? All the talk about Mexicans on the TV and news has polarized people on both sides."

Then Anne said something that made Zack's perspective change. "I get the feeling that Mark and Katie were not like this before all this Trump talk. In a way, they are forced to defend themselves now. You should be a little more understanding."

"Mom, you just don't get it!" He put his head down and said, "Also, since he and Savannah started dating, I have come to realize what a fake friend he is. He's a traitor like Cole says. He knew I liked Savannah, and he didn't care."

"Look, honey, you aren't the first friends who have gotten into a fight over a girl. You will soon realize it and will be great friends again." Anne had a lot of influence on Zack.

"Well, I don't know, Mom, you may be right. Maybe when he gets out of jail." When he said those words, a chill ran down his spine, and he felt responsible. "I hope he will be okay; he isn't a bad person."

"I'm worried. You know what is said on the news about Sheriff Arpaio's jails—they tend to be abusive with their inmates, especially Mexicans. And he is so young and handsome, I don't think that is a good thing in jail." Then with resentment in her voice, she said, "I just don't know why that Arpaio keeps getting elected. He is so hateful, and I have never liked him."

That night, Zack went to bed with a knot in his throat. His mom had made him reconsider his position. When he was called as a character witness, he was upset with Mark, and in his mind, he never considered Mark would be put in jail. Zack had underestimated the whole thing. That night he didn't sleep at all.

CHAPTER TWENTY-ONE

DREAMERS

Mallory's and Cindy's lives shattered when their dad was deported back to Mexico. For Mallory, things got worse after high school ended and her mom decided to go back to Mexico. The two Ochoa sisters, especially Mallory, refused to return to Mexico with Soco. Finally, Soco understood, so she spoke to Anne, who promised to keep a close eye on the girls and care for them as a family.

Soco tried to prepare the girls, explaining how dangerous it would be for two girls alone, in what Soco described as a hostile country for Mexicans. Mallory and Cindy had only known America as their home and country, and because of their parents' illegal status, they could not leave the country, so they had never visited Mexico. They both loved America. Phoenix was their home and they wanted to stay. After Miguel was deported, there was constant fighting amongst the Ochoa women, so Mallory had decided to move out of her house.

Soco and Miguel decided to move to Guadalajara, a large, beautiful, and modern metropolis not far from Tepatitlan, to be able to get better pay and send the girls some money. Anne Mackintosh offered to pay for both of the girls' community college tuitions and to help in any way they needed. The Mackintosh family was a lifesaver for the Ochoa girls.

After Soco left, Mallory and Cindy rented a tiny apartment in the nicer part of La Ponderosa. Although both worked part-time jobs and had school paid for, it was tough to make ends meet. Cindy was three years older than Mallory, both were pretty, slender, and had Soco's green eyes. Cindy was a little taller and the prettier of the two. Soco had been a strict parent and implanted good values, so they were good girls and a little sheltered.

Cindy lived in constant fear of being deported, but she would go to school and study hard to get good grades. There were moments in which she wondered if it was even worth it since she didn't know if she would be deported at any time. Cindy had Soco's emotional strength. Though she tried to show no fear in front of Mallory because she understood Mallory needed her, the uncertainty of her future started to eat at her insides.

During this turmoil, Mallory felt so lonely she started dating a young man from the barrio, Johnny Coronel, a tall and handsome young man whose parents were from Sonora. His dad was a bricklayer, and his mom worked as a babysitter. Johnny's parents were good, hardworking and honest people, but Johnny felt a massive resentment toward society, seeing his parents work so hard and often be abused. Although he was American- born, he still felt like an outsider—unwanted. Like many young people who felt disenfranchised, he became a thug and committed minor crimes.

Mallory was a catch for Johnny because she was well-educated, beautiful, and a positive influence for anyone. Johnny wanted to be a good man for her and decided to stop his life of crime. He would get a job and go back to school. Unfortunately for Johnny, he had been raised in an environment of poverty and crime and had lawless friends who were a bad influence.

One night he agreed to rob a liquor store. The liquor store had high-definition camera surveillance, and soon the police were after Johnny. The next day the police came knocking at Mallory's apartment. They knocked on the door hard and said, "Police, open the door!"

Mallory had no clue what was happening, and she thought it was ICE looking for Cindy. Her head pounded, and she opened the door.

"Are you Mallory Ochoa?"

"Yes, sir, what can I do for you?" Her voice was weak and shaky; she was so frightened.

"We're looking for Johnny Coronel. He's accused of committing a crime, and we know you're his girlfriend, and you may be hiding him. Where is he?"

"I don't know. I haven't heard from him since yesterday morning, and he was at his home. Did you go there?'"

"Yes, his mom said he hasn't been there since yesterday."

The policeman saw that Mallory was sweating profusely and he became suspicious of Mallory. "Do you know anything about the robbery at the El Paisano liquor store?"

"No, absolutely nothing."

"What do you do? Are you a legal resident?"

"I'm a student at Mesa College, and yes, I am an American citizen."

"Show me proof."

"Okay, sir, let me get it." Mallory, with her heart in her throat, walked to her room and started rifling through her papers. She did not remember where her mom had placed her birth certificate when she left, and all her documents were in a shoebox. Going through her head was the thought of not finding the birth certificate and getting thrown in jail and deported. She dumped the contents of her shoebox on the bed and with a huge sigh of relief, she saw the paper.

"Here is my birth certificate and my social security card."

"Okay, let me take the numbers." As he wrote the identification numbers, he said, "Who else lives here?"

Mallory felt her head would explode and realized that Cindy would have to prove her citizenship, but she couldn't because she was not a US citizen. Mallory imagined a life without Cindy, alone, and felt a terrible panic.

"My sister, Cindy."

"Is she here? Let me talk to her."

Mallory's voice cracked, "She must be in her room, let me see." She walked toward Cindy's room yelling, "Cindy, someone here wants to talk to you." There was no response, and she opened the door in a full panic, but no one was there.

Mallory turned to the policeman and said, "She must have left early without me noticing it, sorry." Mallory had been in her room listening to music and had not noticed Cindy had gone shopping.

"Okay. I may be back if we need any more information."

When the policeman left, Mallory sat in a corner and started to cry. She felt she had almost lost her sister and her entire life was about to go up in smoke. At that moment Mallory decided two things: that she would never allow a man to drag her into this type of situation again and that she had to fight for her sister and against the injustice of police being able to profile people and demand proof of citizenship.

A few minutes later, Cindy arrived. When she walked into the apartment, she saw Mallory on the floor crying and got very frightened and asked, "What happened?"

Mallory told her, and they both cried for a long time. They felt completely alone.

Cindy continued to go to college and work part-time; she had a dream of becoming a doctor to help people in need. She studied hard and was scheduled to finish her required classes the following summer. Soon after Trump became president, he threatened to end the Dreamer program, DACA, and leave 800,000 young people without legal protection, thus making them eligible for immediate deportation.

Devastated by all that was happening, Cindy would go home after school and cry in her room from feeling a sense of doom for her future. When Mallory was home, Cindy acted strong, but when alone, Cindy's depression took over. Finally, the internal turmoil started to have external signs, and Cindy gained thirty pounds, her face broke out with severe acne, and she stopped wearing makeup because she began to feel hopeless. People around her did not know what was happening to her because she kept it all inside.

At one point, the Democrats pushed for a permanent solution for the Dreamers, and Trump demanded fifteen billion dollars for the wall or he would not support any resolution. For once, there appeared to be a negotiation happening and a resolution for these kids. There was a breakthrough during the negotiations, and Cindy was so happy! She listened to the news with sustained attention, and a ray of sun started to peek through the clouds of her depression.

During those two weeks, she started to feel better and decided to go on a diet, which quickly cleared her skin, and she felt great. People at Mesa Community College organized a march in support of a resolution for the Dreamers, to create awareness of the problem and show support to the hundreds of students, who, just like Cindy, lived in constant fear and in limbo as to what their futures held.

At the end of negotiations, Trump used his usual trickery when dealing with massive community outcry. He faked real interest and willingness to negotiate, allowed the negotiation to move forward, and allowed the initial passion to fade. Then he started delay tactics, stalls, accused the other side of not negotiating in good faith, and finally, quietly killed the deal. This technique was right out of Trump's book The Art of the Deal's list of tricks.

By now, Jerry Valenti's words were proven correct; Mexican-Americans had no real political or social leadership or organization. His campaign to vilify and devalue the Mexican people was successful, and since the majority of the Dreamers were the children of Mexicans, there was no public will to help or admit them to the country permanently, which left the kids without powerful advocates. No politician was willing to spend political capital on an issue that their voting constituents showed only minor interest in, and Trump only had to stall for a while until the interest disappeared.

Cindy's world was imploding.

The following day, Mallory arrived home from work earlier than expected, because her manager said that business was slow that day. When she walked into the apartment, she yelled, "Cindy, I'm home," and as usual, went to her room. After a few minutes, Mallory smiled and remembered it was almost time for the girls' favorite daytime program, Los Ricos Tanbien Lloran (The Wealthy Also Cry), an old Mexican soap, which had been seen by millions all over the world, and now was being re-done with a new cast. The girls felt it was their way to stay in touch with their parents' roots.

She was happy they would be able to watch it together for once since their work schedules were so different. Mallory went out of her room, and into Cindy's. Cindy was sleeping.

"C'mon, Cindy, wake up, we finally can watch Los Ricos together. I wonder if Veronica finally dumped that rich asshole." She turned the TV on and flipped through the channels.

"Don't be so lazy, Cindy, how often do we get to watch our soap together?" Cindy did not respond. Concerned, Mallory shook Cindy. No response.

Mallory yelled, "Cindy, what's up with you?" Mallory's heart started pumping so hard it felt like it was going to beat out of her chest.

Mallory dialed 911 on her phone. She put her phone on speaker as she was put on hold, and in the meantime, she shook Cindy to get her to respond. She checked Cindy's breathing and fortunately she was, but very faintly.

After two agonizing minutes, she heard, "Operator 911, what is your emergency?"

"My sister is sleeping, but I can't get her to wake up. I know something is wrong, she is barely breathing."

The operator gave her instructions to ensure Cindy's airways were open by checking for obstruction to her windpipes, which helped Mallory stay calm. It took a few minutes for the paramedics to show up, but as soon as they arrived Mallory felt better and not as panicked. They checked Cindy's pulse, put her on oxygen, and rushed her to the hospital.

The doctors found that Cindy had taken too many sleeping pills and they asked Mallory if Cindy had been depressed or if Cindy had ever tried to commit suicide before. Anne Mackintosh showed up thirty minutes after Mallory had called her. Anne was the strength and support Mallory needed at that moment—both girls needed Anne.

After arriving at the hospital, Anne took control of everything. She spoke with the doctors to ensure the best care would be provided for Cindy. Anne was a kind woman. Her heart broke for Cindy when she heard more about what Cindy was going through, with her life feeling so uncertain.

Anne imagined how sad it would be if her children went through something like that, and she felt rage against the politicians who didn't care or think about the irreversible emotional damage the uncertainty caused the young people. This could create a generation of damaged individuals.

When she finally woke up, Cindy found herself in the hospital surrounded by Anne, Mallory, Katie, and Zack who had also arrived. They all were delighted to see her wake up and hugged her and told her how worried they had been.

Cindy was put on a twenty-four-hour hold in case she was suicidal, even though Cindy never acknowledged that she had tried to kill herself. She said she was so stressed out after the effort to pass legislation for the Dreamers was put aside by Trump. She took two pills to calm down, and because they did nothing, she took a couple more. Cindy did not entirely convince everyone that she had not attempted to take her life, but they all acted like they believed her.

Katie felt like she had to do something, and that night while driving an idea came to her mind, and she said out loud, "This is so crazy, it may work!"

CHAPTER TWENTY-TWO
ARPAIO'S JAILS

After Mark's conviction, the Suarez home was never the same. The smell of pancake breakfast on Sundays was replaced by emptiness and silence. The kitchen was deserted, with every pot and pan neatly in its place, looking like nothing had ever been used. No one was ever in the mood to watch TV, or talk about the news or the events of the day as they did before.

Family dinner ended and was replaced by Lorenzo and Elizabeth working late to avoid each other as much as possible. When they were together, they fought incessantly. Elizabeth blamed Lorenzo for everything, and the blame ranged from spoiling Mark too much, to not enough time spent with him, to choosing the wrong legal team or choosing the wrong legal strategy. Katie was the strongest of them all, and she continued to go to school, worked to get good grades, and even tried to reconcile her bickering parents.

While waiting for the judge's sentence, they took turns visiting Mark in jail. They visited as often as allowed, and each time, Katie would come along with either one of them.

They were anxious about the Maricopa County Jail system's infamous reputation. Under Joe Arpaio's leadership, the jail system had received serious accusations ranging from illegally detaining Mexicans and Latinos, to abusive and degrading treatment of Mexican and Latino inmates and intentionally failing to investigate sexual assault in jail. Arpaio's jails were found to repeatedly violate the constitutional rights of the inmates.

The first visit was nerve-racking. The large visiting area had cream-colored walls with no decorations, had a smell of roach killer and bleach, and it felt cold and scary. Elizabeth was used to it, as she had been there many times. For Katie, this was a very depressing place, and it broke her heart to know her brother had to endure it.

Elizabeth and Katie both wanted to be upbeat and talked about how there was hope for a lenient sentence. Katie even made an attempt to joke by saying, "Mark, it's kind of a shame you'll be here for such a short time because I'm becoming a lawyer soon and I would love for you to be my first case."

Mark was somber but strong and said, "Very funny. The thought of being here for a year is awful. The sooner you can get me out, the better."

"Honey, I am talking with friends, and we believe the court erred on several matters, and if necessary, the Court of Appeals should remand the case for resentencing. Trust me, we will do everything in our power to get you out soon. I am hoping for a suspended sentence and probation."

"I know Mom, I love you, you know that. I'm so sorry I did this to the family." Mark started to cry softly. The women's eyes swelled up, but they each made an effort to not cry. They had agreed to avoid making the visit a sad one. The visit ended well and they all were hopeful.

Lorenzo visited Mark every day. Lorenzo's law practice started to suffer because he was ignoring his own cases as desperation and despair settled in. Elizabeth's hands were tied. Her boss had warned her that she could jeopardize the case and she could be in serious trouble if she tried to use her influence to help her son.

With every day that passed, the visits became more and more difficult. After each visit, Katie arrived home crying and went straight to her room and closed the door. Almost every time they visited, Mark had a new bruise, and he was losing weight at an alarming rate. When they asked about the bruises he would only look down and sob, and they stopped asking. The thought of Mark being abused in jail was too much for anyone to bear.

Elizabeth tried to put on a brave face at work, but she hurt terribly because her baby, her boy, was being abused in jail, and she, a lawyer and a prosecutor, could do nothing about it. That fact was eating at her.

She kept blaming Lorenzo for their son's misfortune. Her mind revolved around the idea that it was all Lorenzo's fault. Sometimes she would think that Lorenzo could have done a better job finding a different legal defense team and sometimes she felt Lorenzo had failed them by encouraging Mark to get involved with the football team. Her accusations were never-ending.

"If I had gotten married to Douglas," she thought, "my last serious boyfriend, my son would not have looked so Mexican, and maybe he would not have been convicted." Then she realized what she was thinking. She was prejudiced against her own son, and maybe Lorenzo was right.

All of the talk from Trump and Arpaio and their campaigning for a wall to keep Mexicans out, because they are criminals and rapists, may have influenced the jury. After all, the media had had a field day painting Mark as an "entitled rich kid from Mexican parents, who felt he could do anything he wanted."

This realization softened Elizabeth toward Lorenzo. Maybe it was not all his fault," She thought. That evening she was more agreeable to Lorenzo than she had been in a long time.

The next day, Lorenzo and Katie went to the Maricopa County jail to visit Mark. He sobbed uncontrollably and kept repeating, "Dad, please do something! Get me out of here!"

Lorenzo tried to be composed. "My son, it won't be long. We think the judge will give you a lenient sentence. Just a few more days, we will get you out very soon."

Katie tried, but couldn't stop crying. "I love you, Mark."

When they left the jail, they went to a local Olive Garden for dinner. There was silence for a long time; neither one of them could say a word. Then Katie felt compelled to say, "Dad, I love you, and I am going to make you proud and fight against injustice."

Lorenzo used all the strength he could muster to speak. "I love you too, my sweet. I'm already so proud of you, both of you. Just make sure you help your brother. If I am ever not around, he will have a challenging future and will need you."

Katie hugged him and promised she would.

That night, the phone rang at four in the morning. Elizabeth picked it up. As she listened on the phone, Lorenzo saw his wife's face turn to terror, and she screamed a sound like he had never heard before. The phone dropped to the ground, and so did Elizabeth.

In the background, a female voice could be heard saying, "Hello, hello?" from the phone.

Elizabeth was on the ground in the fetal position, unable to talk.

Katie ran in the room and asked, "What happened?"

Lorenzo's face was distorted because he knew in his bones what had happened. He tentatively picked up the phone, not wanting to hear the voice on the other end. But he had to listen. Katie drew close to her father, sensing the worse.

The officer on the phone told him that Mark had been attacked and fatally stabbed by a gang member in jail. The family was asked to go down to the medical center to make a positive identification. Lorenzo didn't cry; he was too broken to cry.

The funeral was small, and they invited only close family members. With all the bad press, they did not want to have any negativity around. The media reported the news with the banner headline: "Youth Recently Convicted of Sexual Assault Killed in Jail."

The blow was too much for Lorenzo and Elizabeth. They hung together through the funeral, but afterward, the empty space was too much. Katie felt she was adrift in a sea of sorrow and neither her mother nor her father could help her.

After a few weeks, Lorenzo and Elizabeth decide to separate. There was too much pain to deal with. Katie was still underage and had to choose whom to live with. She was torn and loved them equally, so she decided to split her time between them, and lived half the time with each.

Katie found herself ignored, forgotten, and in the middle of awful fights at both homes. Her parents' sadness and inability to cope was overwhelming. Elizabeth stayed at the family home, and Lorenzo moved to the Magnolia Apartments in downtown, a complex of fully furnished apartment usually rented month-to-month to well-to-do recently divorced people, or important guest who needed long term accommodations.

Elizabeth's favorite, her beautiful boy Mark, was gone, and she focused her bitterness on Lorenzo. She buried herself in work concentrated on climbing the ladder of the district attorney's office. When Katie was at home with her mother, there was always a painful silence, only broken up by bouts of anger.

Katie would arrive home trying to be cheerful. "Mom, today I finally got the results on that critical math exam I told you I had to study for last week, and guess what?"

Silence…

"Mom! I got an A!"

Katie's loud voice finally got Elizabeth out of her own mind and she just said with a robotic voice, "Good job, honey."

Katie felt ignored, just like when she was a child, and all the attention from Elizabeth was always on Mark. But instead of resentment, she felt so sad for her mother, realizing the pain she must have been feeling.

When Katie was at her dad's apartment, Lorenzo's overwhelming grief was hard on her. Lorenzo never recovered. His law firm continued to deteriorate because he was unable to concentrate on his cases. Lorenzo became obsessed with clearing his son's name and punishing the authorities that allowed this to happen. Lorenzo was losing weight at an alarming rate, and Katie worried so much about his health.

"Dad, are you eating? I see no food in your refrigerator."

"I'm okay, my love, I'm just working too much, but I am eating. I promise, I'm fine." A smile showed on his face. "I had a great meeting with a Washington law firm. They think we could bring federal charges against the sheriff's office for their terrible failure to protect Mark and other inmates. Also, we think we could bring charges against the prosecutor's office and even the judge, as the case against your brother was extremely flimsy and should have never gone to trial."

Lorenzo's eyes swelled up, "I don't want what happened to Mark to ever happen to another boy, or his family, again."

"Oh, Dad, that would be so good," Katie said, and they hugged and cried for a while.

The next day Katie arrived at her home after school, and heard Elizabeth on the phone screaming,

"So what! Is that lawsuit going to bring Mark back? It is your fault he is dead, and now you want to ruin my life with this stupid federal lawsuit? Do you understand what this can do to my career? Lorenzo, you are just making everything worse! Just go back to beloved Mexico and leave us alone."

Katie was fuming. But she could feel her mother's pain. Giving her a look of disapproval while Elizabeth was still berating Lorenzo on the phone, Katie decided to just lock herself in her room.

Hours passed. Katie expected her mom to come to her room and maybe talk with her, but there was only silence.

While locked in her room, Katie felt sorry for herself. She missed Mark terribly and lost her former happy family life. She had always been under Mark's shadow. In school, he was the popular one, and she, Mark's little sister. She always felt weak under him, protected by him and her loving parents; now she felt more alone than ever before in her life.

When she was at the most profound moments of despair, she resolved to be strong, to be in control, to not allow other people to control her destiny. To fight to protect the weak and fight against injustice and clear her brother's name. And at that moment she felt stronger than ever before. Katie picked up the phone to call her dad and tell him she was going to help him in any way she could on the lawsuit.

The phone rang and rang, but no response. She called again; no answer. Lorenzo always picked up when Katie called. She panicked.

Katie drove to her dad's apartment to find him on the floor unconscious. She called 911, and he was rushed to the hospital. The doctors discovered an undiagnosed heart condition which had been exacerbated by all these events.

Katie's life was spinning out of control.

CHAPTER TWENTY-THREE
2021

In a meeting room at the Phoenix Airport Holiday Inn, a hallway with cheap gray carpet led to the Camelback Room, one of the hotel's smaller conference rooms. The tables were set up in a large rectangle, and the chairs were stainless steel and black plastic. To the right of the entrance was a coffee station with three medium-size stainless steel hot liquid dispensers. One said "coffee," the other said "decaf," and the third said "hot water"; they were next to an assortment of inexpensive teas and a row of white coffee cups. Next to the carafe of half and half sat a plate of Danish, which by the looks of them, could be from yesterday. And below the refreshment station, the carpet displayed many spills.

It was 2021, and a more mature Katie was about to start a meeting she felt in her heart could be the beginning of a new destiny for the Mexican-America community. She called the meeting "Unification for A New Destiny." She wore a style similar to her mom's, a pantsuit and high heels; she looked more like a model than a second-year law student. Although she was only twenty-three years old, her demeanor and presence were that of a person who understood life and activism. The struggles she and her family endured taught her the importance of taking action when the action was needed.

During undergrad and now grad school, Katie proved she was a woman of action, which was why such talented people felt compelled to attend her presentation. Katie was involved in student government and political activism, and was always surrounded by a group of strong allies, including her best friend Blaire, as well as Brandon, Savannah, Mallory, and Zack. Through thick and thin, they had been there supporting Katie's plans as a means to keep Mark's name alive. Katie was a fierce women's rights and social justice advocate.

She prepared for this meeting for weeks, planning to tell her story as a means to represent the consequences of Trump's assault on the Mexican-American community, and how much irreversible damage had been done to hundreds of thousands of families, Katie being a firsthand witness to this.

Her hands were shaking, but her voice was firm and resolute when she started the meeting. "It is my honor to officially start this meeting of 'Unification for A New Destiny,' and I am honored so many important and influential people have accepted our invitation. It is my strong belief that the future of our community, our young people, especially the Dreamers, depends on what happens at this meeting."

Katie stopped for a second to allow people to absorb what she had just said. "I would like to start by introducing the distinguished guests present here today. I will do the introduction, not in order of importance, but clockwise. First, to my right, is Mr. Ignacio Barrientos from California, president of the Chicano Coalition, who has, for several decades, worked to bring culture to Hispanic youth in California. Next to him is Maria Zavala, President of the Latina Business Women Society, based in Chicago, which is an organization that provides guidance to Hispanic women wishing to start small businesses."

She went around the table introducing five more presidents or chairpersons of Hispanic, Latino or Mexican-American Activist organizations, until finally Katie stopped, looked around the room and with a big smile said, "Now, please allow me to introduce two people who have been instrumental in the organization of this meeting. In fact, without them, you all and I may not be here today. Starting to my left is Mr. Zack Mackintosh, currently completing his MBA at Arizona State. Some of you may have cheered for him as the quarterback of the Sun Devils. And last but not least, Mallory Ochoa, an active member of The Student Mexican-American Anti-Defamation Coalition, based in Phoenix, who has been in contact with you and has helped me with the logistical organization of this meeting. Thank you all for being here.

"My name is Katie Elizabeth Suarez, and I am a first-generation Mexican-American from my father's side and third generation lawyer—well, future lawyer." She smiled. "I'm currently GPSA president at Arizona State University as well as founder of the Students Mexican-American Anti-Defamation Coalition.

"I would like to tell you a little about my story to put into context why this meeting is so important to me and why we must work together to advance some issues and laws that profoundly affect Mexican-Americans. A primary goal is to deal with people who have chosen to continue to use defamation and repression to contain the Mexican-American community, which has had devastating effects on millions of people.

"I was born in Phoenix, a city with a long history of repressing Mexicans. I was fortunate to have been born to a middle-class family of educated people--my mother, a fourth-generation Mexican-American prosecutor and my father, a Mexican-born lawyer. I have seen firsthand the irreversible damage caused by the attacks, repressive actions, and defamatory speeches president Trump, and people like Sheriff Arpaio and his successors have had on the Mexican-American community.

"During my junior year in high school, my life imploded when my brother was wrongfully accused of a minor crime, fueled by biases likely caused by President Trump's hate-promoting campaign. My brother was jailed at one of Arpaio's infamous jails, where human rights violations against Mexican-Americans are common. While awaiting sentencing, my brother Mark was murdered.

"The young man who was the star witness against my brother at his trial, Cole Jones, is currently serving time in jail for brutally attacking a young man who he assumed was an illegal Mexican. The young man ended up being a tourist from Turkey.

"After those events, my happy family life was forever destroyed. My parents' relationship could not recover and ended in divorce. My father had a heart attack, which ended his life a few months later. I ended my relationship with my mother because she has refused to denounce and take action against Sheriff Arpaio's jail system.

"My mother is currently a prosecutor for the Maricopa County Attorney's office. To me, she represents the many millions of closet Mexicans who choose to ignore or reject their Mexican background and bury their heads, in the belief that being a good American means integrating, renouncing their ancestry, and ignoring the struggle of the millions of Mexican-Americans in need.

"I was ostracized in high school by an abusive teacher who, although once my friend and mentor, chose to repudiate me, and knowingly derail my efforts to be accepted at Harvard because I decided to show pride in my Mexican culture and ancestry. She called me unpatriotic in front of my classmates. During the past seven years, I have seen families destroyed by the inhumane and unconstitutional arrest, and deportation of good people targeted only because they looked Mexican.

"We all know that, since Trump started his campaign five years ago, poverty has skyrocketed amongst Mexican-Americans. During the same five years, Mexican-Americans as a community have become marginalized and despised, and resentment has led to a dramatic increase in crime by Mexican-American youth. Racist attacks against Mexicans have increased dramatically. An entire generation of Mexican youth is being destroyed with the uncertainty of their future, and the so-called Dreamers are living a nightmare, which is irreversibly damaging them, and harming future generations of Mexican-Americans.

"While the entire country and universities continue to diversify, Mexican-Americans are not included because we lack the role models. My dear fellow Mexican-American leaders, my story is not unique. I know I am fortunate to have been born to a family with money and education. I am well aware that there are people who have experienced worse pain than I have, and I feel for them. The damage to the future of Mexican-American families and communities is creating a generation of damaged people who will perpetuate the cycle of alienation and despair. Unless we unite and do something to reverse this, the damage will be irreversible. Please allow me to share with you my plan..."

CHAPTER TWENTY-FOUR
FIVE YEARS

Despite her youth, Katie had been able to accomplish in the past five years what many people could not achieve in a lifetime. As a socially aware senior in high school, Katie ran for student class president and won, which was not an easy task, as her reputation was severely damaged by Mark's imprisonment and Mrs. Smith's attacks. She ran her campaign with the slogan "It Is Time for Fairness." She ran on the platform that change in three areas was needed.

First, the beautiful athletic facilities at Washington High were mostly utilized by the different boys' varsity teams, and the women's teams were given less than one-third of the available times, and at the worst hours and at inconvenient times.

Second, the past three class presidents had been the children of PTA presidents, showing clear favoritism.

And third, she demanded more transparent grading by the faculty at Washington, as many students complained they did not understand why they got certain grades or how to improve them.

Katie ran for president and Blaire, her usual partner in crime, ran as her vice-president, and Brandon as treasurer. Brandon also ran the campaign. They fought hard against their main opponent Jonathan Durham, a very worthy adversary. He was a 4.0 student, a varsity basketball star, and the son of a high-powered lawyer and a powerhouse of a mom, who happened to have been the past president of the PTA. During the final pre-election rally, Jonathan was extremely articulate, bright, and enthusiastic while presenting how he would bring more unity and progress to the class as its next president.

Jonathan also had a cutthroat attitude, and he knew Katie's main weakness was her tarnished reputation. At the end of his speech, he went for the jugular when he adroitly spoke with great admiration about Katie's scholastic history and her well-crafted presidential plans, and then said, "…and I also respect my opponent tremendously because of her courage to advocate for Mexicans by insinuating that Americans have been abusing the Mexican community. Although, in this case, her loyalties may be misplaced. As Mrs. Smith said in her class, her views are unpopular, historically inaccurate, and may be anti-American. Also, we all mourned her brother and at the same time rejected his actions when he was convicted of sexual assault."

The entire auditorium was shocked. These harsh accusations were delivered most diplomatically as a way to question Katie's character. The tactic might have worked if Zack, who stood in the middle of the auditorium, had not interjected by raising his voice and asking to say a few words; after all, he was the most popular athlete on campus.

At the top of his voice, Zack said, "I know that Jonathan is a brilliant guy and all, but this time his statement is stupid and offensive. I know Katie, and she is the most honorable person I know, and she is from a family who are honest and respectable Americans. Also, everyone knows Mark was my best friend, and everyone here knows he was a good guy, and I will fight every day of my life to show he was not treated fairly.

"Jonathan, whether you win or lose, you will always be a loser in my book for saying such hateful things." Zack's unexpected speech was an enormous boost to Katie's candidacy. Nevertheless, the audience was split.

In the end, Katie defeated Jonathan by twenty votes, and furthermore, she beat him again when she became valedictorian of their graduating class.

After Mark's death, Katie avoided Zack like the plague and had not spoken to him in months. The passion of Zack's speech was a massive surprise to Katie. She was not aware that when Zack received the news of Mark's death, he cried inconsolably and didn't leave his room for a full week. Zack realized the terrible mistakes he made, and that he had allowed jealousy, and hateful speech from people, to cloud his judgment and allowed himself to behave like the man he never thought he could be.

At that moment, Zack decided to do everything in his power to fight to clear Mark's name and fight against injustice. He was relentless in his determination to show Katie he was remorseful and would do anything to support her efforts to undo the damage done. Zack suffered over Soco's misfortune and felt firsthand the suffering caused by Trump's attacks on Mexicans. He became a powerful ally for Katie. Over the years, every time Katie needed his support or endorsement, she knew she could count on Zack. He tirelessly worked to support Katie's efforts for social change.

After high school, Zack became the quarterback for the Sun Devils and had a brilliant college football career, racking up some of the best numbers in school history. He was also enrolled in business school and studied diligently, following the footsteps of his accomplished parents. At every game, Zack glued a tag on his shoulder pads with Mark's name; he played on the field for his friend, and he fought to never again fail the people he loved.

In her first year of college at Arizona State, Katie went to a student film screening event called Popular Culture in Film Series organized by the psychology department. The first movie she saw was 21 Jump Street. In this movie, one of the main characters, played by Channing Tatum, has a scene where his character is forced to impersonate a Mexican-American. As usual, the Mexican-Americans are depicted as gang members and criminals. In his impersonation, Tatum's voice becomes very thin, with an accent that made him sound not very bright.

Katie found that offensive. The movie was scheduled to play again the following week, and this event triggered her decision to hastily form an organization she called the "Mexican-American Student Anti-Defamation Coalition." Katie went around campus looking for the support of Mexican-American socially active students, but sadly, she found very few. Most of her support came from socially active African-American groups, socially progressive white and Asian students, and some LGBT associations who supported the idea of fairness for all.

The day the movie was scheduled to show, twenty people picketed at the entrance with large signs and chanted, "Stop the abusive depiction of Mexican-Americans!" They hoped to stop the movie from showing. One of those at the door was Zack Mackintosh. His presence helped a great deal, as he smiled and convinced people to do something else.

Katie came up with the idea to provide moviegoers with an alternative cream store right outside of campus, owned by a Mexican-American family, and offered them to any person who changed their plans and did not go inside to see the movie. The plan worked, and when not one person entered the auditorium, the film was canceled. Katie's success made her realize that this may be a good grassroots way to build a resistance against the constant character assassination.

One month later, the same Popular Culture in Film Series was scheduled to show Argo with Ben Affleck. In this movie, Affleck, who in real life claims Irish ancestry, plays a brilliant CIA agent, Tony Mendez, who is a second-generation Mexican-American. In the movie, Mendez saves many lives during the Iran hostage crisis.

When the movie first came out in theaters, some minor controversy arose about Affleck taking on a Mexican-American role, but it quickly ended when Tony Mendez, a closet Mexican, said in an interview he did not consider himself Mexican-American, so he was "okay" having Affleck play him.

Katie had her group picket the movie with a sign saying "Stop Excluding Mexican-Americans from movie roles" and "Stop Ignoring the contributions of Mexican-Americans." Katie asked Blaire, who now was a junior reporter for a local TV news station, to see if she could bring cameras to provide attention to this event. Blaire told Katie she did not think she could and would be hard for her to convince her producer to cover the event. Katie understood and did not want to cause trouble for her friend.

At the event, one of the fellow picketers, Jose Chavez, brought a Mexican flag and started to wave it. When Katie saw it, she grabbed it, put it away, and got very mad at Jose. She told him, "We are not fighting for Mexico, we are fighting for fair treatment of Mexican-Americans. Waving a Mexican flag will only enrage people and will make us lose support. Put that away and never bring it again if you want to be a part of this group." She again had vouchers for ice cream, and Zack was there to support her.

Unfortunately for Katie, this time Professor Carrol Peterson came out and demanded that Katie and her group leave or he would try to get her expelled from campus. He had already called campus security. When security arrived, they were very aggressive to the picketers, tore the signs out of people's hands, and started shoving and demanding they go or they would have to use force.

Zack did not want to have a fight with campus police, so he suggested to Katie that she back off this time. Katie was scared as she did not condone violence, but the moment she was about to call off the strike, the cameras of Channel 2 News showed up; it was Blaire to the rescue.

Blaire and Katie continued to be best friends and always supported each other's goals, even though after high school they took different paths. Blaire chose to get an associates degree in journalism at Phoenix College, knowing her grades were not very good. She received an opportunity to intern at a local news channel. Both girls had hectic lives, but never lost touch with each other, even though during finals and tough projects they would not see each other for weeks. But whenever they had time, they would spend time together, feeling like time had not passed at all and they both were back in middle school.

Blaire was more of a free spirit, had many boyfriends, and thoroughly enjoyed her college life. When she would tell Katie stories about the wild times she and her artist and journalist friends were having, Katie would admonish her to be careful and to stay focused on her career, knowing Blaire tended to forget school and focus more on her social life and boys.

At one point, Blaire told Katie she started smoking weed because everyone in school was doing it. Katie once more admonished her friend and told her not to become a pothead because it would make her less effective at school and reminded her of how hard she worked to be accepted to the Journalism program.

The following week, Katie surprised Blaire by visiting her at her dorm.

At Katie's knock, Blaire opened the door. "What! What are you doing here?" Blaire's eyes were red, and she was speaking very fast.

Katie, who knew her friend very well, immediately noticed Blaire's strange behavior. "So what's up with you? I wanted to surprise you and take you out to a late dinner and ice cream."

"How sweet, but I am just ready to go out and meet a bunch of my friends at a party. Do you want to come?"

"But honey, you don't look very coherent to go out. Do you know this crowd well?"

"Not really, but they are super fun."

Katie's motherly instinct kicked in, and, wanting to protect her friend, insisted they go to dinner and ice cream, and reminded Blaire it had been some time since they were together. Katie stayed with her all night.

She spoke like a concerned parent and asked Blaire to be more careful and selective with her friends. Blaire knew that Katie was relentless, and truly spoke out of love, so she agreed to be more careful.

That night Blaire's new friends got into a serious car accident, the police found coke in the car, and most of them ended up booked for drug possession.

Katie's natural wisdom, true love and demonstration of profound interest in Blaire's well-being refocused Blaire and gave her the boost she needed. Katie was a positive influence.

Blaire continued to look at her beloved friend like the cutest nerd she knew, like when they were children in Paradise Valley. She knew Katie loved her and with Katie as a friend, life was always better.

Blaire came charging in with her camera like the cavalry, and she was determined to protect her friend. Blaire immediately put her microphone in the faces of campus police and asked them, "Why are you manhandling these people? Have they committed a crime?"

The campus police's attitude softened when they realize they were being videotaped.

Then Blaire placed the microphone in Professor Peterson's face when she noticed he was yelling at Katie.

Professor Peterson said, "Your behavior is anti-American and ridiculous. The last time you forced my movie to cancel, I let it slide, but this time you have gone too far. You're interfering with my class."

"No, professor," Katie said, "this isn't a class, it's entertainment, and I have the freedom our great country provides us to congregate and make our voices heard when we feel unfairness is being committed."

"What unfairness? This is a movie about how a man's ingenuity and bravery saved many lives."

"Professor," Katie said, "this man you are talking about is Mexican-American, and the movie depicts him as white. We are picketing because this movie clearly depicts the habit of minimizing the contributions of Mexican-Americans in this country." And she then said with indignation, "But of course Trump and his allies have a campaign to devalue the contributions of Mexicans and Mexican-American people to this country and focus only on the bad. How can that be fair?"

"Well, young lady, my choice of movies isn't racially related, and I don't appreciate that you're trying to turn it into a racial problem. I don't care what Mexicans do."

Katie said, "Yes, professor, that is the issue. I know you don't care. Your family isn't being destroyed, and your neighbor isn't wrongfully imprisoned or racially profiled, so why should you care?"

"You're twisting my words, and I'm done talking to you. Leave or face the consequences."

After the altercation, the movie showing was canceled, and Katie and Professor Peterson's exchange was shown on the news. While there was some support for Katie, most people who saw it tweeted hateful things about Katie and her newly formed group. It took courage to be an activist, and Katie had courage.

The next day while Elizabeth had breakfast she saw Katie on the news in an altercation with a professor and almost getting arrested for organizing the picketing. Then, she heard the newscaster mention how Twitter was buzzing with hateful comments about Katie and her group. Elizabeth was shocked and very mad at Katie.

On the other side of town, Katie was getting ready for class when her phone rang. It was her mother, and it had been a while since they last talked. She picked up. "Hi, Mom."

"Katie, what do you think you're doing? I saw you on TV. I thought I was paying for you to go to school, not to do these silly things. And you almost got arrested?"

"Hello to you too, Mom! Why is it that every time you call me, you attack my desire to be socially active and help my fellow Mexican-Americans?"

"Look, I understand you blame racial profiling for your brother's death, but you have to get over it. The world is unfair, and I worry that because of your actions, you may become a target and I don't want you to have a problem. I still blame your father for putting all those thoughts in your head."

Katie's voice got deeper and louder. "Please stop attacking Dad. He was a good man, and he taught me who I was, and where I came from. I'm not embarrassed by it like you are, and I intend to help the mistreated Mexican-Americans in this country."

"Well, first of all, I'm not embarrassed by anything. I am an American, and I have done what Americans should do, assimilate."

"No, you have done what many assimilated Mexicans do—turn your back on who you are! Other cultures have pride, they help each other, and that is what makes them powerful communities."

Katie waited for a response, but there was only silence, so she continued, "You can be a proud American and still embrace your ancestry and culture. That is what this beautiful country is about, and Mexicans should be able to do the same."

"You sound like your dad. I'm just telling you, if you keep on this path, I'll stop paying for school and then you'll see what all of this costs you."

"Mom, no disrespect, but Dad left me a good amount of money, and if you want to stop helping me, I'll use that money."

"You are impossible. Do what you want. But don't expect me to bail you out if you get in trouble."

"Okay, Mom, thank you for your support."

"You have been warned. I don't need any more tragedy in my life."

"Okay, Mom, talk to you soon. Bye."

After that conversation, they did not speak for a long time. Katie's relationship with her mother became even more distant, and on the rare occasion they did speak, it was fast and businesslike.

CHAPTER TWENTY-FIVE
ENLIGHTENMENT

During all these years, Brandon and Katie had been there for each other. When Mark was convicted, Katie received great support from most of her fellow students. She also had to endure abuse in school, from some people who disliked her, had a grudge or felt comfortable showing their prejudice. Some would find ways to get under her skin by saying things like, "Say hi to Mark in jail," or they would say distorted Spanish words to her like "compreendeee," trying to demean her.

After Mark's death, Katie felt hopeless for the future. Katie's parents were overwhelmed, and while Katie tried to avoid adding to their concerns by showing a strong face to them, internally she was shattered. Brandon was always there at the perfect time; his strength and honesty were the emotional air she needed.

Senior year at Washington had been challenging for Katie. Running for class president placed her in a vulnerable position, and while many appreciated her work to make student life better, others disliked her, disagreed with her initiatives, fought her, and made an effort to make her life hard. And again, Brandon was there for Katie.

Brandon knew he could count on Katie's strength and determination to encourage him during the challenging undergraduate years for a pre-med student. Katie helped him study and encouraged Brandon when he was ready to give up his studies. Both thought of themselves as nerds and loved to talk about their respective newfound knowledge, and current events. They admired each other's smarts and saw themselves as a synergistic power couple.

Cindy's suicide attempt happened during Katie's first year of college at

Arizona State, and she was overwhelmed by Cindy's actions. That evening, she bitterly complained to Brandon about the unfairness of the situation.

"Those poor Ochoa girls, I feel so bad for them. Their lives have been turned, and I truly don't know what will happen to them! I don't understand how people like Trump and Arpaio don't care about how much damage they're creating for these people's futures. And the sad part is that they do it only for political and financial gain. How can these people get away with this in twenty-first-century America?" Katie's voice showed the hurt she felt in her heart.

Brandon, who pulled no punches, said, "They get away with it because you guys are weak and have no unity; you allowed that to happen." When Brandon said those words, Katie got up. Her eyes were wide and her mouth opened in disbelief at his insensitivity.

Brandon wanted to encourage Katie, and he felt that the best way to help her get out of her sense of helplessness was to fire her up, because he knew she was a fighter. "Jewish people have been dealing with people much worse than Trump, and we have been able to overcome it. You want to know how?"

"What are you saying, Brandon? Are you trying to help me or piss me off?" Katie's face was red and she was in no mood to hear insensitive advice.

"You're Catholic, and you should know that for over two thousand years, Christians have accused Jews of killing Christ, and because of that, Jewish people have been persecuted and abused everywhere we went."

"You know I'm not a practicing Catholic, but I do know that Jews have been persecuted. What's your point?"

"Well," Brandon said, "this is a long story, but I will tell you the short version. For two thousand years, Jews all over Europe were abused, expelled out of different countries, vilified, and forced to be peasants because they were denied education, rarely being accepted at any higher education institution, which was mostly controlled by the church. Most Jewish people lived in squalor all over Europe, and they had zero rights. During that time, Jewish people survived by keeping to themselves, having strong community support for each other, and maintaining traditions and a strong identity. At the time, there was no other alternative."

Katie's demeanor changed as she became more interested. "So how did your people manage to become so successful and powerful in the US?"

"During that time, Jews in Europe had some periods of peace and prosperity, followed by terrible repression and suffering. One country where Jewish people had pockets of improved rights and prosperity was Germany in the late eighteenth century. During a particularly good time of Jewish tolerance, Moses Mendelssohn, a highly educated and politically influential German-Jewish philosopher, promoted the idea of 'Jewish Enlightenment' and touted the importance of education for a group of people who hadn't had the opportunity to do so.

"With this freedom, many German Jews experienced great prosperity. In the late nineteenth century, large numbers of educated and prosperous German Jews migrated to America looking for greater liberty and civil freedom. Following them was a massive migration of heavily oppressed Eastern European Jews.

"By the beginning of the twentieth century, there were over two million Jewish people in America." Brandon ended, "The freedom provided by America, strong community support, and finally with the influence in numbers, the Jewish community moved from a mostly lower-class community to the wealthiest per capita community in America, in less than a century. Especially after the Nazi experience, Jewish people have been extremely proactive in protecting their civil liberties."

Katie realized that change in the destiny of an entire group was possible. Using her scientific reasoning, and almost as if she was in class, she summarized her learning experience. "So basically, the reason for the amazing Jewish success in America is first, your strong community identity, not rejecting who you are even in adversity, but having pride in your culture and traditions; second, group unity, community support for each other, which allowed your people to protect and encourage each other, including good organizations to protect your civil liberties. And finally, your appreciation for educational 'enlightenment,' good leadership, and role models that promote education and advancement."

"Well, more or less... scholars who have tried to identify why it is that the Jewish experience in America has been unique have many different opinions."

"Thank you," said Katie. "This talk has made me realize that I can do something, and not just feel sorry for myself and my people."

"Honestly, maybe in the 1840s, Mexicans had no power to do anything, but now, you guys are so powerful, or you should be so powerful. Your economic power is enormous. I read there are almost 40 million Mexican-

Americans, about 12% of the population of the entire country. If that turned into political power, you would be unstoppable."

Katie smiled and kissed Brandon. "I see you've done your homework. You have no idea how much your support means to me."

Brandon and Katie continued to be powerful supporters of one another throughout undergraduate school at Arizona State. Their love and support for each other was enviable.

CHAPTER TWENTY-SIX

ART

During Katie's second year in college, she used the attention the media brought to her and the newly formed "Mexican-American Student Anti-Defamation League" to further her plans. She used social media to target Spanish surnames in Phoenix to invite people to participate and support a meeting she was planning that would take place in one of the University's lecture rooms.

She found out very quickly how some Mexicans and Hispanics felt offended if someone assumed they were Mexican or Hispanic because of their last name. She got a lot of nasty responses saying, "Quit sending me this crap, I'm not Mexican.

On the other hand, Katie had been able to secure some support from the dean of the law school, Alan Greenberg, and he allowed Katie the use of a lecture room for her meetings as long as it was after hours, and the room was not being occupied by any class.

In her first meeting, Katie was amazed to see that fifty students and a hundred guests attended the first regularly scheduled meeting. Katie asked Mallory to help her with the organization of this meeting. At the time, Mallory attended community college, so her classes were flexible, and she had become an activist, after her sister's scare.

As usual, Katie was prepared for the meeting, and the most essential part of the agenda was to figure out why there were so few cultural events showing Mexican-American art or culture anywhere in town, when the population in Phoenix was almost one-third Mexican. Katie knew of several young and brilliant Mexican-American artists who were struggling after being rejected and ignored at many of Arizona's leading galleries and art exhibitions, including the Arizona Museum of Modern Art. Katie tried to reach out and speak with the curators to see if they would consider a temporary exhibition of young Mexican-American artists, but her request had been ignored.

She shared this information at the meeting and after much discussion, they found a way to stir up change. At the meeting, it was decided that the first step should be bringing attention to those facts by marching at the entrance of the Arizona Museum of Modern Art. There were a plethora of Mexican and Mexican-American painters, and the museum had not had an exhibition of Mexican or Mexican-American art in years. Katie, being the organizer she was, made a list of requirements for any volunteer who would join the march.

First, all marchers had to be American citizens, to ensure protection in case anyone was arrested.

Second, she asked all the marchers to come nicely dressed to represent the community and show that Mexicans-Americans are proud people.

Third, no Mexican flags would be brought or displayed anywhere during the march.

And fourth, even if people confronted them, the marchers had to be peaceful.

She used social media to attract attention to the march, and once again asked Blaire to see if she could bring the Channel 2 News. Blaire did better than that, and she helped Katie put out a properly written press release and got some other TV stations and a couple of newspapers to show up at the march as well.

The march was short and peaceful. They arrived at the entrance of the museum at ten a.m., the time it opened. It was a large group of fifty well-organized people, waving banners saying, "1/3 of Phoenix is Mexican-American, show our beautiful Art" and "Stop Making Mexican-American Art and Culture Invisible."

Most people entering the museum were not amused and, in fact, were rude to the picketers. There were a couple of young men who, while passing through the marchers, intentionally shoved and pushed one of the marchers to the ground. More than one museum patron yelled at the marchers, "Mexicans have no freaking decent art, go home."

In addition to the TV cameras, Katie arranged to have everything filmed by one of the students, expecting that there might be some useful footage.

While researching for the march, Katie discovered that two of the big donors to the museum were local corporations, with wealthy Mexican-American ownership: The Jimenez Group, a real estate developer, and one of the more prominent injury law firms, Los Abogados Nogales. Katie made a banner, which she personally waved, that said, "The Jimenez Group and Los Abogados Nogales Do Not Support Mexican Art."

Once more, Katie was on the news and gave Blaire the footage of the aggressive man who shoved a marcher and the offensive comments to include in her piece. As on her previous marches, there was a massive wave of extremely offensive comments on social media and some threats against Katie and her organization.

The next day, Katie received a threatening phone call from the lawyers of the Jimenez Group and Los Abogados Nogales. She was told that if she mentioned them again, they would look into suing her for defamation. Katie asked them to have a meeting with her, and they agreed. After some negotiations, they decided to bring to the board of the Arizona Museum of Modern Art the idea of having a Mexican art exhibition, maybe David Alfaro Siqueros, Diego Rivera, or Frida Kahlo.

Katie insisted that at least a small portion of this exhibit should include works from young talented and promising Mexican-American painters, who deserve some recognition. The museum agreed, and three months later an announcement was made on TV of an upcoming Mexican and Mexican-American masters exhibition. This event brought great pride to the Mexican-American community in Phoenix.

Throughout her undergrad year, Katie and her group continued their labor, pushing their way through the different art-related events. Whenever a movie or a play had adverse Mexican representation, they would march and wave banners, always peacefully, always well-dressed, and never waving a Mexican flag. The strategy was working.

After college, Katie chose to stay in Arizona to go to law school at Arizona State because she knew her work was far from over. Brandon accepted an offer to attend Harvard medical school. When Brandon informed Katie he was moving to Boston for five years, Katie was upset; she had assumed he would stay in Arizona for medical school, and in time they would get married.

Brandon was not willing to miss the opportunity of going to Harvard. He insisted that their relationship could withstand the distance and they would make it work. The first year they talked on the phone almost every day, and he traveled to visit her during every school break. By the second year, the visits and the calls became less and less.

At the end of the second year of Brandon's medical school, the jealousy and arguments increased, and they both realized the long distance was hurting their relationship, and instead of ending up hating each other, they chose to end their relationship and see other people. They continued to be close friends and stayed in touch because they knew they could count on each other in the case of real need.

CHAPTER TWENTY-SEVEN
BACK AT THE UNIFICATION

Back at the "Unification for A New Destiny" meeting, all eyes were on Katie. Telling her heartbreaking story and showing her resolution to see things change for the benefit of others had a definite effect on the people present.

"My friends and colleagues, Trump and his followers are causing irreversible damage to the Mexican-American community. Over the years, Sheriff Arpaio and his allies have terrorized the Mexican immigrants and isolated the entire Mexican-American community in Arizona. Most of these families are a mix of American citizens and Mexican immigrants.

"Literally, hundreds of thousands of Mexican-American families who are part citizens, part Dreamers, and part illegal, have been separated. Trump, Arpaio, and their supporters are destroying families and literally robbing millions of Mexican-American people of a chance to live the American dream, forcing them to live in depression and agony every day.

"Do not assume things can't get worse. Let's not forget how in 1930, almost half a million Mexican-Americans were deported by local authorities as a solution during the Great Depression. Many of those were, in fact, American citizens. Leaving hundreds of thousands of Mexican-American children orphaned of fathers of mothers and forcing them into poverty and servitude. Are we to allow this to happen again?

Ignacio Barrientos stood up. "Do you remember when the great wave of Cuban immigrants came to America in 1980? The "Marielitos" came on their boats, and there were over 120,000 in a few months. Some of them were prisoners, and some were people with mental problems who Castro had released from prison. Initially, they were treated poorly, detained, and put in camps; their future looked dim.

"But then the Cuban community united in helping those people. Cuban-American celebrities like Gloria Estefan and Andy Garcia, as well as Cuban-American political leaders, became strong advocates of fair treatment to these new migrants. In the end, each refugee received money for sustenance, money for education, and financial support for years to allow them to join the American life and have a chance to have the American dream. Their strong united action provided a great future for many Cubans, which is now evident by that community's well-being."

"Exactly," said Katie. "We should learn from them. When Mexicans are being abused and mistreated, defamed and oppressed, where are the Mexican-American celebrities, the Mexican-American politicians, the Mexican-American leadership? There are a few isolated voices, but the lack of a unified voice makes us vulnerable and weak."

"But why should anyone listen to our voice?" ask a member of the audience.

"First of all, numbers, In 2016, 12% of the entire American population had Mexican origin," said Katie. "Now, that number has grown to 13%. It is one of the largest ethnic groups in America, approximately the same size as the entire African-American population in America. That should not be surprising to anyone because approximately one-third of the US territory used to be Mexico, and Mexico is our only neighboring country to the south.

"Don't you think Trump's diversion tactics, are meant to weaken Mexican-American's political influence?" ask a young woman.

"Yes, America under Trump is enjoying great prosperity, some good fiscal decisions have yielded good growth, and jobs are being developed, and industries are growing. African-Americans have experienced tremendous social progress as a community," Katie responded.

"We see their well-deserved success everywhere in movies, TV, music, politics, and sports. The gay and lesbian community enjoys improved equality and Muslims, Indians, and many other minorities fill the universities and are treated respectfully and represented well in TV and movies.

"Nevertheless, the life of Mexican-Americans under Trump has only gotten worse. Trump's offensive language and open attacks against Mexican-Americans has polarized people against them and created visible and invisible negative consequences to the social progress of the Mexican-American community. Hate crimes against Mexicans have doubled since Trump took office. Less than 0.1% of university students are of Mexican origin.

"On TV and in movies, Mexican-Americans are almost invisible. Whenever an affluent Hispanic character of any importance is portrayed, it is always Cuban, Chilean, or Colombian. Who would want to see a Mexican or Mexican-American leading role on TV or the movies, when every day we hear Trump on Twitter reminding us how we need a wall to keep undesirable Mexicans out?

"But whenever a Hispanic character is said to be Mexican, it will likely be a nanny, a cleaning person, or gang member. Trump and his allies have revived the systematic character assassination of Mexicans, which started after the Mexican-American war. Consequently, what little progress Mexicans in America had made in 150 years has been lost. That needs to change, for the good of present and future generations.

"Jewish, Italian, Irish, Armenian, Indian, Puerto Rican, and Cuban celebrities are proud of who they are and talk about the tradition with a sense of pride; no other ethnic group feels the need to hide or forget their ethnicity to be consider a good Americans. While there are many successful Mexican-Americans, most are closet Mexicans who choose to blend, conceal their identity, or just keep it quiet.

"Some, like Mitt Romney, flat out say that, while they have Mexican born ancestors, they do not identify themselves as Mexican-Americans. These people's selfish and offensive effort to disassociate from a Mexican-American claim, hurt the youth. Many selfish assimilated Mexicans carry the idea that their lives will be more comfortable if they consider themselves just American.

"I agree with you, Katie." Maria Zavala in the back stood up. "This hurts the Mexican-American youth, and it robs them of role models to aspire to, severely limiting their career choices."

Then Katie jumped in. "My friends, do not underestimate the power of role models. It may be the single most important factor in the future of our youth, the belief that people like them can achieve great things. This was greatly demonstrated by a 2009 article in the New York Times which highlighted a research study showing the "Obama effect as lifting black test-takers scores." They tested African-Americas and whites before the election, and the results showed the historical trend of blacks scoring much lower than whites. Then they tested again after Obama won the election, and the black scores spiked to match whites, without any other altering factor, other than the confidence that people like them can achieve great things." Katie looked around and said, "We must work to provide positive role models for our youth.

"But what exactly is your plan, Katie?" said Ignacio.

"Now is the time for this to be reversed. Change must start within our community. I want to share with you my three-point strategy for the Mexican-American Renaissance:

"One, to have Pride and Unity we must stop diluting our strength and identity by using confusing terms. We must call ourselves who we are: Mexican-Americans and not Chicano, Latino, or Hispanic, it shows a lack of pride, and creates a generational division, confusion and thus lack of unity. Cubans call themselves Cuban-Americans, so do Puerto Ricans, and so do Jewish-Americans. We must understand the root of these names.

"After the Mexican-American War and for the next hundred and fifty years, the term 'Mexican' had been so maligned, in fact used as a derogatory word, people preferred to be recognized by other terms, such as Chicano, Latino, Spanish, and Hispanic. And when possible disassociate form their Mexican heritage. That needs to change.

"Only education will change that. We must develop an educational program to help Mexican-Americans reclaim and recognize their precious, beautiful, and plentiful cultural importance and contribution to this country. This should be done by using every possible educational means, including creative participation in the arts, movies, books, and museums.

"Second, Mexican-Americans must have strong organizations which represent our interest, while we must continue to have strong coalitions with our Latin-American brothers and sisters. Never excluding anyone, and always supporting organizations fighting for fairness for everyone.

"Mexican-Americans currently have severe and unique challenges, which require special attention. Every Hispanic group has their own unique needs.

"When Trump first ran for president, Mexican-Americans overwhelmingly voted against him for obvious reasons, but the majority of Cubans voted for Trump because they felt he had a better plan for the relationship with the island. Puerto Ricans are American citizens and have different political needs, which they champion. Central Americans have their own unique needs, including their refugee status, and they receive different immigration treatment and have unique political and social needs.

"Mexican-Americans are currently the most maligned group in this country and are under attack by Trump and his ilk. A unified Mexican-American organization must fight for our unique needs; for example, to protect the unity of the family, and a good future for the youth, we must fight for fair immigration laws, which will protect Mexican-Americans family unity. End the discriminatory immigration practices aimed against legal Mexican immigration, which separates families. More than 800,000 Dreamers, mostly Mexican-American, are living in fear and depression. We must fight for them and find a path for citizenship. We must fight to regain the respect of our name and culture, no longer allowing abusive speech to go unchecked. This organization must be vigilant and immediately strongly denounce abusive and derogatory speech. Fortunately we have great untapped power due to our large numbers. Trump knows this, and this is why he has worked to suppress us again.

"Third, Mexican-Americans need to work hard to have educated leaders and role models who declare with pride they are Mexican-American. Promote education. Remember the power of role models. We must fight to have more successful Mexican-Americans depicted in movies and industry.

"Education should be focus on re-gaining our stolen reputation, remembering our community is economically depressed not because we are less capable but because of the forced repression and denied opportunities we suffered for over 150 years."

"We must scorn the closet Mexicans who choose to selfishly hide their identity and deny the Mexican-American youth positive role models. We must repudiate Mexican-American industries, which, instead of supporting Mexican-American culture, choose the easy path of blending in. Companies like Corona beer cowardly cater to the American mainstream, when they could use their considerable influence to show the positive side of the Mexican-American culture.

"We must spotlight the exceptionally high number of Mexican-American Congressional Medals of Honor recipients, the many thousands of successful professional and entrepreneurs who graduated from the most prestigious universities, and the achievements of the many hundreds of Mexican-American elected officials at many levels. Not forgetting the countless successful people in the arts.

"When there is a lack of positive role models, some type of role model will appear, and we must reverse the negative, low standards uneducated Mexican-Americans stereotypical role models for our youth, people like

'Paquito El Peludo' on the radio. We must promote education, find and highlight the great role models, and strive to represent the good values of the Mexican-American culture."

Katie looked everyone in their eyes and said, "Let's not be embarrassed to have an organization that is working for the betterment of our people. The African-Americans have shown us the way, the Jews have them, the Evangelicals have them, and the LGBTQs have them. And they all are still proud and loyal Americans. Why can't Mexican-Americans have a group looking out for their interests?"

"By our inaction, we are allowing an entirely new generation of Mexican-Americans to be forced, once again, into poverty, servitude and despair, just like after the Mexican-American war and the great depression. Are we going to allow this to happen again?

Katie took a big breath and said, "My friends, after this long speech, I would like to introduce Mr. Zack Mackintosh, who is here to share his perspective as an Anglo-American who cares about our work."

Zack stepped up to the front of the room. "I just want to say that I was raised by a nanny who is Mexican, and I loved her. She is one of the kindest, most proud and honest people I'll ever know, and I lost her to Arpaio's abusive and unconstitutional roundups of Mexicans. I saw the suffering this brought to her lovely family. I also lost my best friend to injustice spurred by Trump's hateful speeches. I will not get into details of that because I will cry."

His eyes immediately welled up as he saw Katie's mouth quiver. "And while I am not Mexican," he continued, "I have firsthand suffered from these attacks. I will not even pretend to know what it's like for the people who've actually suffered through this. But I can tell you that Americans are fair people and the vast majority I know, and have spoken to, hate what is happening. We want to see fairness and justice, and I am pledging my undying support to you."

"Thanks, Zack. It's people like you who have helped me through so much, and I truly appreciate your support." Katie turned back to the audience. "I propose we form a coalition and call it 'The National Coalition for the Advancement of Mexican-Americans.'"

The room was silent.

"Okay, the table is now open for more questions and discussion. I have written an agenda which will allow us to tackle all the issues I know you want to discuss."

Maria Zavala spoke up. "Okay, Katie, I accepted your invitation to this meeting because I can see you have been doing a nice job here in Phoenix and I wanted to see how we could help you. I am in full disagreement with your statement that the use of certain terms like the one my group uses, 'Latinas in Business,' means we're embarrassed by being Mexican-American. We use the term Latina to be inclusive to all Latin American people.

"Ms. Zavala," Katie said, "I admire that your group does a great deal of good, and that is very inclusive, keep up the good work. I also know that many of your members are Mexican-American, as I know you are. We are not asking you to change, we are asking your group's support, becoming a member of this coalition of groups, with the intent of helping the Mexican-American oppressed people."

Katie stopped and looked around, and said, "Do we agree that an effort to help the oppressed Mexican-American community, does not conflict from a desire to help everyone else?"

Katie waited to see the response, and everyone nodded or said a resounding "Yes."

"Do we agree that it's time to stop the scapegoating and character assassination of the Mexicans in America, and the devastating effect this has on our youth's self-esteem?"

Everyone said "Yes!"

"Does everyone agree that the Mexican culture is rich and beautiful, and it has a powerful and positive influence in this country, and our children need to know that?

Everyone said "yes'

"And if all the successful Mexican-Americans stopped hiding and became better role models, they would greatly influence the future of our youth?"

Again, everyone said "Yes."

"Well, my friends, I move to form this coalition."

And thus it began.

CHAPTER TWENTY-EIGHT

THE STRIKE

The success at the Phoenix Modern Art Museum and the strength of a national coalition made Katie ready to tackle their most challenging project yet: to bring a resolution the Dreamers' plight.

After Trump's success at blocking the effort of the legislature to resolve the Dreamers' legal situation, he used the strategy of silence on the matter. No more attention was given to the issue. Trump did not renew the DACA program and thus left those Dreamers vulnerable. He followed his well-calculated plan by doing little about it and keeping quiet, which allowed the issue to disappear from the public eye.

Finally, in his fifth year in office and after his reelection, he ordered the quiet deportation of the Dreamers. No one received warning letters, and, randomly, ICE would show up at their homes, apprehend them in front of their crying families, and detain and deport them as fast as possible to prevent a family's time to react. Once deportation became known, a new outrage started, and some students protested, but once more, there was no real appetite to help the Dreamers.

Katie, her Mexican-American Student Anti-Defamation League, and the newly formed National Coalition for the Advancement of Mexican-Americans got to work. Ever since Cindy's suicide attempt, Katie had been plotting and thinking about how to bring attention to the plight of the Dreamers. She understood Trump had done such a great job of vilifying and devaluing Mexicans that by and large, the public was not interested in legalizing hundreds of thousands of young Mexicans, regardless of their suffering.

At the meeting called to tackle this issue, Katie shared that she had been thinking about a plan for a long time. Katie proposed a two-pronged action, but when Katie explained her ideas, the reaction of all who were present was, "You are crazy."

The first prong of her plan was to create a compelling public relations campaign, including a TV commercial, depicting the heartbreak of the deportation of this youth, and the heartbreak to the family, and to find sponsorship for these commercials from some wealthy Mexican-Americans. Katie said she had a close friend, Savannah Birkeland, who attended USC's School of Cinematographic Arts, where she had been working on some projects with the Oscar-winning director Alejandro Urchueta—a native of Mexico City. They might help.

"For the second prong of the plan," Katie said, "I will go on a hunger strike to bring attention to the terrible plight of the Dreamers."

People at the meeting thought that she was kidding, but when they noticed she was entirely serious, the group strongly opposed the idea, but Katie was relentless.

Mallory knew Katie's determination and said, "I will do it as well." She knew of the suffering Dreamers and what their families were going through firsthand.

Cindy, who was also at the meeting, said, "Me too, I'll go on a hunger strike."

The group was stunned but saw the passion in these three young women. Katie thought the idea was powerful and that three beautiful young women on a hunger strike would have to attract attention.

The group finally agreed and pledged their full support for the plan and agreed that for the time being, they would keep the idea of the hunger strike in strict secrecy. They would all reach out to their supporters to raise money for the making of the commercials and to have them aired at the appropriate times. They also agreed on correctly timing the commercials and the hunger strike, and with the group's support, they would bring national attention.

Katie started the plan by reaching out to Savannah. After Mark's death, Katie and Savannah had little contact, but they had a strong bond created by the tragedy. Savannah had always told Katie she would do anything to clear Mark's name and to fight injustice. Savannah was happy to arrange a meeting with Urchueta to ask for his support.

Katie traveled to Los Angeles for her meeting with Urchueta. Katie had never been to Los Angeles, and when she landed at LAX, she saw a city that never seemed to end. Katie did her research and found out that well over 30% of the inhabitants of Los Angeles, the capital of the entertainment industry, were of Mexican descent. She wondered why they were almost invisible in the movies and TV.

She met Savannah outside of the Warner Brothers studio lot in Burbank. She was very excited and hoped she would see George Clooney or Tom Cruise. They walked past the sets and into an office where Savannah announced, "Savannah Birkeland and Katie Suarez to see Mr. Urchueta."

He didn't make them wait long.

Urchueta kissed Savannah on the cheek and then shook Katie's hand and said, "Savannah tells me you are an unstoppable activist for the Mexican-American people. How can I help you?"

"Mr. Urchueta, it's an honor to meet you, and I think there could be no more urgent time than now to have this meeting." Urchueta was immediately impressed with Katie's passion, her fire and intensity, and that she went straight to the point.

"Savannah was right. I can see you are a woman on a mission. She mentioned a little about your family's history…so tell me, what is this urgent time and what action is needed?"

"Sir, I know you're an artist, but I'm sure you've heard what's happening to hundreds of thousands of Mexican and Mexican-American families in this country—that they are permanently damaged by this massive deportation of young Dreamers. I am here to ask for your help."

"Katie, my heart goes out to all those families and the youth, but I am an artist, not a politician, and I am not inclined to get involved in politics."

"I understand, but maybe you can help us by recommending me to a great filmmaker who would be willing to create three commercials. What I really have in mind is three separate, super-high quality, one-minute movies about the plight of this youth and their families."

Urchueta smiled. "A one-minute movie?" He was intrigued.

"Yes, sir, I'm not looking for thirty-second commercials, I'm looking for three one-minute movies that tell the stories of the Dreamers, their families, and how it's hurting so many Mexican-American families in irreversible ways. I am representing the National Coalition for the Advancement of Mexican-Americans, and we have some important sponsorship to help air these commercials. We believe this may help people understand. I know this is difficult, and that's why I needed to meet one of the best movie makers of our time." Then she smiled and asked, "Can you help?"

Urchueta realized that Katie was a force to be reckoned with and she had ideas and the ability to make unimaginable things happen. He was extremely interested in helping her and, of course, helping the poor Mexican families who lived in a state of constant doom. Although he chose to stay behind the scenes, he instructed Savannah to work with Katie, gave her the names of his best writers, casting director, musical director, and cinematographer to create productions, which would be of movie quality, but would tell the stories in one minute.

Katie approached some wealthy Mexican-American business people, as well as companies interested in doing business with the Mexican-American community and got the money to fund this project, especially after she mentioned Urchueta's name and the people involved in the production.

At a Hollywood set, Rodolfo Manriques, an up and coming director and protégé of Urchueta, said, "Action." Two patrol cars with ICE logos appear at full speed, and with loud screeching tires they stop in front of a pretty middle-class house in a cul-de-sac.

Loud and aggressive door knocks; the ICE officer yells, "Open the door immediately, it's the police."

The music and cinematography are perfect; it feels like a drug bust is taking place. Then, an attractive Mexican-looking woman in her mid-twenties holding a baby in her arms, with a four-year-old next to her, opens the door. She is immediately handcuffed and informed, "You are being deported."

The baby is crying, and the camera zooms to the beautiful four-year-old Mexican-American boy who says, "They are taking my mommy away from me."

It ends with words on the screen, "Is This What the American Dream Is About?" A disclaimer below reads, "Paid for by The National Coalition for the Advancement of Mexican-Americans."

A second short film depicts a med student being pulled out of class and handcuffed, and the third movie takes place in a courthouse where a seven-year-old girl is being separated from her mother and is being told by a child services counselor that she will have to be put up for adoption because her mom will be deported. The movies ended up being masterfully made with powerful stories.

In preparation for the second prong of her plan, Katie approached Blaire and asked her to spread the news about her new plan.

Without much thought, Katie spat out her plan to Blaire with the same intensity she did everything. "Blaire, I need you to help me put out a press release that I will be going on a hunger strike to bring attention to the plight of the hundreds of thousands of Dreamers suffering all over the country."

Blaire coughed and said, "You what?"

Katie said, "Sorry I didn't warn you. I'm going on a hunger strike, and. Cindy and Mallory are doing it with me."

"Katie, you've lost your mind! You're going to put your health at risk. You're a young woman, and you can damage your health permanently."

"Blaire, this has already been decided, and I am determined and will not change my mind. If you don't want to help me, I'll do it without your help."

Blaire could see the absolute determination in Katie's eyes. By now, Blaire knew that when Katie made up her mind, there was no stopping her. She loved Katie and would do anything to help her. Once Blaire was resigned to the fact her friend was going to do this, she switched into a planning mode, as she strategized how to help Katie put the message out, hoping the news would work fast and the hunger strike wouldn't have to last very long.

Blaire was put in charge of publicity and spreading the news about the reason for the upcoming hunger strike. She called Zack, as she knew he would be very concerned, and he made no effort to change her mind because he knew it would be futile.

Instead, he called Katie and said, "Hi, Katie, I heard about your insane but brilliant plan,"

"Who told you? It's a secret."

"Don't be mad. Blaire told me because she knew I'd be concerned about you. She told me it was an absolute secret and I will never violate that secret. In fact, I'm offering to join the hunger strike and now that I'm out of my football team commitment, I want to be more involved."

"You're crazy! Nooo, you can't!"

"Why not? I've also suffered a great deal, and I hate what's happening to the people I love. Plus, I owe this to Mark and to Soco!"

Katie's eyes filled with tears and she said, "Zack, we are serious, we will go all the way. You don't need to do this."

"I want to. I must. Plus, I want to be there with you. You matter a great deal to me."

"But Zack, you must understand that people will hate you, and will think you're a traitor. You're a celebrity and have an amazing future ahead of you. This could put it in jeopardy."

"I know all of that, and I don't care what other people think. I know what the right thing to do is and I promised myself that I wouldn't turn my back on you or the people I love again."

And, for the first time, Katie felt affection for Zack. All the resentment she felt toward him for all those years melted away and was replaced by a new feeling.

CHAPTER TWENTY-NINE
VALENTI'S REACTION

On the agreed-upon day, the small 500-square-foot dorm room with white walls, posters of Katy Perry and Coldplay, two beds with light blue comforters, and a few pieces of IKEA furniture, was filled with members and volunteers of the National Coalition for the Advancement of Mexican-Americans. The nightstands and desks had been pushed to the side to make room for two extra cots. And these four brave young activists— Katie, Mallory, Cindy, and Zack—started their hunger strike.

One of the volunteers videotaped the initiation of the hunger strike and posted it on social media. The room was full, and people gathered outside and in the hallways. Blaire had prepared press releases, and at the designated time, she started sending them everywhere.

Within a few hours, news cameras arrived at the scene of the strike. Katie chose to do it in her dorm because she felt proximity to the university and all the students would be helpful. Blaire wanted to be the first news reporter to interview them, and she was prepared.

Blaire arrived with her cameraman and said, "We are here with four Arizona students who have gone on a hunger strike. They say they intend to bring attention to the suffering of the young Dreamers and their families, as well as to bring attention to what they say is president Trump's assault on Mexican-Americans."

She continued, "Today is day one of their hunger strike. Their leader is Katie Suarez, a law student. Joining her are two sisters, Cindy and Mallory Ochoa, and the admired former quarterback of The Sun Devils, Zack Mackintosh."

Blaire brought the microphone close to Katie's mouth and said, "Katie, could you please explain to us what you're trying to accomplish with a hunger strike?"

"In this beautiful country of ours, some terrible injustices are being committed to hundreds of thousands of young people who live in fear every day. And while they want to live the American dream, study, work hard, and move up, they can't, because they could be deported tomorrow. Most of these young people don't know any other home than America; as you know, they were brought to this country by their parents illegally, and mostly from Mexico.

"The irreversible damage to these young people's lives is shared with their families, and now some of them have children. This is happening to an entire generation of Mexican-Americans. Why is there no resolution to this problem? We want to make it very clear that we do not condone illegal immigration, and we do support a strong border control, but we support a humanistic immigration reform, which will protect the rights of Dreamers, children, families, and law-abiding people."

Blaire then brought the microphone to Zack and said, "Zack, last year you were breaking records on the football field as one of the most acclaimed quarterbacks in Sun Devils history. Why are you risking your health for this hunger strike?"

"Blaire, although I'm not Mexican, I've personally seen the lives of people I love destroyed by the injustices done to Mexican-Americans by people like Arpaio, whose cops detain and deport innocent people, and then by people like Trump, who are using Mexican American lives as pawns to consolidate his power. Americans are good people, and the four of us are American Dreamers who know that the American dream will prevail."

Blaire then turned the microphone to the Ochoa girls. "Cindy and Mallory, why are you risking your life to do this hunger strike?"

Cindy said, "I am a Dreamer, and personally know hundreds of Dreamers like me who live day to day scared and depressed. I was in school and had good grades and was working hard for a degree, but the stress of it all damaged my health, and now I struggle in school, and I feel like I have no more hope. I guess if I die, it will be for a good cause and maybe some other people will benefit and live better lives."

Mallory cried when she heard her sister's heartfelt statement and when

Blaire asked her about her intentions, she said in a muffled voice, "My sister is my life after our parents were deported. I'm an American citizen who has lost hope."

Blaire ended her report fighting tears and said, "Following the four American Dreamers, I'm Blaire Carter for The Eye on the News channel 6, Arizona State campus, Phoenix."

There was a lot of attention that day, and many people came to see what was going on. On the second day, the crowds got larger. Social media buzzed, and many people showed sympathy and started to call the four strikers the "4 American Dreamers," but were quickly overwhelmed by trolls' aggressively negative comments. There were a lot of hateful tweets and comments like, "Let them die," and "Go back to where you came from."

One tweet read, "I think Zack Mackintosh got hit too many times in the head, he is turning against his own country, fuck him."

Katie was not surprised. She'd learned early on that when she stuck her neck out for what she believed, there would always be people willing to cut it off.

The next day, the group woke up with the campus police knocking hard on their door. They were being evicted because the school did not condone such actions. Katie had a contingency plan and called a friend who was a licensed lawyer, who showed up with documents proving the dorm was, in fact, not inside school property.

The school did not directly own the dorm, and since she was current on her monthly payment, she had the right to stay in her dorm room. The school lawyers quickly looked into the matter and found out they were within their right to remain.

On that same day, Elizabeth showed up at the strike zone and demanded to speak with Katie. She was allowed in when she said she was Katie's mother. Elizabeth was crying, but her tears did not appear to be of sympathy, but of rage, the moment she saw Katie.

"You stupid child. I did not raise you to be so reckless. You are putting our entire family to shame and destroying your future. Are you crazy?"

"Mom, you're not welcome here, especially with that attitude. I'm following my heart and what I believe is the right thing to do to honor my brother and my dad's sacrifice. You're the one who turned your back on your son and your husband to avoid hurting your career and acknowledging who you are. I will not follow your servile example."

Elizabeth was terribly hurt by her daughter's words, and tears streamed down her face as she turned around, speechless, and left.

By the third day of the strike, the local Phoenix news media was no longer at the site and had lost some interest. Suddenly, a hostile group of agitators showed up at the strike zone and started demonstrating outside of the dorm, against Katie and her group. They were chanting, and holding sign that said, "If you don't like our laws you can leave" and "We don't need more lazy people clogging welfare and bringing crime."

The demonstrators were aggressively shoving the strike supporters, trying to gain access to the dorm and the strikers. The police did not appear to be doing anything to control them, and turned a blind eye.

Katie was scared and called Blaire to ask her for help. "Please bring the news cameras." Katie thought that if the media was watching, the demonstrators might become more reasonable. Blaire quickly scrambled to the strike zone and found a real melee going on. Some of the strike supporters had created a barricade to protect the strikers, but the attackers were gaining ground, hitting and kicking people.

Blaire showed tremendous courage and bravery. She put herself in harm's way and pushed herself to the middle of the attackers and started interviewing them.

"Sir, what are you trying to do? What group are you with?"

Blaire turned to a policeman standing next to all of this, and asked, "Sir, why aren't you stopping this aggressive demonstration?"

The policeman on camera gave all sorts of excuses, "We can't do much, as each side has the right to demonstrate and speak."

"Yes sir, but people are bleeding, and the protesters have pipes in their hands."

The cameraman panned out and showed people with shaved heads and pipes in their hands.

Finally, the police started to demand people to disperse. It took some doing, but finally, the demonstrators left. By the next morning, national news media began to show what was happening at the University of Arizona.

And then, at the scheduled time, the mini-movie commercials started showing around the country, each showing the plight and suffering of American citizens being damaged by the treatment given to the Dreamers. The mini-movies were very successful in humanizing the reality of what was going on, especially showing how American citizens were being hurt.

Many at home watched for the first time and understood what was happening as they saw a face and the consequences of the political inaction; the good-hearted American people started calling their representatives and asking why nothing had been done about the Dreamers.

In a corner office at Trump Tower with a beautiful view of Central Park, Jerry Valenti sat at his desk on a phone call with the boss. "I'm sorry, boss, I know you're mad. I'm not sure how my team has allowed these stupid college kids to create such a fuss."

Valenti's face was red and he had to move the earpiece away from his ear to decrease the heat that was coming out of the phone.

"Yes sir, I know I told you that Mexicans are submissive, not fighters, and they wouldn't give us any real resistance. I honestly don't know where this group came from but trust me, boss, I'm on it. I'm leaving immediately for the airport, and I will get to the bottom of this. They will be sorry they attempted to defy you, boss."

Valenti was in full damage-control mode. He had his entire team look deep into each and every one of the people involved in this catastrophe. Valenti was in one of Trump Corporation's limos on his way to the airport, barking orders to his subordinates.

"By the time I reach Phoenix, I want to know every single detail about these people: their families, their dreams, and their families' dreams. I want everything! No dam excuses." Then he tried to remember who his contacts in Phoenix were and who might be able to help him.

Once in Phoenix, Valenti already had meetings scheduled. The first one was with his top media contact in town who had previously helped him leak information about Mark's arrest. He arrived at Arraviati Cucina, a trendy Italian bistro, and Sebastian Romer, his connection, was already seated.

"It must be nice to have a private jet at your disposal. You arrived here from New York so fast!" said Sebastian.

"Well," Valenti said, "this is an important issue. My boss was preparing to launch his latest budget proposal, and the mess you've made here is casting a shadow. Somehow these stupid kids have started to get the nation's attention on the immigration issue, and my boss does not want to go there."

"You won't believe that the ringleader is the sister of Mark Suarez, the rich Mexican kid who got in trouble with a girl and I helped you spread leaked information from your cop, what was his name…" and his eyes looked up, trying to recall, "oh yes, Summers."

Valenti said, "What the fuck is wrong with this family? They didn't raise those kids right or something."

"Yeah, or something. She is a troublemaker. Previously, she did some minor activism and forced the local museum to do a stupid exhibition of some Mexican-American artists. It was crap anyway." He looked irritated and continued, "But this time she has gone too far and has somehow gotten more people around her and has launched an all-out attack on your boss's policy on the Dreamers."

"Stupid people, they don't learn. Well, I'm here to crush this shit one way or another." He looked at Sebastian, expecting him to suggest something.

"Well, one of the first things I would do is damage her credibility by linking her to the criminal brother and paint her as an instigator and troublemaker. I'm already working on an article creating that connection."

And then, as if reading Valenti's mind, he said, "She is too young and clean, I don't think you're going to find much dirt on her."

"Look, everyone has a weakness," said Jerry.

"You know I'm here for you if you need me."

By the next day, Sebastian had published an article exposing Katie's family's secrets, which painted her and her family as disloyal to America. No sooner had the article hit the street than nasty tweets poured out against Katie and the other strikers, and some were very menacing.

At the strikers' headquarters, the team of volunteers kept careful tabs of the social media reaction to the strike. They immediately brought to Katie's attention the news piece and the online reaction. Katie was not surprised, as she had expected a negative response. She had experienced people's efforts to discredit her before.

The entire group decided to be more vigilant and beef up security, as the expectation of aggression became more real.

Valenti started the next day watching the news, and the first thing he saw was Blaire on the screen saying, "It is day four of the hunger strike at the Arizona State campus…"

Valenti was very interested in what was being told to the public, and then one of the one-minute mini-movies aired: the ICE patrol, the crying boy. Valenti was fuming. He turned the TV off and threw the remote to the ground. "Mother fuckers."

Blaire used her media know-how and influence to keep attention on the strike. She convinced the news director to allow her to do a daily update on the condition of the strikers.

Valenti continued his assault by going to meet with the Maricopa County attorney, who was an older, bald-headed man with a huge swollen nose, the type people with liver cirrhosis get. His name was John Cleaver, and he was a man with a short temper and a "god complex." He agreed to meet with Valenti because he received a call from very high up. He decided to meet at a small café far from the office because he knew that this discussion should be kept private.

"Okay, Jerry," Cleaver said, "what the hell brings you to Phoenix? The last time you were here, you looked like you couldn't wait to get the hell out."

Valenti was smooth when he wanted something. "Mr. Cleaver, we love Phoenix, and my boss has tremendous support and affection for this town, and so do I."

"Cut the bullshit. I know what you're here for, the hunger strike at Arizona State, but what do you want me to do?"

"Mr. Cleaver, my boss is very interested in silencing these people. They're stirring up the Mexican-American people and making my boss's policy on the Dreamers and immigration more difficult."

Valenti paused and tried to think how to bring up his next point. "Look, we uncovered that the ringleader Katie Suarez is the daughter of one of your prosecutors. We need you to have a talk with her."

"Are you freaking kidding me? And what do you suppose I tell her?"

Valenti's voice and demeanor changed from one of conciliation to one of demand. "Look, John, you'll be up for reelection next year, and this is coming from the top. Get your house in order or…" Valenti stopped short and gave Cleaver a look that said it all.

Cleaver, not used to being told what to do, said, "You guys can go fuck yourselves. Who do you think you are?"

Valenti used his bright blue eyes as a lethal weapon and said, "John, do you really want to go there?"

Cleaver looked at Valenti's eyes and felt a chill down his spine, gulped and walked away.

Message received.

At the County Attorney's office, John Cleaver sat in a leather chair. Behind him were rows of leather-bound law books, nicely organized in floor-to- ceiling cherrywood bookshelves. He was sipping his coffee when the phone rang.

Cleaver said, "Yes, Mary?"

Cleaver's assistant Mary said, "She's here."

"Ok, let her in."

Opening the door very slowly, trying to make minimal noise, Elizabeth Suarez peeked her face in and smiled. "Hi, Mr. Cleaver, you asked for me?"

Cleaver, with his booming voice, said, "Yes Elizabeth, I keep hearing that you're doing a fine job in the trenches. Sorry I haven't had time to speak with you in a while, but I've been watching, and I think soon you'll be moving up."

Elizabeth was flattered and surprised to hear that, as she had thought that Cleaver didn't really like her and had avoided giving her any incentives or praises. "Thank you. I have been a junior prosecutor for several years and have been working hard. Thank you for noticing,"

"Well, Elizabeth, there's actually another item I need to talk to you about," and he went straight to the point because he was a man with power and expected people to do as he said. "Your daughter is creating a big stir. People are starting to get uncomfortable, and I'm worried this could become something serious. I need you to control her and put an end to this."

"Excuse me? With all due respect, this has nothing to do with my work. My daughter is an adult, she doesn't live with me, and in all reality, she does not listen to me. What exactly would you want me to do?"

"Well, she's creating a serious problem, and I have instructions coming from the highest levels of government to put an end to this. If you could help, I would personally be very appreciative."

The pressure and feeling this conversation created in Elizabeth made her more incisive. "And what if I can't help? What will you do?"

Cleaver, drunk with the power of knowing he could control people's destiny, said, "Elizabeth, it's up to you. Your destiny and your daughter's destiny are in your hands; there will be serious consequences." He stood up and walked around his desk to open the door.

Elizabeth said nothing, got up quickly, and exited the office. Her head spun, and she felt fear in her heart for her daughter. Hearing that the higher levels of government wanted and were determined to see an end to her daughter's action sent a chill down her spine. At that moment, she became a mother again, and her own future became of less importance to her because she was more worried about her daughter's safety. The same sense of doom she had experienced before with Mark came upon her.

She kept repeating in her mind, "This is not going to end well."

CHAPTER THIRTY
DAY 5 LOVE

When Elizabeth walked into the dorm, she found Katie looking very pale and not talking at all. It was now five days of no food, just liquids, and her energy was starting to falter. Elizabeth's motherly instincts sharpened, and she felt love for her daughter. "Katie, my love, I'm sorry for my behavior last time I was here. I was trying to protect you, and I know I did it the wrong way."

Katie looked at her with an empty look on her face, partly because she was hungry and exhausted, and partly because she did not want to get into an argument with her mom.

"Honey, I am worried for you. I had a terrifying conversation with my boss, the county attorney. He was very concerned and told me that very high in the government, there is deep displeasure for what you guys are doing and they intend to put an end to it, one way or another."

Katie's eyes opened as though she had woken up and said, "Mom, this is great news! It means it's working!"

Katie called the other strikers and said, "We just found out that very high up in the government, people are upset and want to put an end to our strike!"

Zack and the Ochoa girls, with equally small amounts of energy, did a faint cheer.

Elizabeth started to forcefully hush them. "Shush, guys, this isn't a cause for celebration. We have to be scared. They don't mean to end this in a friendly way." And then, as Elizabeth recounted her words, she realized she included herself when she said "we." She was now part of the team.

"Mom, we know, we have zero expectation that Trump and his guns will just grow a conscience and want to help the Dreamers or us. We expect a fight, we expect attacks, and we expect many people to hate us. Change never comes easy, and we are prepared."

"But honey, aren't you guys scared? You're all so young and with such bright futures ahead of you. This could screw that up."

"Mrs. Suarez," Zack said, "we know, but we also strongly believe we're doing the right thing, and we're on the right side of history. This may mean we have to sacrifice ourselves, but we know millions of people will benefit and our country will be all the better because of what we're doing."

Katie looked at Zack with such admiration and affection, Elizabeth noticed and smiled to herself.

"Yes," Mallory said, "we believe in our hearts that change is inevitable. It has come to the point that the millions of people here today, and those yet to be born, will either grow up with fair and equal opportunities and enjoy the freedom and chance of a better life our country stands for, or, if we fail, those same millions of Mexican-American people will continue to face a future of rejection, exclusion, poverty, and hopelessness. I can tell you, I've never believed in anything as strongly as I do now for what we're doing here."

Cindy nodded the entire time, and at the end of her sister's comment she said, "Amen."

Elizabeth left the dorm with an entirely new understanding of what was happening. Elizabeth had never been very interested in her Mexican background, nor had she ever identified with it, or cared to do so. In fact, the more Lorenzo used to talk about Mexican issues, the more she became disinterested.

Nevertheless, the passion these young people had for helping the millions of people affected by this struggle made her think about her own story and how her father worked quietly and never got the recognition or respect he deserved because he was a Mexican cook and not a French chef. She also thought about her mother, who felt her only choice to get out of the ghetto was to hide that she was Mexican and teach her children to hide their Mexican background. Elizabeth began to view things in a different light.

After Elizabeth left, the hunger strikers felt a combination of excitement, fear, and exhaustion.

"What do you think Trump would do to us if he could?" Cindy asked.

"Oh, I am sure he is scheming something—most likely he has his team developing a smear campaign against us, and every dirty little secret we may have will be exposed." Katie smiled and asked, "Zack, do you have any secret children somewhere? With all those women throwing themselves at you, I'm sure you have a few secrets to hide."

Zack started to laugh and said, "I'm not falling for that one."

"Come on, Zack, come clean."

Zack realized Katie expected an answer. "Yes, there were many women, but I have nothing to be ashamed of, and I have always treated women with respect."

When he said those words, the tarnished reputation of his beloved friend Mark came to him, and he said, "I know for a fact our beloved Mark was equally as respectful to women, and I would give anything to clear his name." He looked at Katie and said, "You know I am doing this to honor him."

Katie's eyes closed for a few seconds to recall memories and to hold back tears, and then her eyes opened, and she said, "I know, Zack, I'm so grateful you're here with me... with us," she corrected. Then she smiled and looked straight in his eyes and said, "You're our knight in shining armor, defending us—your fair maidens—from the dragons outside."

Zack looked back into her eyes and said, "I would do anything for you. I'd give up my life."

He extended his hand to grab Katie's. She clutched his hand with force and passion.

The Ochoa girls suddenly felt like they should leave the room, but there was nowhere to go. After a minute of staring into each other's eyes, which felt like an eternity, Zack and Katie realized their love would have to wait; there was a big battle with evil people ahead of them.

CHAPTER THIRTY-ONE
ICE

Entrenched in the Arizona Biltmore's presidential suite, Jerry Valenti was on the phone. His eyes were red, and there were two veins on his forehead that looked ready to burst, as he said, "Sir, I promise I have my entire team working on this. The dam county attorney was of no use. These country people here have no diplomatic skills. He bullied the mom so hard, she ended up quitting her job as a prosecutor." The curse words coming out of the earpiece were so loud, Valenti had to pull the phone away from his ear.

"The media and social media campaigns are in full force," Valenti said. "So far, we have uncovered little we can use, but we're working to shed light on what a bunch of freaking opportunistic agitators those mother-fucking kids are."

Again, loud curses came out of the earpiece.

"Yes, sir, I will intensify those campaigns and get results, I guarantee it." And then a hint of a smile showed as he said, "Boss, I'm working with the local ICE field director and the DOJ to see if we can use a loophole and deport one of the strikers. She is a Dreamer, and they're looking into the legal details. We want to be sure when we do it, we will have all our ducks in a row."

No more curses came out of the phone, and the boss appeared pleased with the idea of using force to remove at least one of the strikers and break their spirit. Valenti knew his boss's mind and knew he liked the idea of showing overwhelming power to strike fear in his enemies.

Valenti called Manuel Herrera, the local ICE field director, to get an update on his plan to deport Cindy. He was delighted when he heard they had confirmed that the deportation could be carried out legally and they were preparing to do the operation. Valenti reminded Manuel that the operation had to be done the way they had planned it.

The following morning, at five a.m. on the dot, at the dorm, a dozen ICE officials and Phoenix police combined force in full gear. They woke everyone with extremely loud door knocks and loud cries, "United States Immigration and Customs Enforcement, we have an order for the arrest and immediate removal of Cindy Ochoa. Open the door."

ICE had made a last-minute call to a local news reporter and asked him to bring his camera team and be sure there would be a video of the operation, even though no one was allowed to go inside the building.

Inside dorm room 105, there was chaos. There were no volunteers, only the strikers, who were caught by surprise.

The girls started to cry. Mallory said to Cindy, "I won't let them take you!" But their muscles were weak, and they could present very little resistance. They refused to open the door for ICE, so the officers used the door breach to shatter the door and ram it open.

They found Cindy behind the three other strikers who valiantly tried to defend their friend. Although they offered no real resistance, the officers had been instructed by their command to arrest anyone who stood in their way and showed the slightest resistance. All along, Valenti planned to arrest all four.

Before she was arrested, Katie had the clear mind to text Blaire, who once more heroically risked her job to rush the cameraman and herself out of their assignment and arrive just in time to see all four strikers walking out, in handcuffs, led by ICE and Phoenix police.

Blaire looked at the camera and said, "A few minutes ago, exactly one week after the initiation of the hunger strike, ICE officers and Phoenix police officers have arrested The Four American Dreamers. At this point, it is unclear what the basis is for this arrest."

Blaire pointed the microphone to one of the policemen who was standing by. He pushed it away and said forcefully, "Not now."

Social media went on a frenzy, with extreme opinions being shared. Some condemned the arrest and called it an attack on freedom. Valenti was prepared to manipulate social media by sending a massive attack on any supporters, having an army of people send joyous, congratulatory tweets about the arrest, with comments like, "Finally, action against these Anti-Americans" and "Deport all 4, we don't need people like that."

What Valenti had not counted on is that Katie and the National Coalition for the Advancement of Mexican-Americans were prepared for the social media attacks, and they had planned a counter-attack strategy. All over the country, an army of volunteers had been prepared to respond politely and articulately about the offensive attacks. There was a vicious social media war…but this time, it was not a one-sided fight.

A few hours later at a press conference called by Ice and the Phoenix police, Manuel Herrera said, "This morning a combined operation by ICE and Phoenix police detained Cindy Ochoa, who is in this country illegally. During the operation, three other subjects were arrested for interfering in police operations by resisting and fighting the police and ICE officials."

Blaire was present and asked the first question. "Mr. Herrera, could you explain why Cindy Ochoa, who has lived in the country for almost twenty-four years, was all of a sudden targeted for arrest?"

Herrera responded, "This individual had already been identified as eligible for deportation and the notoriety she brought on herself only helped us to identify her location and perform a perfectly legal operation."

"You know that the other three American citizens, who you arrested, have been on a hunger strike for almost a week. They have lost a lot of muscle mass and are very weak. Are you saying these people presented resistance to your officers?"

"They interfered with our actions, and they had to be arrested. That is all." A loud "Boo" was heard from a group of bystanders.

Once in police custody, the three American citizens were threatened that if they didn't eat, they would be force-fed. They were told that once in custody, it was within police discretion to do so. Katie was so weak she had a hard time thinking straight. She hoped her volunteers would find them a good lawyer to get them out before they were force-fed.

To her surprise, Elizabeth showed up and presented bail and declared herself lawyer for all three, demanding a stop to any interrogation and any attempts to force-feed her clients; she knew the law and the rules better than anyone.

In another part of town, in a cold, dark and damp cell, Cindy was alone and scared. She had been sent to a different facility, the ICE detention center. Here, the ICE officers were less concerned with her rights and immediately forced her to eat, threatening they would force-feed her if she didn't. The office in charge told her, "Don't get too comfortable. We've been given directions to deport you immediately. You'll be with your people in a couple of hours."

Within a few minutes, she was in severe pain. Her stomach was not used to food and did not take well to the food they gave her. The pain and sadness were almost too much to bear, and she started to cry. She was scared to be sent to Mexico, a place she had never seen, and even more scared that she might never see her beloved sister and everyone and everything she loved and held dear. Dark thoughts came to her mind.

The moment Katie, Zack, and Mallory were out on bail, they told Elizabeth they had to rush to Cindy's aid. Coalition volunteers had already done their due diligence and knew where Cindy had been taken. All four rushed there, and when they arrived, they found a large group of protesters demanding the immediate deportation of Cindy, holding large signs saying, "We don't want these criminals, send them to their home."

But this time there was a considerably larger group of counter-protesters demanding Cindy's immediate release, and they were not just Mexican-Americans; in fact, the crowd had far more white Americans, African Americans, and Asian Americans than Mexican-American people. They held signs saying, "America is a land of immigrants" and "We are all human, we are all Dreamers."

There were cameras all around. The screaming between one group and the other was so loud, it got scary at times. Elizabeth, once again, wanted to declare herself Cindy's lawyer, but other volunteer lawyers had already requested a legal stay of her deportation.

Fortunately, Elizabeth called every contact she knew, and, as part of the team of lawyers, was able to stop the deportation. In fact, Cindy had to be taken off of the bus that was taking her to the border. The country's conscience was now being put to the test.

The next morning, newspapers and TV worldwide covered the strike and reported an international outcry of support. Video of the handcuffed "4 American Dreamers," together with clips of the heart-wrenching mini-movies, were shown around the world. Headlines from the largest newspapers, like the French Le Figaro, said, "Is this the American Dream?" The London Times proclaimed, "In the land of the free, Dreamers are waking up to a nightmare."

Other European newspapers followed.

Emboldened by the world's attention, some Mexican and Mexican-American celebrities finally started tweeting and giving interviews in support of the "4 American Dreamers." The first were the most socially conscious ones, Salma Hayek, Eva Longoria, and Gael Garcia Bernal. A sense of duty pushed others out of the closet, and many Mexican-American celebrities voiced their support and told stories of how their parents or grandparents had come to the US legally or illegally looking for a dream.

The tide was turning.

That same evening at the Arizona Biltmore, Jerry Valenti received a call from his boss. Valenti was insulted in the most humiliating ways possible, and at the end of the call, he heard the words, "You're fired." That evening he did not return home on the Trump private jet; he had to fly coach.

CHAPTER THIRTY-TWO

RECONCILIATION

With the national outcry, a judge approved a one-year stay on Cindy's deportation. She rejoined the other three, and they resumed their hunger strike. They had already achieved great success by creating all the media attention, and it was evident there were tough conversations all over the country about what to do about those Dreamers.

Back at the dorm, the four considered whether they had achieved their goal and if they should end the hunger strike.

"I think we've done our share," Mallory said. "People are talking, and I feel something good will happen."

"I'm afraid that," said Katie, "as with many other almost-achieved goals, if we stop now, sentiment may cool, and all will be for nothing. I want to continue, and now that we have come this far, we can establish a more defined endpoint. I vote we continue our hunger strike until a motion to enter a bill on Congress is placed."

It was day nine of their fast and their muscles were starting to hurt.

"How soon do you think someone can introduce a bill? I don't know how much longer I can do this," said Mallory.

"There are already a number of people who have bills drawn up, so as long as the Congress is in session, if someone wants to do it, it can be done in one day."

Zack agreed with Katie, and they decided to continue a little while longer.

The next morning Blaire showed up with her news van as usual, to do the daily update. "Here we are on day ten of the '4 American Dreamers' hunger strike."

Blaire looked at Katie and said, "You guys have gained nationwide, well, more like worldwide, attention for your cause. Do you feel you have done enough?"

"Blaire, we are very thankful to the American public for their support. We see and read thousands of supporting messages, and of course, we also see some very hurtful comments. As you know, that is what makes this country great, freedom of speech. We plan to stay on our fast until legislation is entered in Congress, offering a final resolution to the Dreamers' plight. We are so close."

Katie asked her volunteers and all the members of the National Coalition for the Advancement of Mexican-Americans to contact every member of Congress they knew to see if they could convince someone to enter legislation.

Elizabeth, who was now out of a job, spent all her time with the strikers. She made sure they were hydrated and slipped some electrolytes and needed vitamins into the fluids they were taking. She also started calling every contact she had, urging them to have a Congress member introduce a bill; her daughter's life depended on it.

Elizabeth and Katie started to interact and smiled at each other. Finally, they were looking eye to eye, and they began to reconnect. Zack noticed how happy Katie looked, happier than she had been for a while.

"Mrs. Suarez," Zack said, "Katie looks so happy, although she is looking very skinny." And he laughed, "All joking aside, I want to tell you that I'm in love with your daughter, and if we survive this, I will ask you for permission to marry her. Seeing how happy it makes her to have you here, I hope you will always be around in our lives."

Elizabeth's eyes welled up. She had been alone and bitter for so many years— suddenly she felt there was a family again, and she cried.

Katie's eyes also teared up and she said, "Mom, I love you so much. Never leave me again. Zack and I are in love, and we will have a family, and we want you to be a part of it."

"Zack, you know, secretly I always liked you for Katie, ever since you were a boy playing soccer with Mark. You were always so polite and caring for others, I have no doubt you will be an amazing husband and father, as you are an amazing man today."

Tears streamed down Elizabeth's cheeks. "I only wish Mark were here to see this."

Everyone in the tiny room was in tears. They all hugged each other and then talked about their favorite memories of Mark. That evening lasted forever, and the room was full of love.

The following day, thousands of Mexican-Americans began contacting their legislators and representatives demanding action. Once the American public realized the damaging effect the inaction was having on the Dreamers, the great suffering of their families, and the permanent damage inflicted on American-born children, there was an outcry of support for a permanent solution for the Dreamers. That same day, Congressman Ian Liberman entered a bill to resolve the Dreamer issue permanently.

At the dorm, there was a celebration. Katie and Zack hugged and kissed. The strike was finally over.

The bill was modified several times, but it finally passed Congress, and it also had modifications in the Senate.

As usual, Trump used his tactics to delay and stall, hoping people would quickly forget and he could move away from this deal, but this time, he found a newly organized National Coalition for the Advancement of Mexican-Americans led by Katie, which was loud and relentless and did not allow the matter to be forgotten.

The pressure from the coalition was unyielding. Katie was there at every point to remind the group not to give up, and not to allow people to forget. For the first time, many of the forty million Mexican-Americans were unified in a mission to help their most vulnerable. Once they were energized and with good leadership, their political influence was enormous.

During meetings, Katie reminded them that ultimately only the Mexican-Americans care about Mexican-American issues. It is human nature, there will always be conflicting interests, and there will always be groups who want precisely the opposite, and that is why it is so important to have a voice with social and political representation to protect the interest of the Mexican-American community.

For the same reasons, African-Americans, Christians, Muslims, and Jews have organized representation to defend their interests. The millions of Mexican-Americans who were once without voice or organized representation, now had the National Coalition for the Advancement of Mexican-Americans.

With the relentless pressure, and after weeks of negotiation, a bill was finally passed and arrived on President Trump's desk. He signed it and congratulated himself for finally resolving such a difficult problem, which none of his predecessors had been able to do.

Three months after the bill passed, Zack and Katie got married; it was a small event, only for close friends and family. Katie went on to finish law school and became a civil rights lawyer, while Zack started a successful dot-com business, and funded a watch group to monitor the conditions of incarcerated teenagers convicted of minor crimes.

Exactly one year after the Dreamers bill passed, Zack and Katie had a baby boy. They named him Mark Lorenzo Mackintosh.

The End

JL RUIZ

Born in Mexico City, JL attended university at UNAM, one of the oldest and most prestigious universities on the continent. JL relocated to the U.S. as a young man and experienced the unique challenges and opportunities of a Mexican immigrant. He observed similar experiences by other immigrants as well as witnessed the life and perspective of countless U.S.-born Mexican-Americans. With hard work and dedication, he became a highly respected dentist, researcher, and educator.

Author of the textbook "Supra-gingival Minimally Invasive Dentistry" published by Wiley-Blackwell, he has also published many research papers and clinical articles on adhesive and esthetic dentistry. Ruiz regularly lectures at all major dental meetings, nationally and internationally.

JL enjoys a clientele of many stars and entertainers and has made numerous television appearances for his dental expertise, including NBC Channel 4 News, ABC's News, Good Morning America & Vista La, VH1 and Channel 52's Telemundo and 34 Univision. A lover of history, psychology, and culture, his socially charged novels offer a fresh understanding of how historical events shape the present and the future. A big fan of music and the arts, JL is a past member of two rock bands.

CPSIA information can be obtained
at www.ICGtesting.com
Printed in the USA
LVHW021704010719
622876LV00018B/981/P